Black Dawn

by

William Blackwell

Paperback ISBN: 978-1-0697318-4-5
Published by Telemachus Press LLC
Second Edition
Version: 2019.04.13

Acknowledgements

Heartfelt thanks to my loyal and supportive friends, family, readers, and editor

To laugh is to risk appearing the fool.
To weep is to risk appearing sentimental.
To reach out for another is to risk involvement.
To expose feelings is to risk exposing our true self.
*To place your ideas, your dreams, before the crowd is to risk
loss.*
To love is to risk not being loved in return.
To live is to risk dying.
To hope is to risk despair.
To try at all is to risk failure.
*But risk we must, because the greatest hazard in life is to risk
nothing.*
*The man, the woman, who risks nothing, does nothing, has
nothing, is nothing.*
—Mother Teresa

Revenge is a confession of pain.
—Latin proverb

Life begins at the end of your comfort zone.
—Neale Donald Walsch

Prologue

In a celestial sphere of existence unimaginable to most mere mortals, the gatekeeper of the crossroads between the living and the dead sat cross-legged with his head bowed. Through the all-encompassing thick gray mist, the powerful Voodoo spirit couldn't see them. But Kalfu knew they were there. A jury of his peers. There to judge him. To punish him. Maybe even banish him from the spirit world entirely. He cringed. Although he was master of the malevolent spirits of the night, there were others more powerful.

And they knew.

Kalfu allowed himself a slight raise of his head. It would be a severe breach of protocol to hold his head high during these proceedings. He was not there to be worshipped or revered. Through his peripheral vision he saw a small glowing white dot appear, perhaps fifty feet ahead. The dot grew to a full moon. Gray misty streaks swam across it, painting elongated eyes and a garish grin. Bondye, The Supreme Being, spoke: "You have transgressed your boundaries, boundaries that are paramount to keeping the natural order and peace on Earth. You have been meddling in the affairs of humans to such a degree that you threaten the very balance of this natural order. Our governance over the earthly world does not allow wanton pleasures of the flesh with humans for self-serving reasons. With your blatant lasciviousness and debauchery, you crossed the line. And for this you will be punished."

Next to The Supreme Being, another small dot materialized and glowed ominously. It slowly formed a skull with empty black eye sockets and cotton batten stuffed into the nose cavity. A lit cigar dangled from the mouth, blue smoke twirling up, barely visible in the suffused gray light. The Baron Samedi, the spirit of resurrection and the dead, said, "Not only has Kalfu wantonly fornicated with humans, but he has also interfered with my role in the natural order, Your Highness. He has been telling me, according to *his* whims, who shall be resurrected and who shall not. It is not his decision to make." The Baron glared at Kalfu directly. "Stay out of my affairs. There are others more qualified than you to judge. Nobody died and made you God around here."

Head bowed, Kalfu remained silent.

A thunderous boom echoed through this otherworldly dimension of reality.

Bondye's eyes met the Baron's. "You watch your tongue in my presence," he snapped. "Unless you too wish a severe reprimand."

Kalfu tried but couldn't contain it. A small smile pursed his lips. He wiped it away quickly with a flick of his serpent-like tongue.

"I beg your forgiveness, Your Highness," the Baron said. "I'm sorry."

Bondye's eyes darkened and shrank to tiny slits. They drilled into Kalfu. "You dare smile at such a time? You mock these proceedings? Are they such a joke to you?"

His head still bowed, Kalfu said, "No, Your Highness. I beg your forgiveness."

Another glowing white dot emerged and magically enlarged, transforming into a face not unlike The Virgin Mary. It was Erzulie Freda, the spirit of love. She eyeballed Kalfu scornfully. A lone tear snaked down her face. A white hand appeared and brushed it away. "You are not the council concerning love and lust on Earth," she said. "I've seen multiple transgressions. The earthlings, in consultation with spirits like myself, make their own decisions in these matters. You are an intermediary between the spirits and humanity. You stand at the spiritual crossroads and merely grant or deny permission to speak with the spirits. But you have abused this power. You have made yourself judge, jury, and executioner."

There was a brief silence before Bondye spoke. "We are not here to discuss specific details of Kalfu's transgressions. He knows what they are, we know what they are. There is no question he is guilty. We are here to mete out punishment. And to decide on the severity of the punishment we need to know why Kalfu committed these intolerable breaches of spirit protocol. We need to know if he is repentant for his sins."

Bondye stared daggers directly at Kalfu. "Can you atone for your sins? Are you remorseful? Are you capable of ever becoming a dutiful and law-abiding spirit? Why would you commit such sins? Speak now, for this is your one and only chance at redemption."

Kalfu raised his head. He knew there was no point in denying the accusations. This wasn't a civil or criminal court where you were presumed innocent until proven guilty. This was a jury of his peers, far away from the boundaries and limitations and laws of Earth. He had already been found guilty. In the strange and mysterious world of Voodoo, his peers could see his transgressions, usually as they happened. They didn't need proof.

He applied a properly repentant frown. "I want to apologize to Your Highness, Erzulie, and the Baron for my crimes and transgressions. I am deeply sorry and wish I could turn back the hands of time so those things would never have happened. I realize by straying from my duties I interfered with the duties of all of you. I overstepped my bounds in the spirit world. I know the severity of this and am deeply repentant and remorseful. As my excuse, I can only say Satan got inside my head and I was no longer conscious of my actions. But the Devil has been exorcized from my being and I am once again in full control of my faculties."

"Are you absolutely sure about this?" Bondye said. "You won't leap off the cliff of temptation again? Because if you do, you will plummet to a fate worse than death. Of that I can assure you."

"No, Your Highness. I promise you, if it happens again, you can banish me from the spirit world forever." *Why the hell did I say that?*

"What makes you think I won't banish you indefinitely now?"

"I pray you won't, Your Highness. Please don't. I promise to stay the path of righteousness." *There, that sounds better.*

There was a brief silence as Kalfu waited.

The gray mist turned black, pitch black, enveloping the rising sun. Black dawn, sentencing time. A time for punishment. A time for retribution.

The scene was familiar to Kalfu. He had witnessed this darkness before. It was not the first time he had been disciplined, nor would it be the last.

A thunderous boom clapped through the heavens and reverberated into silence. Finally, Bondye spoke. "I hereby strip you of all your spirit duties and sentence you to three years of pain and suffering in the underworld. One year for the affront to my unquestionable power and absolute divinity, and one year each for your affronts to Erzulie and the Baron. You claim the Devil made you do it? Well, you can cavort with his minions in a torturous existence until you atone for your sins…"

"But, Your Highness, that's too—"

"Silence your lips, sinner," Bondye snapped. "Would you rather I banished you to Hell for all eternity?"

"I'm sorry, Your Highness. Forgive me, please."

"At the end of three years, you will come before the council. We will decide then if you're worthy to resume your role as spirit of the crossroads between the living and the dead. In the meantime, I will appoint an interim gatekeeper. Is that clear?"

"Yes, Your Holiness."

"This meeting is over. Disperse."

Bondye's image vanished in a flash, leaving only a faint shadow of his former presence, silhouetted against a black curtain. Then the Baron's glowing white skull shrank to the size of a pin before vanishing entirely. With a popping sound, Erzulie also disappeared.

Spiraling down a dark tunnel into the bowels of Hell, Kalfu grinned. *They don't have a clue what's coming. Not a fucking clue.*

Chapter One

Nothing, nothing, nothing. But no, that was something, Saul Climer thought as he turned his chainsaw off and set it down on the forest floor. He looked to where the noise had originated. A tree bluff close to the ocean. Some small bushes. He had heard a hollow rattling noise first, then a loud hissing sound, like a snake. He wiped sweat from his eyes, adjusted his black baseball cap, and stared at the chainsaw for answers. *How could I hear anything over that?*

Instead of moving toward the noise, he scanned the clearing for something else: his Alpine Lager can of beer, still half-full if memory served. He lumbered toward it, gingerly moving his right shoulder, sure that he had torn a rotator cuff during a fall in the forest a few days ago. Beer had gotten the better of him and his brush-clearing efforts had become haphazardly dangerous at best and downright reckless at worst. The following day he'd been hungover, and while examining his efforts at creating a usable clearing near the Atlantic Ocean on his Prince Edward Island acreage, he'd noticed a few downed trees outside of the orange spray paint of his proposed perimeter. By law on the Island, local authorities wanted to see about 50 feet of tree bluff separating clearing from water's edge, a buffer against erosion and other environmental concerns.

He reached the beer, lifted the can, drained the contents, and looked back at the patch of bush where the disconcerting sound had originated. The bush was still. All was quiet, but for the chirping of birds, the odd skittering of a chipmunk, and a gentle breeze hissing through the trees. Familiar sounds. *Forget it, you're drinking too much. It's the beer, nothing else.* For the moment, he forgot the noise, approached his well-worn 1979 green Ford pickup truck, opened the cooler, cracked open another Alpine, and thirstily swilled a third of it. It was his seventh, but who was counting? Certainly not Saul. He belched loudly, chuckled at the resounding echo, and peered at the sea through a clearing. The sun had just set. The glassy smooth water reflected perfectly the brilliant cloud colors above. Pink-orange layers illuminated the bottom half and misty purple-gray layers blanketed the top portion of the sky.

Beautiful. But it means nothing with no social life. Deadbeat. Loser. Stop.

Saul set his Alpine on the hood of the pickup, rotated his aching shoulder—*I should get that checked out—ahh, fuck it*—and surveyed his progress. With the help of a hired hand, a man much more skilled than he with the chainsaw, he had measured a clearing, about 75 feet wide by about 150 feet deep, marked it with fluorescent orange paint, and cut all the trees inside the circle, allowing for the obligatory tree bluff separating clearing from ocean. The idea was to create a usable beachfront area, accessible via a winding road that he had cleared the previous year. He had to admit he was pleased with what he saw, aside from the drunken foray where he'd mistakenly breached the no-go zone. Half of the felled trees were neatly cut and stacked into an organized wall of wood at the back of the clearing. Smaller branches were positioned in the center of the clearing inside a makeshift fire pit that now smoldered due to inattention. He had maybe another thirty felled trees to cut up and stack, a few more slash burns to go (burning off the useless stuff) and then he'd be ready to call in the bulldozer to remove the stumps, pile them somewhere away from the clearing, and smooth out the red dirt, making it traversable by vehicle and on foot.

"Looking fucking good," he said to no one. He took another swill of beer and staggered toward a plastic lawn chair positioned fireside. It was July 1st, Canada Day, and the weather was a pleasant 16 degrees Celsius. He set his beer on a large log coffee table, perhaps two feet in diameter. He'd fashioned it from an older long-dead Maple tree. He had three such coffee tables positioned around the fire and had even oil-stained the tops blue to prevent further rot and ruin.

He checked his watch: 8:44 pm. *Good. Still time for some more cutting, and getting this blaze going good again.* He gathered small branches and threw them into the fire, then located a five-gallon plastic container of gas and doused it. Flames leaped seven feet in the air with a whooshing sound.

Saul felt searing heat on his face and suddenly realized he was standing too close. Too late. He smelled something foul and familiar. Burning hair. His hair. "Shit-fucking shit," he said, stepping back a little too quickly. He tripped on a small branch and face-planted into the dirt.

He uttered a muffled gasp and started rolling toward the blaze that was now burning full-tilt, threatening to engulf his drunken moving body. A few feet from the fire, dizzy and disoriented from the fall, he put his right hand firmly on the dirt and stopped. Hot pain shot up his arm from the injured shoulder.

"Fuck sakes, you idiot. Get out of here." He started crawling away from the blaze as the wind picked up, showering his moving body with hot embers. He kept crawling on all fours, finally reaching a safe distance some thirty feet away. He stopped, rubbing the aching shoulder until something foul assaulted his nostrils. Burning hair. And burning clothes. He looked down. His steel-toed shoe was on fire. Flames licked up his right pant leg.

Screaming bloody murder, he pounded the shoe and pant leg flames out, and examined the damage. The shoe was charred black, but had not burned through to the foot—although part of his sock was burned in a ragged V-shape that clung to shriveled leg hairs. About six inches of the pant leg had burned away. Wincing, he examined the leg. It was red and swollen, singed and burnt. Beginning to blister.

He removed the shoe. Although his foot was hot, most of the sock was undamaged. He put the shoe on, tied what was left of the laces, and gingerly touched the injured leg. A patch of about eight inches continued to swell and redden.

Narrowing his eyes and balling his fists, he stood up, staring at the fire. "You can't beat me, you fucking thing. You can't, so get used to it."

He tested the foot and leg. They worked just fine, although the burned calf smarted like a hundred hornet stings. He gathered up a few bigger logs and tossed them in the fire, keeping a respectful distance from it. He quaffed his seventh beer, opened the cooler, and cracked Alpine number eight. He took a long pull, then raised it up. "Happy fucking Canada Day, motherfuckers."

He had no idea who he was talking to. Himself? Maybe forest critters? Maybe the seals that occasionally swam in the little bay bordering the waterfront? Maybe the trees? But who the words were meant for didn't matter to Saul right now. He focused bleary-eyed on the flickering orange flames, licking higher as the gentle breeze transformed into a more formidable wind. He decided that the chainsaw work, at least for tonight, was done. He had just about toasted himself extra crispy in the bonfire, and wasn't about to tempt fate by cutting timber that was slowly turning black with the blanket of nightfall. He absently rubbed his right eyebrow, simultaneously realizing two things: the eyebrow was almost singed bare, and there was a small cut above what remained of it—a result of the face-plant onto God's red Earth.

He wiped wetness away from his eyebrow and examined his hand. A little blood. *Must not be that deep. Who fucking cares.*

Canada Day, the country's birthday, he thought. Over a hundred and fifty years old. *A lot to celebrate for some people, but not me.* Since returning from the Dominican Republic two months earlier, Saul couldn't help but compare the island of Hispaniola to Prince Edward Island. Too many laws here. Not enough there. But where would you have more fun? Not here, certainly not. Go to practically any Canadian beach and read the signs—*Sign, sign, everywhere a sign. Blockin' out the scenery, breakin' my mind. Do this, don't do that, can't you read the sign?*—No dogs allowed, no open fires, no alcoholic beverages, no vehicles of any kind, no lifeguard on duty, no inflatable objects permitted in the water, no barbecues, no camping, open during these hours, closed during these hours.

"Why the fuck don't they add no swimming allowed, laughing and having fun prohibited, and all people prohibited on the beach? What about no walking or talking?" Saul said. Some Canadian laws and bylaws were completely nonsensical. He had been to many public parks across the country where NO SMOKING signs adorned the greenery. The city council in Calgary, in its infinite wisdom, had passed a bylaw declaring that all cats must be on leashes. What? And smoking in bars was restricted on outdoor patios, but permitted in tiny, specially designed rooms inside the establishments. What the hell was that? City bylaw officers towed vehicles on private residential driveways in certain municipal districts because of invalid license plates. Goddammit, it was private property.

That was just the beginning, but Saul didn't want to think about it anymore. Too damned depressing. Since returning from his Dominican adventures, he'd been unable to curtail his alcohol abuse. In Costambar, where he'd stayed, alcohol was just part of the culture, particularly among expats. What do you do when you're at a beach bar, enjoying a nice breeze and the gentle lapping of ocean waves, not to mention the varied and entertaining mix of foreigners and locals alike? Drink water? Yeah, right.

So Saul had stayed with the booze, something that was now part of his everyday existence. And he had rationalized it in just about every way possible. *I'm just easing myself back into Canadian culture. A drink a day keeps the doctor away. I need it to get over the culture shock. I can stop anytime I want. I don't need a drink. I want a drink. Alcohol makes the world go around. Society can't function without a few good drunks.*

After some time, the rationalization stopped, but the drinking continued as it had in the DR. There, it was eat breakfast, hit the beach, and start drinking. Carry on, with a tour of no less than ten and no more than twelve bars, until maybe three or four in the morning. The next day, if you weren't too hungover, you started all over again. Why the fuck not? What else was there to do there?

But what else is there to do here? At 59, Saul was dead broke. He had blown what little savings he had in the DR—the savings were left over from his job as a public relations officer for a large oil company, a position he'd held for five years before being laid off due to an economic downturn. He'd left the company two years earlier and relocated to Prince Edward Island, intent on becoming a great Canadian bestselling author. After spending fifty thousand dollars on renovations and taking two tours of drunken debauchery in the DR, he went to work on *The Final Hour*, a post-apocalyptic tale about savages surviving in a wasteland created by humankind's stupidity. Four months later, he'd completed an 80,000-word, full-length novel. But, while doing edits and rewrites, he'd grown to hate the manuscript. He thought its best use would be either as ass wipe or kindling for a bonfire. Focusing on the latter and more sanitary option, one drunken night, he actually tossed the manuscript into a raging blaze. The paperclip-bound pages landed on the edge of the fire, and just then a freak thunderstorm erupted. Looking at it as some kind of divine intervention of fate, he'd collected the manuscript, threw it in a file box, and tucked it up in the attic. Out of sight, out of mind.

Maybe *The Final Hour* wasn't the problem. Maybe it was the money. Financial stress, the root of all evil. While writing, his cash reserves had dwindled. First he was in the black. Then he was in the red. And as the colors changed, so did his moods. He kept second-guessing his talents, believing he never had any in the first place. *And how can you pretend to write a book if you can't even support yourself?*

Then he hit rock-bottom.

The money going out had far exceeded the money coming in. He refinanced his only material asset, the Prince Edward Island home, into a $120,000 line of credit, which now sat at $19,000 remaining. He was living on credit. This road would eventually dead-end. He'd crash into a concrete wall, or maybe crash and burn in the bonfire one night, whichever came first.

So he had a plan, however weak-minded it might be. He wanted to finish the beachfront clearing and slap a FOR SALE sign up. He had to try and bail himself out of his debt-ridden, alcoholic existence. He might scratch together fifty thousand dollars after legal fees, which would go toward a new-and-improved life in the DR. The beachfront clearing and beach access were key to getting a good buck for the property. Typically waterfront property rose at ten times the rate of rural real estate sans waterfront.

He sat silently, watching the fire, and felt the pain, emotional and physical. He felt dizzy and disoriented from the face-plant and his self-diagnosed torn rotator cuff ached.

The arm felt weak and he had even lost partial sensation in his two middle fingertips. *Gotta be a torn rotator cuff. Gotta be.* His calf stung from the bonfire barbecue and now even a rear upper molar was starting to smart. A Dominican dentist had done a root canal on it and fashioned a crown. The fucker must have missed a canal, he thought, gliding his tongue over a spongy, sensitive, probably infected gum.

Saul finished his beer, crushed the empty, and tossed it next to a log pile. He staggered to the cooler and grabbed another one. *Alpine number nine.* He cracked it open and took a deep pull, reflecting on the tooth. *I better get that looked at.* He had read somewhere that if left unchecked, gum infections could actually spread straight to the brain and kill a person—though documented cases of tooth infection death were pretty rare.

Lost in reflection, Saul sat still for a while, contemplating all the ways he might die. The sky grew black as the moon rose over the horizon, the stars twinkled, and the coyotes began to howl off in the distance. But Saul was oblivious, as his thoughts now turned to his emotional pain. It was all because of her, he thought. Wasn't love the root cause of all emotional pain?

After the usual tours of drunkenness and debauchery in the DR, he'd met twenty-nine-year-old Joella Rosario in a supermarket cafeteria. Although Joella had a basic command of English, Saul had a very good grasp of Spanish. Generally, they communicated in Spanish and the language barrier was practically non-existent. And in the beginning, it appeared there would be no barriers at all.

Joella was different than all the others. Timid, sensitive, quiet, honest, with a good sense of humor, and he believed she actually loved him. Her body was perfectly proportioned, Saul thought. Small, perky breasts and the most beautiful little ass he had ever laid eyes on—not to mention her long, slender legs. She had blemish-free mulatto skin, small facial features, a bright, infectious smile, and nice white teeth. And that she had three kids didn't bother Saul either, though he was childless.

She'd been a breath of fresh air. Being with her, every day had gotten better and better, with no arguments worthy of even mentioning. It had taken him four months, but he'd found the proverbial needle in the haystack, one of a small percentage of the women in the Puerto Plata area who wasn't a predator, didn't have a money agenda, and didn't have five foreigners simultaneously sending her money via Western Union. He had found the single most important thing in life, the thing that eluded so many. He had found true love. He should have been happy.

But no.

Like many things before the Joella relationship, he had fucked it up. Not royally, perhaps not irreparably, but fucked it up nonetheless. During their three-month intensely passionate and happy union, he'd lied to her, saying he was a prolific and commercially successful novelist, and was always working on a project or two. They talked about the future and how one day they could live together (the kid issue had not been factored into this equation) in near-perfect bliss and harmony, totally and happily in love. In the DR, of course.

He had left on a good note. But when he returned to PEI, the lies started pounding him like so many headshots from a mixed martial arts fighter. He felt guilty. Soon the guilt festered and infected his mind. What had started off as daily phone conversations slowed to once a week, once a month, and then nothing at all. The river of love ran dry, at least on his tributary. Her texts and calls went unanswered. And she, like any rational person, began to lose interest.

Her last text: *I know you don't love me anymore, if you ever did, because you won't even return my calls. I hope you enjoy your life and I'm sorry if I caused you any grief.*

That had been two weeks ago, and Saul couldn't even bring himself to respond. The phone had grown silent, at least as it concerned Joella communication. How could he face her after so many lies? He had told her initially he would be returning to the DR after two months, the amount of time it would take him to write another bestseller, take care of some unrelated business matters, and then it would be bye-bye Canada. Forever. But now it was two months and maybe a week, and aside from his physical injuries, increasing daily, he had leapt into a black alcoholic abyss of self-pity, depression, even self-loathing.

Wallowing in this emotional black hole, Saul retreated into the comfort of his imagination. At least he had that. He closed his eyes and began to drift off. He called up an image of Joella. She materialized, nude apart from a pink G-string, dancing around his bed in his DR apartment. Saul lay on the bed, grinning, knowing, waiting. The lighting was subtle and romantic. Gray with spears of yellow. The air conditioning hummed. The bedside candles flickered.

Bob Marley sang, *I wanna love you and treat you right; I wanna love you every day and every night; We'll be together with a roof right over our heads; We'll share the shelter of my single bed.*

Joella gyrated, raising her arms in the air, snapping her fingers, her perky breasts bouncing in flawless harmony with the beat, shaking her impeccable derriere rhythmically like only Dominican women could do. Saul was becoming more aroused by the second. It was the best day of his life, bar none.

He dozed off and the mental image transformed into a bizarre dream. Joella was dancing, inching closer to the bed, then retreating at the last second, just out of reach. Saul was pleading: "Come here...I wanna love ya." This went on for a few minutes before the landscape changed. Joella vanished and another woman appeared—a Russian seductress, clad in black dominatrix boots, panties, and a matching black vinyl bra that barely concealed voluptuous breasts. She held a whip and flicked it teasingly at Saul as he lay...*Where? The same bed, the same apartment?* The dream fast-forwarded and transformed into a love affair montage. He and the dominatrix were doing things together: taking walks in the park, having wild sex, whispering sweet nothings to each other, the whole gamut. Then a giant gloved military hand appeared, snatching them away, taking them into protective custody. A steely-eyed general announced the end of the world, but promised to deliver them to salvation. They were on a large ship in a swelling sea. It overturned and left Saul and the nameless Russian woman floating helplessly in the ocean, clinging to a flotation device. Small, smiling children on canoes appeared and started shooting arrows at them. They were somehow rescued again and suddenly on the streets of a large city. Massive explosions penetrated the sky and a brilliant fireworks display began destroying multiple buildings, a vividly spectacular display of death and destruction.

It was the heat from the explosions that Saul first became cognizant of. It started at his leg, then raced up and flashed through his entire body and into his head, causing multiple, intense hot flashes. He opened his eyes and saw red. He felt intense, searing heat, and smelled the sweet smell of burning flesh. His flesh.

He screamed in agony. And as he pounded out the flames licking up his body, a lone thought entered his troubled mind: *Maybe it's a good day to die.*

Chapter Two

San Marcos is a dangerous barrio of Puerto Plata, Dominican Republic. It's dusty and full of noise pollution, shantytown shacks, beggars, petty thieves, murderers, and all manner of con artists. To some it's a ghetto. To others it's one of the most impoverished barrios in a third-world country. To some it's a vibrant community with friendly, hard-working people, plenty of lively bars, beautiful women, and a great place to party late into the night.

Still others might say it's just a shithole and always will be.

But to Joella Rosaria, it was home. On a noisy street, in the thick of the barrio, somewhere up on a hill, she shared a one-floor, three-bedroom bare-bones house with eleven others: her three kids, Evelyn, 12; Jennifer, 8; and Carlos, 6; her two sisters, Gisella, 32; Isabella, 31; her brother John, 24; and the assorted offspring of her siblings.

Privacy wasn't an issue.

It wasn't possible.

Sheer blinds draped over door openings separated the rooms; even the bathroom had an almost translucent curtain, a damp moldy smell, a cracked and uneven concrete floor, and a dark feeling of decay and misery. The house was plagued by frequent power outages and no running water, let alone hot water. Water was gathered in rain barrels that supplied cooking, laundry, shower, and toilet. Flushing meant dumping buckets of water in the toilet bowl. Forget about internet, although they did have a television, with two hundred plus channels, connected to Puerto Plata cable. But that was perhaps the only luxury the family had.

Twelve inhabitants meant four to a bedroom, crammed into double beds and on haphazardly scattered blankets and mattresses cluttering the tiny bedroom floor space.

Joella awoke that morning (July 2, at precisely 6:55 am) with a heavy heart, an uneasy sense of impending doom, and an unpleasant stinging pain in her ear. Little Carlos, on his way to the bathroom, had accidently kicked his mother in the ear. If he hadn't, Joella might have had the luxury of another hour or two of much-needed sleep. But long ago she'd given up the small double bed, opting for an old mattress on the floor so her three children might have a more comfortable sleep.

She frowned at the bare back of her little boy as he flung open the curtain on his way to the bathroom. "Carlos, please watch where you're going," she said in Spanish. "You kicked me."

The boy turned his head, eyeing her with a mischievous grin. "Why don't you sleep closer to the wall?"

"Why don't you show some respect for your elders," she said as he disappeared into the bathroom.

"I want some milk," Carlos called to her from behind the curtain. "And I'm hungry."

Joella got up, grimacing as she briefly eyed the squeaking ceiling fan, and looked at her two daughters. Jennifer slept on her stomach, her head tilted to the right, a thin blanket covering part of her face. Evelyn slept in the fetal position. She stretched, opened her eyes slowly, smiled at her mother, and closed them again.

Joella smiled. "Don't worry, honey, you have a few more hours before school. You can sleep."

Evelyn slowly opened her eyes. "Thanks."

Joella went to the kitchen and made coffee, then went into the living room and sat on the couch. She took a few sips and reached for her smartphone, a gift from Saul. She quickly checked it for messages and lowered her head when she saw none. She stared at Saul's face, the wallpaper of her phone, and contemplated deleting it. *But to delete it would be to delete him. I can't do that.* She refocused on Saul's image. Smiling amicably, he stood in the kitchen of his rented Costambar apartment, holding up a foam cup containing a rum and Coke mix. She studied the brown eyes and was sure she saw adoration in those eyes, a sort of twinkle and intensity that could only be love. Sure, he had a bit of a beer belly, but could hardly be considered fat. In her eyes, his tousled gray-black hair and distinctive facial features gave him a kind of George Clooney look. Other people might not think so, but beauty was in the eye of the beholder.

She thought of calling him, though he might still be sleeping. She didn't want to wake him. Yet a nagging feeling of impending doom told her she should call him. After debating it for a few minutes, she speed-dialed him. To the rolling thunder of speeding motorcycles, bodies stirring and moving about the house, dogs barking and roosters crowing, she left a voice message: "Honey, I know you don't want me or love me anymore, but I'm worried about you. Please at least let me know you're okay. I had a bad dream about you last night. Something is terribly wrong, I just know it...

anyway, take care." She was about to click END CALL, but on impulse added, "I love you" before hanging up.

Joella rubbed a moist left eye with her right hand and thought about the dream. In it, she had been dancing topless for Saul, something she knew he loved, when a figure with a venomous red face, big black and red eyes, a serpent-like tongue, and evil grin with large fang-like teeth, surrounded Saul. "No, no, no," she had screamed, but to no avail. The beast cackled with laughter and Saul burst into flames and vanished—spontaneous human combustion. She had abruptly woken up, sweat-soaked, more from the nightmare than the intense summer heat. Her heart was pounding furiously in her chest. The feeling of impending danger lanced her heart like a spear penetrating a wild boar. She had never had a premonition dream. Didn't understand it. But of this she was dead certain. Saul was on a path of destruction, both by his own actions and the actions of some unspeakable evil she dared not give voice to, for fear it would endanger her and her children.

"You are the Devil," Carlos said, stepping out of the bathroom and heading for the fridge.

Like a rabbit sensing a predatory coyote nearby, Joella recoiled and snapped out of her dark reflection. "What?"

"Nothing, Mom. I want to eat. Make me some food."

Of her three children, Carlos was the most demanding and least appreciative. The children shared the same father, Elido, Joella's one and only boyfriend and husband before Saul. But where the girls showed respect for father and mother, this trait was evidently missing from Carlos's DNA. If he didn't get the proper guidance—or perhaps even if he did—Joella knew on some level that he could turn into a real monster.

If he hadn't already.

"Don't you have the word 'please' in your vocabulary?" she said, getting up and approaching the little boy.

Carlos ignored the comment and stretched his arms out. "I want a hug."

Joella obliged perfunctorily. "I'll fix you some breakfast. Then you can get ready for school."

Carlos pouted. "I don't want to go to school."

Joella started to speak but just then her elder sister Gisella entered the room and glared at Carlos with steely eyes. "You do what your mother says, young man, or I'll smack your face so hard you won't even remember your name anymore."

For a second, Carlos stared at Gisella, his brow furrowing, his hands balling into fists.

"Sit down, shut your mouth, and wait for your breakfast," Gisella said, raising an open-palmed hand. "And don't even think about giving me that look."

Carlos dropped his gaze, said nothing, and sat obediently at the kitchen table. He bent his head, stared at the kitchen table, and sulked.

Two hours later, Joella had prepared the children breakfast—rice, beans, chicken, and salad—gotten them off to school, showered, and walked down the sweltering hot, sunlit street in search of a motorcycle taxi, motoconcho as they were known, to take her to university. She was in the third year of a nursing degree program and had decided to take a few summer school classes to give her a leg up when she started back full-time in August.

It didn't take her long to find a ride. Fifteen minutes later, she was outside the campus, a few blocks from Costambar, where Saul used to live. Just being there brought back memories of their happy but short-lived union. Joella struggled to prevent darkness from getting a debilitating grip on her heart. With an effort, she plied the tight grip of darkness loose.

An elderly Haitian man walked past, leading a donkey, a makeshift cart overflowing with coconuts holstered to the animal. Squeaky wheels made steady but slow progress. The man smiled and waved. Joella did the same.

Another young Dominican man pushing a wheelbarrow full of empty beer bottles ambled past. Motoconchos honked horns as he crossed the street. Dogs parked, one yappy Chihuahua starting after the man. He picked up an empty bottle from the wheelbarrow and waved it angrily at the dog, shouting Spanish obscenities. It ran off.

A classmate, Monica Morales, sat on the stairs of the Universidad Autónoma de Santo Domingo (UASD). Spotting Joella, she smiled brightly and waved. Monica's long black hair was tied back in a ponytail. She wore flesh-molded red shorts and a low-cut white blouse. Large breasts pushed out, exposing plenty of cleavage, as if wanting to be unleashed. Joella still had a few minutes before class, so she sat down on the entrance steps beside Monica, although unsure how to take this woman who seemed to have such an unorthodox—or maybe here it was orthodox—opinion on how to get ahead in life. A few days ago, Monica had told

Joella she had met a middle-aged Canadian in Costambar, fucked his brains out, and had been rewarded with 2,000 pesos. But that was only the beginning. Monica had lured him with the promise of a relationship and was receiving a monthly allowance. She had two such foreign boyfriends who had left the country and sent money every month. She was trying to school Joella in what she called "the ways of the world."

After the cursory greetings, Monica focused intent black eyes on Joella. "Have you heard from Saul yet?"

"No," Joella said, looking away.

"I'll tell you how to get him back."

Joella knew all about the predatory nature of many Puerto Plata women. Even her sister Gisella had tried to brainwash her once, urging her to ask Saul for money to buy her a house and car. House and car? The relationship was only a few months old, and already she was supposed to be asking for a house and car? After a long lecture, Joella, her economic situation desperate, had been oh-so-close to complying. Cuddling in bed one night with Saul, she had stopped herself moments before making the suggestion, realizing finally how ridiculous it was, how predatory it would sound, and how it would certainly lower her esteem immensely in his eyes. But desperation does strange things to people. Particularly when they have four mouths to feed. *But I asked him for money for books. Now he won't talk to me. But I need the books, and have no money to buy them. Doesn't matter. You messed it up, girl. Messed it up big-time.*

She looked at Monica sadly. "I don't think you'll tell me anything new."

"He likes your daughter, Evelyn, right? Isn't she like a daughter to him?"

"Told me he loves her. Told her that. And she loves him to death."

"That's what you want to play with. His emotions. Men are so stupid when it comes to that. They can't control their emotions any more than they can control the pecker in their pants. Does he answer your calls yet?"

Joella shook her head.

"Well, leave a message. Tell him Evelyn is sick in the hospital and urgently needs to speak to him. Tell him to call at eight during visiting hours. When he does—and he will, trust me—say she's sleeping, but needs her appendix removed and ten thousand pesos will fix the problem. Say she's in a lot of pain, suffering terribly."

"He's not going to fall for that. Everyone does that. And I'm not going to lie for the sake of money."

"But would you tell a white lie to get him back?"

"What do you mean?"

"You could leave a message that Evelyn is sick, and when he calls back, tell him you just said that because it was the only thing you could think of to get him to talk to you."

Joella wanted to believe she'd never even entertain such an idea. But hadn't things changed? Her gut said Saul was in danger. If she really loved him, wouldn't she do anything to save his life, even tell a white lie?

She pushed the thought away, telling herself deceit was never justifiable. Yet she wasn't sure. Was it, at least in this case? Before she could decide, a black pickup truck rolled in front of the university and stopped.

Two beer-toting gringos waved to them.

"That's Rick driving, the guy I told you about," Monica said, pulling Joella's arm. "Come on, let's go with them."

"Are you kidding? We have class."

"Who cares," Monica said, striking a pose, adjusting her cleavage. "These guys will get you ahead in life faster than some stupid education. And faster than your deadbeat ex. Come on, Joella. Let's go have some fun."

"Hey Monica," said Rick. "Bring your hot friend. My buddy wants to meet her."

"Let's go," Monica said. She wouldn't let go of Joella's arm. "I need you. It'll be fun."

Joella struggled and finally yanked her arm free, almost dropping her books. "No, I'm not going." She turned and started walking up the stairs.

"You think you can find true love with one gringo? You're sadly mistaken, girl," Monica said. "You have to love them all."

Joella glanced back at Monica, who ran to the waiting vehicle. "Be careful, that's all I can say," she called after her. She doubted Monica had heard her, and even if she had, the woman wouldn't listen. That wasn't the first story Joella had heard from Monica. A few others involved multiple, drunk male sex partners. She not only loved exploiting foreigners for money. She loved sex—hard, fast, and often. She was flying by the seat of her pants, and in a few hours probably wouldn't be wearing any.

Joella hurried down the hall and entered class. She was a few minutes late and it had already begun. Heads turned and followed her. The female instructor stopped talking.

Joella sat.

Fernando Rodriguez, two seats in front of her, turned around, ran his tongue across his lips, grinned, and eyed Joella's breasts. He had been asking her out ever since Saul had stopped returning her calls, but she wanted nothing to do with him. She had flatly refused his solicitations three times. He had bad breath, body odor, rotten teeth, and a lecherous attitude that suggested he wanted nothing more than to sample Joella's attractive assets, then spit her out like the unwanted pit of a sweet mango. How he had found out that she and Saul were splits was anybody's guess. Probably Monica, Joella thought, opening her textbook and focusing on the teacher's words.

Bur it wasn't the teacher's words that she heard. It was Saul's pleas for help: "Help me, somebody help me, for fuck sakes, I'm burning up."

Save him, Joella thought. *Please, God, save him!*

Chapter Three

"God save me," Saul shouted, but quickly realized where he was, and that no one could hear him. He had passed out drunk in front of the fire last night, leaned forward, and pitched himself into it. Luckily, the chair had tilted slightly to the left and he hadn't face-planted directly into the blaze. Instead, he'd landed on his shoulder, just on the left boundary of hot ash and not into fanning flames. But the hot embers quickly began singeing his long-sleeved shirt. Soon it burst into flames. Again, it was the pain, and the smell of burning flesh mixed with burning clothing that made him open his eyes abruptly and stare straight at the flames licking up his shirtsleeve.

Yelling and screaming in panic mode, he rolled around in the dirt. It wasn't long before he extinguished the flames. He got to his feet. Still smarting from burns, he grabbed his work gloves and patted his smoldering arm down some more until the smoke dissipated.

But for a full, glowing moon and a shock of brilliant white dots, it was a black dawn.

Saul fumbled around in the darkness, found his flashlight, and pointed it at the fire. The chair burst into flames with a whooshing sound. "Shit... I keep this up, I'm never gonna get outta here." He found his keys on a log table, flashed the beam at the truck, and approached. It wasn't until he got in the vehicle and started it that he noticed how badly his pants were ripped. *Wait a minute...that's not a fire burn.* Starting from just below the belt, his jeans were shredded all the way down to the cuff. Panicking, he grabbed the flashlight and shone it at his shredded pants. He gently lifted away a piece of blue jean material and noticed claw marks starting at his ankle and stretching to just a few inches from his groin. The marks were crusted with blood, but tiny red rivulets still spider-webbed down his leg.

Suddenly he heard a loud guttural growl, the kind a vicious guard dog makes when it means business. Hands trembling, he slammed the truck into drive and floored it. Spinning tires and weaving down the windy road, he hightailed it back to the house. He had no idea what kind of animal—or monster—would attack him in the middle of the night and rake claws down his legs. Based on the claw marks, he was pretty damn sure it wasn't a coyote. This injury appeared to be the mark of a larger animal. With larger claws.

It was almost two hours later that Saul's hands stopped trembling. After a cold and painful shower, he had disinfected his burns with rubbing alcohol and peroxide, and used three tubes of topical antibiotic on the worst burns, the blistering patches. He also disinfected and applied bandages over the two-inch cut above his right eye. It didn't look deep enough to require stitches. He wasn't a doctor, but he suspected—at least hoped—he wouldn't need medical attention for the burns. A Google image search of first and second-degree burns satisfied him to some extent that most of his were first-degree.

Either way, he had no intention of going to a hospital, not now or anytime soon. Sometimes, he wasn't even sure he wanted to live anymore, never mind seek medical attention.

Sleeping was another problem. Every which way he turned brought fresh pain. His mind kept conjuring up images of a ferocious beast that now had his scent and would soon come crashing through the door and kill him. At every little creak of the old house or sudden gust of wind, he would bolt upright in bed and nervously shine a flashlight around in the darkness.

By the time he did fall asleep, the sun was coming up.

******

Opening sleepy eyes, Saul glanced around the room. Unfamiliar. *Where am I?* A double bed. On PEI he had a queen. He saw a flat-screen TV mounted on a whitewashed wall. A lampless bedside table. A whirring ceiling fan. An old, wall-mounted air conditioner. A built-in closet. A wooden vanity dresser, an assortment of neatly arranged toiletries. A bathroom door ajar, spears of sunlight poking into the room from a small window.

Rubbing tired, hungover eyes, he sat up, feeling his heart rate quicken and his head begin to beat to the tune of its own painful drum. A pounding headache, pain intensifying with each pulsating blow. *Where the fuck am I?*

A rooster crowed. He ran an unsteady hand over his right eye. No cut. *What?* Adrenaline took over, dulling the headache. He jumped out of bed, opened the bedroom door, and entered a small, bare-bones kitchen. He slid the curtain away from the sliding-glass door and peered outside. Bright sunlight assaulted his eyes and it took a moment for them to adjust. When they did, he saw a balcony, a few chairs, and a plastic table with an empty rum bottle on it. Below, a pool. Dominican children were playing in the water, smiling, laughing, and screaming.

Dominican children. I'm in the DR. My old apartment.

He closed the curtain. Returning to the bedroom, he stopped and examined his legs. Nothing. No burns. No claw marks. A dream, nothing more. But no—this felt too eerily real.

A smartphone on the vanity beeped. He whirled around, slipping on white ceramic tiles. He stumbled toward the vanity, grabbing it with both hands to steady himself. His right shoulder throbbed with pain and the drumbeat in his head commenced a second set. The room swelled with waves, rolled, and tumbled. He closed his eyes for a moment, fought an urge to puke his guts out, then opened them. The swelling waves diminished to a ripple. It would have to do. He picked up the phone and read the text message:

Nothing, nothing, nothing, nothing, no, no, no, no, no....Yahieeeee, yahieeeee!

Recollection slammed him like a freight train. Clenching the phone in both hands, he reeled back and dropped onto the bed, trying to digest the information. The message was from a woman named Monica, who he'd met during his stay in the DR. She'd turned into a stalker. Judging by the last message, she had also turned suicidal. Without realizing, he said aloud: "That fucking woman is suicidal."

When he'd first met Monica at a Puerto Plata bar, Saul was totally pie-eyed and remembered little. But he did remember the hungover morning after—he remembered it verbatim. Waking up beside a nude, slender, big-breasted woman, his first thoughts were: *What happened? Who is she?*

Saul sank into the memory like it was happening for the first time.

*****

"Where did I meet you?" he said.

"Raffi's."

"How old are you?"

"Twenty."

"What's your name?"

"Monica."

Goosebumps crawled up his spine. He got out of bed and opened the bedroom door. Morning light flooded into the kitchen through the sliding-glass door. He grabbed his pants and checked for his money and cell phone, sighing in relief when he found both intact. He surveyed the scene in the kitchen. The counter was littered with plastic and paper cups, some containing rum and Coke remnants. He closed the kitchen curtains. Too much light. Re-entering the bedroom, he scooped up two soiled condoms and wrappers, deposited them into the bathroom wastebasket, and turned toward the bed. He wanted to get rid of Monica, but as gently as possible.

But she wasn't on the bed. She was rummaging through his dresser drawers. She pulled out a phone and looked at him, childlike and quizzical. "You have a spare phone."

"Yes," he said, gently removing it from her hand and placing it on the dresser.

A knock on the door. Saul went into the kitchen, peered through the curtains of the sliding-glass door, and his heart almost skipped a beat. In his mind's eye, he saw Joella. Hurt. Crying. How could that be? He'd met Joella months after the ordeal with Monica. But somehow, in this surreal state of reality, events of the distant past were merging with events of the recent past. Events of the memory of Monica were fusing with his memory of Joella.

It was only Angie, the cleaning lady, wanting to know if she could do her twice-weekly routine. "Give me a few minutes," Saul said, swinging around.

Monica was sitting at his kitchen table, playing with his computer, going through some files. She touched buttons at random, trying to figure out how to work it. Multiple windows were open and the computer had started beeping, as if she were hitting the same command repeatedly.

"Please," Saul said, "don't touch my computer."

"Why not? I want to listen to music and go on Facebook."

"Later, maybe." He gently took her hand and led her into the bedroom. He told her to get dressed, although his still throbbing member clearly had a different plan.

A few minutes later, they were swimming in the pool of nearby Toucan Two, thanks to his buddy Marlon, who'd luckily answered the phone and left the main gate open. Saul needed the swim to clear his head, to wash away the night's alcohol abuse and debauchery.

Monica loved the water and splashed around playfully like a child. The sky was blue and cloudless, the weather hot and muggy.

Saul's plan was to have a short swim with her, maybe return to the apartment for another sex session, pay her, and get rid of her. They played in the water for fifteen minutes, then retreated to the bed-style patio chairs in the shade.

"I'm hungry," Monica said, before long. "And thirsty."

There was a mini-market a half block away, so Saul handed her 500 pesos, told her to pick up some Coke, a few beers, and whatever she wanted to eat.

She returned with a half-empty bag of Doritos that Saul suddenly realized had probably come from his apartment. She also carried a bag containing beer and Coke. "Where did you get those?" he said, pointing to the Doritos.

"You bought them for me last night. I left them in your apartment."

Goosebumps crawled up Saul's spine. *I need to get rid of her. And fast.*

Then the phone rang. It was Edwardo, Saul's landlord. "Listen," he said in perfect English, "There was a woman wandering through your apartment while Angie was cleaning and I thought I'd let you know. If she's your girlfriend please let me know so I won't get in her way. But this girl, I've never seen her before."

Saul thanked him for being security-conscious, told him it wouldn't happen again, and hung up, not entirely pleased with the way things were turning out. After a half hour of swimming, and some conversation with Monica, Saul began to understand a few things. For one thing, Monica had an extremely limited vocabulary, and didn't seem to know right from wrong. And the way she ate the chips. Crumbs stuck to her lips and chin, covering her bra and panties, littering the ceramic tile all around her. Like a Neanderthal. Or maybe just gut-poor and starving. Or maybe it was all part of the game, all part of the con.

She went to the store twice more, once for water and another time to satisfy a craving for cheese. Both times she had returned with his exact change. Now, an open bottle of water and an open bottle of beer, both untouched, sat beside her on a small, round table, along with the chunk of cheddar cheese, also still in its wrapping and uneaten. Was this woman a thief, a con artist or just a little mentally unstable? Saul believed the latter, but either way it was time to be done with her. She still had a few articles of clothing at his apartment, so the plan was to return there, gather her things, pay her, and get rid of her. Fuck the fuck session. Things were getting a little too weird. He also wanted to check the apartment to make sure she hadn't robbed him.

But when they arrived at his apartment, she started filling pots with water, pulling out pasta and sauce, and cooking.

Saul put a gentle hand on her. "No," he said. "I'm tired and I need to sleep. I'm gonna give you some money and call a motoconcho. You need to go. Now."

Her eyes became sad. "No. You told me last night you wanted me as your girlfriend. And I accepted. We're a couple now."

Saul's aching head spun as he searched for a way out. "Listen, you have to go now. I don't want any problems here."

"No," she said defiantly, plunking her wet, panty-clad ass on a chair. "I'm not leaving."

"Listen," Saul said, trying a different tact. "How about this?" He extracted 1,500 pesos from his pocket and put it in her hand. "If you go now, give me a couple hours sleep, I'll call you tonight. How's that?"

Monica's crinkled brow straightened and a small smile pursed her pouty lips. "You'll call me later? But you don't have my number."

He quickly took her number, dialed her when she insisted on confirmation that it wasn't fake, and saw her phone illuminate and ring. She entered the number into her contact list and agreed to leave. A few minutes later, Saul kissed her goodbye and watched her shapely ass turn into a little red dot as the motoconcho sped away.

******

He stepped out of the memory and into the present of what he was still trying to convince himself was a dream. His hands still tightly clenched the phone. He set it down on the bedside table, wiping away beads of sweat sprouting on his forehead. *This feels nothing like a dream. It feels too real...* He pinched himself. It hurt. "Oww."

Nothing changed.

Is this a dream? Or was that animal attack at my waterfront a dream?

Dumbfounded, Saul let his eyes wander around the room for some time, looking for answers. There were none to be found. He closed his eyes for a few seconds and reopened them. The same room, the same dust-sprinkled spears of light poking in from the bathroom. He sighed. *I'm stuck back in time. I'm fucked.*

He went into the kitchen and made some coffee. When it finished percolating, he filled a cup, lit a smoke, and went out to the second-floor balcony, listening to the incessant crowing of roosters.

The sky suddenly turned gray, and then a fiery red color. *What the fuck is happening?* The crowing of the roosters grew more intense, slowly becoming a cacophony—ear-splittingly loud. Putting his hands to his hears, he winced as the agonizing drumbeat in his head resumed—*Boom-boom-boom-cock-a-doodle-do-boom-boom-cock-a-doodle-do!*

I'm losing my mind. He crushed out his smoke and spilled his coffee on the way inside. He retreated to the bedroom, slammed the door shut, and curled up in a fetal position. He covered his ears, wondering if he might actually be dead. His heart raced. *That's why I can't wake up. Yer dead, cowboy. Lights out.*

"No, no, no," he shouted. "Nooooooooooooooo..."

******

Then he did wake up, his t-shirt and underwear drenched in sweat, the pain of burn blisters clinging to his clothing reminding him grimly of last night. But there was some other stain on his shirt. "What the fuck," he said, realizing with terror that it was a coffee stain. "Where the fuck did that come from?"

It took a cold shower, another disinfecting and dressing of the injuries, and a cigarette and a coffee before he could bring himself to think about the dream. For now, he wasn't ready to address the coffee stain. He sat on his porch, smoking, drinking coffee and thinking.

The frightening experience with Monica was something that had really happened to him in the DR. He recalled the night it had all started, the night and the morning after, so vivid and real in the nightmare. About two hours after Monica had left that day—sometime in February, if memory served—Saul had received about fifty calls and about thirty blank texts from her, with only a date and time stamp. All of them went unanswered.

The next day there were more text messages intermingled with blanks: *Call me... I miss you... How are you, my love?... Why don't you answer?... I want to see you today.*

At least she had figured out how to text.

Saul had initially thought he should just answer the phone and tell her he had a girlfriend, but in the end figured it wouldn't do any good. This woman wasn't processing information normally. So he had sent one text message: *I'm busy right now and can't see you*, then entered her number into Mr. Number, a call-blocking app. Several calls were blocked. When she tried calling him from a different number, he promptly blocked that one too. While the app effectively blocked calls and texts, it also stored them, allowing the user to view the quantity of blocked calls and the quantity and content of blocked texts. It was this feature that allowed Saul to realize that in only two weeks, Monica had called and texted him nearly 500 times. He had started to think maybe she would call the cops eventually and claim rape or something. *Is this a money extortion scheme? Is she really twenty? What if she's underage? Is she gonna show up one day with a butcher knife? With the cops?*

While he felt afraid, part of him actually felt sorry for Monica. Was it really her fault? It was her mother, the bartender later said, who'd introduced her to Saul at Raffi's that night. How many times had he heard that story? Mothers and fathers (or in some cases, even older brothers and sisters) introducing their children to gringos, peddling them into prostitution, exploiting them, oftentimes long before they reached the legal age of eighteen.

Given her perceived state of mental incapacitation, she likely just didn't know any better. And in many ways, she was also doing it out of economic necessity. Saul was probably her first trick. Unaware of any of this in his shitfaced condition, Saul had agreed to take her home for the night. He felt a pang of sympathy and guilt curl up in his stomach. She probably had the mentality of a ten-year-old, and instead of seeking help for her daughter, her mother had exploited her. And Saul, in many ways, had facilitated this exploitation.

Saul scratched his head. He listened to the birds chirp and felt the hot mid-afternoon sun beat down on his face. Gazing out at his well-manicured lawn, bordered by natural green of the surrounding forest, some things started to become clear. Monica's attempts at securing him as a boyfriend, even dropping by unannounced a half dozen times or more, were likely born of desperation. Look at how she ate. She'd been starving.

Thankfully Marlon, Saul's middle-aged Canadian expat friend, had bailed him out. Seeing Saul's increasing anxiety over Monica's persistent stalking, Marlon had one day answered one of Monica's calls. He had a conversation with her, raising his voice angrily at times, and told her in no uncertain terms that if she continued calling, there would be big problems and cops involved. Marlon, as a result of frequent pay-offs, had a few officials, many of them cops, in his back pocket. And that was that. The calls ended, fortunately before Saul had met and started dating Joella.

The ringing of Saul's phone startled him. He checked the incoming number. Joella. He rubbed his aching head and stared at the phone as if it were a rabies-infected monster.

Should I or shouldn't I?

Chapter Four

Some of his friends called him Ricky Ticky Talky for obvious reasons. Others called him Rick the Prick, or just Prick for short, the reasons perhaps not so obvious. A sixty-something Canadian expat living in the DR permanently, Rick Dobson had the habit of using his prick quite often around the Puerto Plata area. He was a whoremonger, and often bragged about his conquests. A retired police captain, he could also be an ornery son of a bitch when drunk; hence, the double meaning of the moniker Prick.

It was early evening in Puerto Plata. He sat at a caseta on the malecón, drinking beer. He was pretty drunk. So was his buddy Mark Poloney, who sat beside him. Middle-aged Mark had just arrived yesterday from Toronto and only had two weeks in the Caribbean before he would return to his job as a streets maintenance worker. He wanted to make the best of his time here. Mark's friends called him Bark, because when he got angry—which lately seemed to be more often than not—the spittle-coated words spewing from his mouth sounded more like a barking dog than anything resembling the English language. Some combined his first name and surname, calling him Bark Baloney. As foreman of a streets maintenance crew in Toronto (the crew also affectionately called him Foreskin, but never to his face), Mark loved barking out orders. To him, control was a pretty big deal.

Monica Morales and Cathy Ortiz, a barely legal hooker friend of Monica's, sat at the gentlemen's table, smiling at all the right times and drinking one of the most expensive drinks on the menu—strawberry margaritas.

Earlier, Rick and Mark had taken the women to a cabana in Puerto Plata and rented the presidential suite—accessorized with Jacuzzi, gigantic round bed, disco light, surround-sound stereo, and striptease pole. These cabanas catered to illicit affairs and all manner of discreet sexual encounters. Dozens of such establishments dotted the Puerto Plata landscape.

Debauchery ensued. The women performed admirably. Two hours later, when the men were about to drop them off at a street corner near the university, they'd changed their minds, largely due to Monica's coaxing. Gliding her tongue teasingly across her pouting upper lip, she suggested that round two would be much more stimulating should they decide to gratify their libidos later that evening.

What the fuck, we can take them for drinks, and if they piss us off, dispose of them like yesterday's trash, Rick thought.

"Waitress," Mark shouted, holding up an empty beer bottle and squinting as he often did when demanding attention. "We need more beer over here."

Rick also held up a hand and pointed to a table littered with empties. But the tiny caseta was packed, and the only waitress was busy. She stood at another table, listening to the largely incomprehensible come-on of an old, balding, fat, shitfaced foreigner.

Monica stood. She knew a few English phrases—probably more than she let on—and her male company knew barely any Spanish. "I do it," she said, pointing to the bartender. "I get bartender."

Mark uttered a low, guttural growl. "They need more staff here. What the fuck is going on?"

"Get used to it, buddy," Rick said. "It's the DR, not Canada."

Monica held up a hand. "Don't worry, be happy. I do." Before they could respond, she was already at the bar, ordering drinks: two Bohemia grandes for the men, a pair of margaritas, and just because she could, a Presidente grande for the lovely and efficient bartender.

Shaking her tight little booty, she delivered the drinks in two trips. She paused to pour the men's beers into glasses, offering them extraordinary views of her ample cleavage. She finished and sat down. "Where is me tip? Propina?"

"I'll give you a tip," Rick said, pointing to his crotch. "A big fucking prick in your mouth."

Monica grinned and licked her lips. "To your casa. Now."

Cathy laughed, cocked a neatly trimmed eyebrow, and gave them a look. *Let's go*, it said. *You won't regret it.*

"In a minute," Rick said. "In a minute. I'm almost ready for a bottle of rum. Then we go."

Cathy held up her drink. "Salud."

"To your health," Rick said. "You're gonna need it when I finish with you. I'm gonna fuck you so hard it's gonna hurt."

Mark grinned, gooned. He turned to Rick. "How many years did you say you've lived here?"

"Seven."

"That's a long time. Ever consider moving back to Canada?"

"What the fuck for? Too many laws and regulations there, and this comes from a former cop, don't forget. Do you think we could do this in Canada without someone thinking we're a couple of perverts, maybe even pedophiles? Not to mention the price. Hell, hookers in Canada want three hundred dollars an hour, not thirty-five dollars a whole fucking night. Anyone ever told ya you can't buy love, they're full of shit. You can down here."

"We paid these girls seventy bucks each."

"Yeah well, they're worth it. Wouldn't you say?"

A panhandler with a wretchedly deformed and infected leg limped spasmodically to the table. He pointed to the injured leg and held out his hand. Everyone at the table looked at him.

"We got no money for you," Rick said, waving him away indifferently.

The man scowled and limped over to another table.

"Well, wouldn't you?" Rick said.

Mark nodded. "They *were* worth it."

"Well, you have to be careful with some of them," Rick said. "I've seen some of them start off at, say, a thousand pesos, and then when you're done start demanding more. Worse, I had one bitch ask for twenty thousand pesos one time. She said her son was sick and needed some operation. Wanted to be my girlfriend, move in with me—all kinds of shit."

"What did you do?"

"Paid her for her services, kicked her out, and never called her again."

"I heard about shit like that."

"You ain't heard shit. You haven't been here long enough. Every time you think you got them figured out, they invent a new scam."

"I've heard a few stories."

"Have you heard this one? Some lame-brained Canadian—I don't know, the guy must have had some serious self-esteem problems or something—he used to come here every winter for four to six months. Anyway, he's leery as hell about the women around here, okay? For months wouldn't even go near a hooker, after some bad experiences. One girl stalked him for months after a one-night stand, standing outside his apartment with her pimp, serenading him and shit. He finally gets rid of her, and next thing he knows he's dragging home two fat Haitian women while shitfaced one night. The women get up in the morning, clear out his cupboards and fridge, steal his camera and phone, then demand more money."

"Did he give it to them?"

"Yeah, they threatened to call the cops, claim rape. He got scared and flipped them—I don't know, maybe another two thousand pesos each or something. Then in an unrelated incident, one crazy hooker performs like a sack of potatoes, demands three thousand pesos, eats him out of house and home—I mean, this bitch left a mess—and then relaxes on his couch all night watching James Bond movies. He was too afraid to kick her out so he sat up all night watching her watch movies."

"Three strikes yer out, right?"

"Well that's what you'd think. But it gets better—or he gets stupider, depending on how you look at it."

Mark lit a cigar and puffed out a blue plume of smoke that slowly rose and dissipated. "I'm waiting for the punchline."

The women had either become bored with the story, or simply couldn't understand it, and fidgeted with their smartphones.

Rick gulped his beer and plopped the bottle on the table. The waitress finally came over, cleared the empties and butt-stuffed ashtray, and returned with a fresh ashtray.

"I'm not sure you're gonna like it," Rick said.

"It'll be an education."

"Well, this guy—Rod, I think his name was—finally hooks up with the worst hooker in Costambar. I mean, everything that comes out of this bitch's mouth is pure garbage. But she's good at what she does, maybe so-so looking at best. I'll bet she has maybe a dozen guys sending her money from different parts of the world. Anyway, that's an aside. She hooks him in and moves into his apartment in short order. They have a few spats. Out she goes. He gets drunk, in she goes, that sort of thing. Long story short, one night she shows up at his apartment hammered—and man, could she pound the rum back—starts muttering some incomprehensible Voodoo chant and paints sideways crosses above every opening... I mean windows, doors, the whole nine yards. Then she gets a bowl with water and herbs, puts it under the bed, kneels down and continues with this ritualistic chant. He doesn't know what to do, so he lets her sleep on the couch. He sleeps in the bedroom and kicks her out the next morning when she's sober. I guess she has a car, and he didn't want her driving drunk for fear she might kill herself and then he'd have it hanging on him."

"Did she leave without a problem? Or the punchline is she killed him?"

"No, she left without a problem, but it gets better. A week later she's back. They're in love again. How the fuck can anyone fall in love with a mainstream bloodsucking hooker? Anyway, everything's bliss for the next week. Finally he goes back to Canada. A week later, he fucks up his back. Then he sprains his ankle badly. Then some teeth get infected and he gets oral surgery to fix them. He starts on all kinds of painkillers, but they do fuck all. So he medicates himself with alcohol. Turns into a complete piss-tank..."

The waitress returned and Rick ordered a 26-ounce bottle of Brugal rum, two bottles of Coke, ice, and two more drinks for the ladies.

"Anyway, where was I?" Rick asked.

"Piss-tank."

"Right... now everyone's starting to think this bitch put some Voodoo spell on him. I don't believe in any of that shit myself, but I *am* starting to wonder. Anyway, two weeks later, I find out he's bought her a plane ticket to Vancouver. She arrives and a week later, walking home from a bar I guess, he steps off a curb and gets mowed down by a bus. He's dead, can you believe it? And she's living in his house, and probably drained all his bank accounts by now."

"Holy fuck. What's this woman's name?"

"Pearla, I think. But that's only her stage name. No one knows her real name."

"Do you think she killed him?"

"Don't know. No proof."

"Shit, man, I start acting like that guy, just shoot me."

Cocking his finger and thumb like a handgun and pointing at his friend, Rick winked. "Don't worry, bud, I won't hesitate."

Monica grabbed Cathy's hand. They stood.

Rick looked at them. "Where you two going?"

"Baño," Monica said. They walked away.

"Fucking chicks, eh?" Rick said. "Always have to go the bathroom together. What the fuck's with that, anyway?"

Mark shook his head.

"That means they'll probably end up holding hands and pissing on the beach together," Rick said. He pointed to a small white building nearby. "That's a baño that costs ten pesos, but they're too fucking cheap to pay that. They'll piss on the beach, mark my words."

"No pun intended?" Mark said.

"What?"

"Nothing."

The waitress returned with the drinks, poured two stiff ones, and left.

The fat bald man who'd hit on the waitress earlier stood up, staggered a few steps, and fell off the two-foot high wooden patio. He landed flat on his chest with a whooshing sound, winding himself. Two Haitian women who were seated at his table helped him to his feet.

Mark and Rick watched the action while their dates, holding hands, urinated on the beach.

"Watch this clown," Rick said. "I've seen him before. Total piss-tank. Eric's his name. Always hammered. Starts early in the morning. Hardly eats. Just drinks."

Eric managed to get to his feet. "Leave me alone. I wanna take a piss." The Haitian women returned to the table and sat. Eric staggered a few feet and, with his back to the growing number of spectators, started pissing. But he lost his balance and, pecker in hand, fell on his back. The female recipients of his generosity rushed to his aid and got him standing again. One put his pecker back inside his pants. He had evidently finished. They got him up the stairs and onto the patio. With some effort, they sat him down. There was a dark, wet circle covering the crotch of his jeans, a dark meandering wet trail extending down one pant leg.

By this time Cathy and Monica had returned. They giggled at the display. Three of the women at Eric's table rose and, drinks in hand, left; but one thin, attractive woman stayed. Eric looked down at his pants and frowned. "Fuck it all, anyway." He looked at his lone companion. "Let's go, baby."

Rick and Mark returned to their drinks.

"See what I mean," Rick said. "Wait 'til he leaves, he'll probably wipe out a few more times. And he's driving, believe it or not."

A black Humvee pulled up to the caseta and parked. A sixty-something, tall, skinny gringo stepped out and shut the door. He took a few steps, almost wiped out, and steadied himself on a palm tree. He eyed the caseta customers, a silly grin playing across his lips.

"Oh fuck," Rick said, spotting him. "We need to go. That's Bob the Knob. One of the cheapest motherfuckers around here. Owns his own waterfront house here, retired with a huge oilfield pension, but you'll rarely see him part with a dime. Fucker brags about paying hookers two hundred pesos, for fuck sakes. I'd be embarrassed if I ever did something like that, let alone tell people. I've bought him many drinks and he's never returned the favor. Matter of fact, you turn your head or go to the bathroom and he'll steal your fucking drink; or at least take a couple big mouthfuls. He always wants to sit with me."

"Just tell him to fuck off," Mark said, squinting.

Rick stood up and waved the waitress over. "Not that easy. Costambar is a small community. He and I have mutual friends. Have to try to get along with everyone around here. The people I don't like, I just avoid the bars they frequent. Or if they do sit down, I always have the option of paying my bill and leaving. Free will, man. That fucker will steal your women, never mind your drinks."

The Knob spotted Rick. He grabbed a vacant plastic chair and plopped it right in the middle of Cathy and Monica. He smiled at the women and turned to Rick. "Hola, amigo. Long time no see." He eyed the half-full rum bottle and scanned the table, perhaps looking for an empty glass.

The waitress approached the table and handed Rick the bill. She also offered them plastic to-go cups.

"We were just leaving," Rick said, motioning for the women to stand up. They did.

"Just leaving?" the Knob said. "I wanted to talk to you about residency here. I hear you're going through the process."

"Another time, buddy," Rick said, waving the women curbside. Mark handed Rick some money, snatched up the rum bottle, and poured his drink into a plastic cup. He nodded perfunctorily at the Knob, left the bar, and waited on the curb with the women while Rick paid.

A short time later, they were parked outside of Rick's third-floor Costambar apartment. Mark and Rick discussed the plan.

Monica fiddled with her smartphone.

En route, they had not only finished their road pops, they'd polished off the take-out bottle of rum.

The plan was simple. They would bring the women inside. Rick would have some fun with Monica in the bedroom while Mark did his thing in the living room. When they were done, the old switcheroo.

They stepped out of the black pickup.

Monica was the last one to enter the building. She closed the gate and then, when the men had gotten some distance ahead of her, unlocked it again.

They reached the third floor.

Two motorcycles pulled up to the building, stopped and parked. Two men dismounted, looked around, and approached the building.

Inside the apartment, Rick got drinks for everyone, put on La Materialista's *La Chapa Que Vibran*, a song about sex, and told the girls to strip-dance to it.

Monica turned up the volume and discreetly unlocked the apartment door.

Rick and Mark sat on the couch and watched as the women peeled their tops off, slowly and seductively removed their bras, and tossed them haphazardly away. Monica's landed on the ceiling fan and began a slow rotation, while Cathy's landed on Mark's head.

Mark sniffed the bra and grinned. "She smells good. I wanna smell her panties." He pointed to Cathy's rapidly gyrating ass. She was down to a pink G-string.

Cathy slid a chair near Mark, bent down, and grabbed the seat with two outstretched hands. She thrust her butt in his face and began shaking it in perfect timing to the frenetic beat. Monica followed her lead and the women shook their booties a few inches from anxious bloodshot eyes and anticipating mouths.

Rick turned to Mark. "Cheers, buddy. This is the life, ain't it? It never fails, that song. Something about the beat just throws the girls into a sexual frenzy."

They touched the Styrofoam cups to their lips, but never got the chance to drink.

The door burst open and two Dominican men rushed in, small knapsacks slung over their shoulders. There was a taller man, lean and athletic, with a goatee; and another shorter one, stalky and muscle bound, with a black beard.

Goatee set his empty knapsack on the kitchen table. Then he turned the music down slightly.

Blackbeard quickly drew a handgun and aimed it at Rick. Cathy and Monica retreated behind the granite kitchen island, where they could still see the action, but also duck should stray bullets start zinging around the room. Monica continued shaking her booty, while Cathy stood frozen to the spot.

The plan had been well-rehearsed. They knew what to do, where to go, what to say.

Goatee pulled out a combat knife and a plastic zip-tie, and approached Mark, who had spilled his drink all over his shirt and shorts. He motioned to Mark to extend his arms. Mark produced two quivering hands and Goatee zip-tied them tightly together.

Blackbeard moved closer to Rick, training the gun at head-level. He spoke perfect English. "Keep your hands up and don't try anything. Unless you want a date with the dirt."

"Fuck you," Rick said, but kept them up. "You're in deep shit. I got cop connections down here. They won't lock you up, they'll kill your ass."

"Shut up."

Rick stood up quickly and head-butted Blackbeard in the chest. He grunted, winded, and staggered back.

Cathy screamed.

Mark tried to stand up. Goatee punched him hard in the jaw. Head spinning, he slumped back on the couch.

As Blackbeard staggered back from the head-butt blow, Rick stepped forward and punched him in the nose. It snapped and blood splattered around the room.

Cathy screamed again.

"Shut up," Monica said, her dance number momentarily interrupted.

Blackbeard hit the wall and stretched out an arm for support. His eyes swam in his head.

Rick turned to Goatee a little too late. Goatee plunged the knife right though Rick's neck, slicing through the jugular vein. Blood sprayed out. Rick made a gurgling sound. With draining strength, he punched Goatee's knife-hand.

Monica gagged a screaming Cathy with her hands. "Shut up, I said."

"Yeoooww," Goatee shouted, his wrist snapping. The knife dropped to the floor. Goatee stepped back. Rick floundered forward and head-butted him in the chest. Goatee fell on top of Mark on the couch.

Blackbeard fired two shots. Both bullets penetrated the back of Rick's head. He dropped dead on the tile floor.

Mark wrapped his zip-tied arms around Goatee and started choking him.

Blackbeard stepped forward, aiming the gun.

A few dogs started barking and neighborhood lights illuminated.

Monica released her hands from Cathy. She narrowed her black eyes, two inches from the petrified woman's face. "Shut your mouth if you know what's good for you."

Monica went into bedroom. She knew where the safe and safe key were.

In the living room, Blackbeard aimed the gun at Mark's head. "Release him or you die."

Mark cradled Goatee's head and neck in his arms. He tightened his grip. Goatee gasped, his eyes beginning to bulge.

"Release him," Blackbeard said.

"Fuck you," Mark said. Applying a headlock, he tightened his arm around Goatee's neck. He grunted, reefed, and snapped Goatee's neck. It made a loud cracking sound. Goatee's head went limp and his tongue dangled out of his mouth like a thirsty dog.

Blackbeard fired two shots. One went through Mark's right eye, the other right between his eyes. Mark slumped on the couch and twitched a few times before becoming still.

"Good shooting, Manuel," Monica said, returning from the room with a knapsack full of goodies.

Manuel picked up his knapsack and frowned. "Fuck! This went all wrong."

"Never mind," Monica said. "Fill your knapsack quickly and let's get out of here." She pointed to the corpses. "And make sure you check their pockets."

Manuel did what he was told.

Monica picked up her clothes and started dressing. She retrieved Goatee's bloody knife, wiped the blood on Rick's t-shirt, and tucked it in her bra. Then she turned to Manuel. "I'll take Victor's moto." She pointed to Cathy, still frozen in fear. "And I'll drive her." Removing the knife from her bra, she approached Cathy. A drop of blood fell from the blade, hit the tile, and splashed into a dime-sized circle. Cathy watched it.

"What are you looking at?" Monica said, waving the knife. "Get dressed. We need to leave. And fast."

Less than a minute later, they left the apartment. They reached the ground floor and headed to the main exit door.

A window from a nearby apartment slid open and a man stuck his head out. "Hey, what're you doing? I'm calling the cops."

Good luck with that one, Monica thought.

They ignored him, mounted their respective motos, and sped away. A small Chihuahua chased Monica's moto, barking angrily and snapping at her heels. She slowed and kicked the yappy dog in the chops, using the spiked heal of her four-inch pumps.

She got it right in the eye. It skidded on its side, its high-pitched, pig-like squeals punctuating their departure into blackness.

Chapter Five

Spiders are among the most efficient and ferocious killers of the insect kingdom. Although rare, technically a spider's neurotoxin can kill humans.

Often portrayed as macabre monsters, they have eight legs, sharp fangs, razor-sharp claws, a hairy exterior, and eight eyes. First constructing an entrance and exit bridge, the spider then spins its deadly web and waits in the middle, monitoring external vibrations. Sometimes the spider will leave the center of the sticky death tentacles and monitor the vibrations through a connected signal line, thereby extending its kill zone over a much wider radius. Once an unsuspecting insect gets caught in the web, the spider attacks swiftly; its retractable fangs strike quickly and inject the prey with a paralyzing or deadly venom. A spider can paralyze or kill multiple insects with this neurotoxin, leave them stuck in the web, and carry on immobilizing more victims. When they're hungry, in most cases, they eat by liquefying the insect's entrails and injecting it with digestive enzymes. Later, they suck up this liquefied goo and leave the insect quite literally a mere skeleton or shell of its former self.

Much like the spider (she preferred the term Black Widow) Antonella Rosario, aka Pearla, was a master at leaving her victims a shell of their former selves—ruined financially, emotionally, and spiritually. But in this case, she had gone a step further, throwing sixty-nine-year-old Rodney Balkwist under a bus and killing him. She had spun the web of deceit and false promises to perfection. And the insect—in his case she thought The Cockroach applied—was ensnared helplessly in her web. By the time she'd flown into Vancouver, the fool was hopelessly in love with her. He doted over her. He kissed her often, made love (if you could call it that) to her twice a day, and his heartfelt words were replete with terms of endearment. "I love you, muffin. Pearla, you are my little jewel. What would you like for breakfast today, my sweet? Can I get you anything, dear? Are you comfortable enough, my angel?"

He would do almost anything for her. It was almost enough to make Pearla want to puke. After a month, she'd not only gotten bored with Rod, he'd started to make her feel sick to her stomach. More times than she cared to remember, the gag reflex had kicked in and she tasted acidity, partially digested gooey food particles clinging to and racing up her esophagus.

Rod left a bad taste in her mouth, and it was more than just his ejaculate. So one evening, walking home from a night of barhopping in downtown Vancouver, she acted on impulse. She was helping a limping, drunk Rod home at about two in the morning. A speeding bus approached. It seemed like the stars had aligned perfectly. Or maybe it was Voodoo spirit Kalfu, master of the malevolent spirits of the night, the gatekeeper of that crossroads between the living and the dead, who had answered her call. Pearla didn't know, although she liked to believe it was the latter.

As the bus approached, she loosened her grip on Rod. When it was within about thirty feet, she'd released his hand. He'd staggered toward the bus—how perfect was that?—helped by a strong shove, of course. As he stepped off the curb, she made a feeble attempt at trying to rescue him. Of course, she arrived too late. He fell off the curb and the bus struck him, squashing his head into the pavement and flattening his skull and gray matter into a neat little circle, which, to Pearla, almost resembled a puke stain.

She sighed, looking around Rod's apartment that sunny afternoon. *At least it was his puke stain and not mine.*

She'd murdered Rod almost two weeks ago, located the passwords to his bank accounts, and drained them. She'd also pilfered three thousand in cash that he'd stashed in the house. Through a translator, the police had interviewed her extensively (Pearla had a decent command of English, but reserved its use for special occasions), but without enough evidence, did not have probable cause to hold her. A handful of witnesses traveling on the bus had also stepped forward, saying they had seen Pearla trying to prevent the fateful fall. Indeed, Kalfu was looking out for her. Of that, she was becoming convinced. The police had phoned her two days earlier, claiming that as far as they were concerned, it had been a tragic accident. "But on a side note," Detective Bill Stepper had said in understandable Spanish, "Please don't leave the country for at least two weeks until we officially rule it an accident. Be available for questioning if we need you again."

Pearla stuffed the last of her belongings in a carry-on bag and looked around to see if she had forgotten anything. Satisfied that she hadn't, she left, waited outside for the taxi, and started to mentally plot her next moves.

Rod's sister would be stopping by in an hour and Marlene had told Pearla in no uncertain terms that when she arrived she did not want to see Pearla or any of her belongings in the apartment. "I have an extra set of keys," Marlene had said the day before. "So leave yours inside and lock the handset lock. I don't want you living here anymore, and I don't trust you as far as I can throw you."

Pearla had claimed innocence, but also said she understood. "I leave here. I visit friend."

"No, you don't visit friend, you stay with friend," Marlene had said.

But Pearla had already planned for this eventuality. She had called one of many Vancouver contacts, in this case a Mike Simmons (she preferred the surname Simpleton) saying she was in the city on vacation and would love to finally meet him. A big surprise. She knew he would be beside himself with joy. They had started a liaison on Badoo, an internet dating site. Three months later, it had progressed to Skype video and phone sex.

Men are so stupid, Pearla thought, checking the latest text message from Simpleton. *I can't wait to see you, baby. I have a special romantic night planned.* Well, he was right about one thing. It would be a romantic night, for him. For Pearla, it would be another step toward acquiring the commodity she knew would give her complete domination and power over the lesser male species—material wealth. Pearla planned on using her charms and physical endowments (not to mention talent in bed) to her advantage. What did men like to call it? The power of the pussy.

She wasn't like the other Dominican women she knew who exploited men for their money. To her, most of these women were stupid, and needed to be educated. They couldn't save money, and were always living from one trick to the next. They relied on stupid ideas to extort more money from their male victims. "My mom is sick and needs a pill that cost 5,000 pesos to cure her." "I need to go to the clinic today but can't afford the check-up. Can you loan me 2,000 pesos?" "I would love to see you, but I need to pay my babysitter. Can you give me 1,000 pesos first to pay her?" "I'll bring my daughter if you pay an extra 3,000. You'll like her." "I need a new bikini. Can you buy it for me?" "I'm hungry." "I'm thirsty." "Can I have more money?" "I want to be your girlfriend. Can I live with you and cook and clean for you?" The stupidity went on and on. That was where they failed and she succeeded. They didn't understand first-world cultures. They didn't realize that most foreigners were wise to these lame lies and blatantly obvious money agendas. They didn't realize the huge difference in the cultures. How could they? Most of them had never been on a plane, and never would.

They didn't know that in other, more advanced countries, the citizens learned the value of saving at a young age. Most had it ingrained in their heads to work hard for their money and sock away some for the retirement years.

And then there was the women thing, which Pearla's many foreign boyfriends were quick to educate her on. Many American, Canadian, European men—at least the ones who had money to extort—had been through divorces. They were super-sensitive to the subject of money, particularly when a request for too much of it came from the mouth of a woman whom they only wanted casual paid sex with.

Or worse still, a woman who had led the man to believe that she was relationship material. Pearla knew most of these men would turn and run at such an obvious money agenda. And they would find another woman. And when that other woman did the same thing—and in most cases, it was not a question of *if* but *when*—they would discard her and move on. And they could do just that in the DR. There were many poor women who would do almost anything to put food on the table for their kids.

But what these women were missing, Pearla had an understanding of. She knew why these men sought out foreign women. They were young and beautiful and performed admirably in bed. A man could easily find a woman half his age or even younger and, if he managed the relationship well, put the woman on a monthly allowance and live happily ever after. Bought affection. The man is happy, and so is the woman. She has money, the prestige of a gringo boyfriend, and an opportunity to make a better life for herself and her family. In exchange, he has the sexiest girlfriend on the beach; and, if he's lucky, a woman who never fails to turn him on in bed.

What he doesn't have, according to Pearla's understanding, is a woman who has lost interest in her personal appearance, become lazy, and his request for another beer might be met with, "Why don't you get off your lazy ass and get it yourself?" Men chose foreign brides or girlfriends for obvious reasons. She thought many of their country's available women had become independent, career-driven, self-absorbed snobs who were looking for a picture-perfect, financially and emotionally stable knight in shining armor to rush in and sweep them off their feet. But these men, at least the ones who spent many months abroad or had abandoned their countries permanently, were reluctant to be that knight in shining armor. Oftentimes it was out of fear—maybe they'd suffered in their last relationship. In their minds, it wouldn't be long before the women would be vying to wear the pants. And that power struggle rarely existed in the DR. The women recognized their place in the household, and accepted and embraced it for the most part. Loving, tender, subservient little angels; such a contrast.

This was exactly the image Pearla had become hugely successful at portraying. But this was just a façade. Deep down, she hated all men. It was her father, raping her at the tender age of ten, who was responsible for that hatred. She had taken her revenge. He had paid for his vicious assault with a spear through his neck. But that wasn't enough. She blamed all men for her pain, and suffering at Ortiz's hands and other body parts. More than that, she blamed foreigners in her country for much of the misery of the female population. The foreign men shamelessly exploited women, waving their dollars around and demanding that the women perform all kinds of lewd sexual acts for money. With their ignorant views and expectations of a subservient—"Yes, honey, anything you say"—trophy girlfriend, they needed to be taught a lesson. They were responsible for stripping DR women of their dignity, self-respect, and self-esteem. And, left unabated, this kind of behavior would create a generation of women who couldn't think for themselves anymore.

Foreigners had fucked up her country enough. It was high time it stopped. And Pearla had a plan to make it stop. Amass enough money to protect herself from harm and deal with these fools legally: get them locked up in her country. And if not, well, as she had already discovered with The Cockroach, there were other ways to do get revenge. *The times, well, they are a changing, dear Pearla.*

Clawing her way up from a small dirt shack in a poverty-stricken Haitian village, Pearla's plan at one time seemed clear to her. But somewhere along the way it had become mired. Mired in her hatred for men, mired by the thought that she perhaps had succumbed to and become corrupted by greed. Mired by her thirst for blood and money, and by her need to please and make sacrifices to Kalfu, the great and powerful Voodoo spirit.

She forced a smile as a taxi pulled curbside. The taxi driver got out and opened the door and she bent down to pick up her knapsack, exposing long shapely legs and just a peek of black panties.

"How are you this fine afternoon?" he said, grinning and making a show of holding the door open.

He's too happy. But she held her smile. "Just wonderful." She gave him the address. He pulled out of the parking lot and drove off, glancing at her in the rearview mirror occasionally, the shit-eating grin widening. She thought about her answer: *wonderful.* Yes, everything was wonderful. The plan, although in a modified form, was still intact.

She extracted a small make-up case, applied a few dabs of bright red lipstick, clicked the case shut, and put it in her purse. She pulled out her smartphone and made a quick call. Time to check on DR progress.

Monica answered on the first ring.

"Everything all right?" Pearla said.

"Yes."

"Good." She pressed END CALL and opened her TO DO list contained in the phone.

Six names. Rodney Balkwist, The Cockroach, was number one. Things had been prioritized. She deleted him.

Her brow furrowed as she reviewed the list of names, people she had to deal with, now rather expeditiously. Two weeks. Detective Stepper might decide there was something a little unusual about The Cockroach's death that warranted perhaps a little more interrogation. And come hell or high water, she couldn't let herself get detained before her mission—Kalfu's mission—was complete. She looked at the last name on the list. It brought a fresh pang of grief. That scumbag had brought her more pain than many of the others. And he had done it recklessly and with no regard for her feelings. She frowned. But then she heard that soothing voice, and this time she was sure it was Kalfu speaking inside her head: *Don't worry, my love. Follow the mission. I will help and protect you.*

It brought her renewed hope. The Black Widow spider returned. The web was being spun again. She re-read the last name on the list and grinned. *You will get your comeuppance, Saul Climer.*

Chapter Six

It took three days before Saul felt well enough to drive down to his waterfront. His tooth hurt, his bad shoulder was getting worse, and the burns were more troublesome than he'd first thought. So, along with the alcoholic self-medication, he'd started a kind of recovery. He had managed a visit to a nearby dentist, who confirmed the upper molar was infected and needed a root canal. But the dentist wouldn't do the work, claiming those back molars often have extra canals that are difficult for general dental practitioners to find. It was a job for a specialist. So, the dentist had put him on an antibiotic, Amoxicillin, and referred him to an endodontist in Charlottetown. And while Saul waited for the dentist appointment, a week away, he was also self-medicating with a codeine-based painkiller called Oxaforte, purchased over the counter in the DR.

He had no idea what other chemicals might be in the Oxaforte, or even if they mixed well with the antibiotic. And as he parked his pickup in the waterfront clearing that overcast afternoon, he made a mental note of just what types and quantities of chemical influences he was under. *Let's see: seven beers, two three-ounce shots of rum, three 500 mg antibiotic pills, and two 500 mg Oxafortes.* But rather than worry about how queasy his stomach felt, particularly since it was now almost five in the afternoon and he had only eaten a banana for breakfast, he was more concerned about what had caused the growling noise the other night. And, he reminded himself, the nasty scratches on his leg demanded a logical explanation.

He shut the truck off, got out, cracked a beer from the cooler, and took a long pull. Feeling a sudden disorientation, combined with a booze and pill buzz, he stopped and let his mind wander.

Ted Nugent's *Cat Scratch Fever* popped into his head. He grinned maniacally and sang some lyrics:

"They give me cat scratch fever

Cat scratch fever

I got a bad scratch fever

The cat scratch fever

It's nothin' dangerous

I feel no pain

I've got the choo-choo train

You know you got it when you, you're going insane

It makes a grown man cry, cry, oh won't you make my bed..."

He stopped singing, suddenly feeling hot flashes racing up his body, settling into his forehead, pumping, causing him to sweat. He wiped his brow and laughed. "I've got fucking cat scratch fever..."

Get a fucking grip! He pulled out a rake from the truck bed, and walked over to the small patch of brush, the subject area. With the rake, he started poking around. The wind suddenly accelerated. Waves crashed on the nearby shoreline. The treetops swayed and hissed.

Undisturbed, Saul plodded and poked, not sure what he was going to find, but now more determined than ever to know. The coffee stain, he suddenly remembered. *I went to bed drunk as a skunk. I put that shirt on clean before I left the house. I didn't drink any coffee when I returned home. Did I? No. How did it get there? The dream. The dream was real. I spilled coffee in the dream. I woke up with a coffee stain. What the fuck is wrong with me?*

Goosebumps were already crawling up his spine when he heard rustling brush a few yards away. Startled, he cocked the rake like a spear and aimed it at the bush. *What are you doing, you clown?* He lowered the rake and moved slowly toward the sound. His beer dropped from his hand, hit the ground, and bubbled forth its contents. He ignored it. That was a first. Nearing, he thought—or was his drug-induced mind playing tricks?—he heard a low hissing sound. *Just the wind, you idiot.*

He tapped the bush. A chipmunk skittered out, stopped, and chattered at him long and loud, then disappeared up a tree.

Saul could feel his heart pounding in his chest. "Fuck sakes. A fucking chipmunk."

He looked up in the tree. The chipmunk stopped and looked back. It chattered angrily.

"Yeah, well, I didn't know it was you. What do you expect me to do?" *Now you're talking to the animals?* But it wasn't the first time. *Probably won't be the last. You're losing it, brother. Go back to bed.*

Instead, he returned to the subject bush, put down the rake, and crawled under a small opening. What he saw made his eyes widen and his heart skip a beat. Bear-sized claw marks in the red dirt. Something *was* there. But there were no bears on Prince Edward Island. After examining the tracks for a few seconds, he crawled out.

Possibilities ran through his mind. Could be a raccoon. Maybe a coyote. A white-tailed fox, maybe. But these tracks were as big as a human hand. Did any of those animals have claws that big? He doubted it, but wasn't sure. It definitely called for some research.

So before he started acting too stupid, he tossed the rake in the truck bed and drove the winding half-mile road to his house.

He did laundry. He force-fed himself a Swanson Hungry Man TV dinner and he did some internet research. Two hours later, he was sitting on the back porch, drinking beer and watching tiny flashing yellow bursts of light as fireflies buzzed around in the pink, gray-blue light of dusk.

The wind swayed the treetops. The leaves hissed.

The tracks were definitely not raccoon, which looked more like tiny infant handprints than adult-sized hands with claws. Nor were they coyote tracks, which were only about two and a half inches long and show separation between heel and toes, unlike the ones Saul had seen. And he was able to quickly rule out fox tracks, which are also much smaller and have separation between heel and toe.

So what was this beast that had attacked him in the night? He set down his beer and pulled down his sweatpants to examine the marks it had left. Fortunately, and after a number of topical antibiotic applications, the scratches did not look infected. They weren't even that deep, just barely enough to cut the skin. Had the beast retreated at the last second, deciding to spare his life? Surely something that big could have ripped his throat out if it wanted to.

Did the beast have an infection? *Am I infected?*

While watching the flashing fireflies, he lit a smoke and contemplated this. His gaze drifted up to the sky. It had cleared, and thousands of white stars punctuated the blackness—the Milky Way, the Big and Little Dippers. The full moon rose slowly above the surrounding tree line.

The dreams. The post-apocalyptic nightmare that had occurred fireside. The dream with stalker Monica that seemed as real as if he'd gone back in time. And it had played out exactly how it had happened on his recent trip. *Did I go back in time? Strange days indeed.*

"But, wait, I missed a dream." A rabbit, apparently startled by lone words in a lonely forest, dashed out from underneath the porch, sprinted into the black trees, and disappeared. Saul started and almost spilled his beer. The dream he hadn't initially recalled now came to him. Dreams were like that, he thought. If you don't write them down, they vanish rapidly from the mind. Unless they're based in reality. Then, sometimes they linger for days, weeks, or a lifetime. He winced and took a long drag on his smoke. The dream had involved Joella. Maybe he'd blocked it from his mind as he'd tried to block her. *Just delete her, wouldn't that be nice.* She was gyrating around his bed, nude, except for a pink G-string, shaking that beautiful ass, those perfect little titties. She had done that. He had enjoyed it. So why was he ignoring her? Then it came to him like a ball peen hammer striking him upside the head. It wasn't only that he'd lied to her about his writing career. It was something else as well. After his return from the DR, the conversations and texts were lovey-dovey. Then one day—not that long ago—he called her just to say hello and hear her sexy voice. It had sounded strange, strained. Then she came out with it. "I need to buy some books for school and don't have the money. Can you help me?"

Knowing the predatory nature of many Dominican women, milking men for money, this had hit Saul like a ton of bricks. "How much do they cost?" he stammered.

"I think around 2,000 pesos."

"Okay, no problem."

But, after hanging up, he was devastated. Was this not love? Was it just about money? He didn't know anymore, and many of his friends' warnings resurfaced with painful meaningfulness. "Oh, they're the best con artists in the world, trust me. Many Oscars have been won down here. They start off small, then the money demands come fast and furious, the amounts higher, until you're bone-fucking-dry. I doubt she loves you. Sure, she's content, content with your money. I don't really like her. But I'll be polite and put up with her for your sake."

Even though Saul had agreed to send the textbook money, he knew Joella knew there was something wrong. That night, although they went unanswered, she sent two more texts: *I would do everything for you, my love, because I love you.* And, *Since I met you, I only think of you.*

Saul forgot about the texts and began numbing himself with alcohol, masking his feelings and emotions. Two days later, he recalled, he had another conversation with Joella. Although she didn't mention the money request, she strongly hinted at the possibility of more. "If you love me you will do anything for me, unconditionally."

After some small talk he'd hung up.

Two texts followed: *Are you sure you love me? If you are sure you love me, then show me.*

Saul remembered now. He had suppressed the memory with alcohol and put the blame on himself for lying to her about his success and being unable to face her or his lies anymore. But there was more to it than that, he now realized. She had, after three months, begun to ask for money. Sure, it wasn't as if her kids were sick and she needed 10,000 pesos to miraculously cure them. Or she was terminally ill and needed the famous 5,000-peso wonder drug to cure her. But she had begun to ask for money. Although 2,000 pesos was not a lot of money, maybe $70 Canadian, as it was Saul was living on borrowed money, namely the line of credit secured against his one and only asset, his house. He didn't have any money. It was as simple as that.

And maybe that $70, even though it was supposedly to better her education, was just the beginning. Where would it lead? Where would it end?

He was confused and hurt. Was it worth it to take a big risk on someone who offered no guarantees? He didn't know anymore. Not if he believed his friends' warnings. So he had given up on Joella, refusing to answer her calls, listening to the voicemails before deleting them, occasionally reading endearing text messages before wallowing in the bottle. He was numbing his pain, numbing his vulnerability. *Isn't vulnerability the gateway to happiness? Fuck that.* He tried to compartmentalize his emotions and lock them away forever.

Wasn't that the real ticket to a healthy and happy life? Put your emotions in a coffin, bury them six feet under, have a funeral service mourning their loss, then move on with your life and forget about their death. But wouldn't their death mean your death?

"Fuck that," Saul said, taking a long pull on his beer. He looked at his hand and realized it was clenching his smartphone tightly. He felt like throwing it away. *Who ya gonna call? Ghostbusters?* He laughed loudly and studied the text messages as his index finger scrolled through them. He stopped the screen suddenly. There was a voicemail from Joella, one he had evidently missed. He listened to it:

"Honey, I know you don't want me or love me anymore, but I'm worried about you. Please at least let me know you're okay. I had a bad dream about you. Something is terribly wrong, I just know it... anyway, take care." There was a second or two of silence before she added, "I love you."

"You love my money, fucking bitch," Saul said, crushing his empty, tossing the can in an outdoor steel garbage can, and returning inside for another. He stepped outside, cracked it open, took a long pull, and started singing: "I may be going to Hell in a bucket baby, yeah, yeah, but at least I'm enjoying the ride, yeah, least I'm enjoying the ride."

The phone rang.

He looked at it as if it were a demon. "Not again. Will you leave me alone?" But it wasn't Joella. It was his friend Samantha Reese, the successful author from Charlottetown. Lately, she had been one of the few positive influences in his life, encouraging him to revisit his novel and submit it to a publisher. He'd had coffee with her twice since returning from the DR.

He struggled with external and internal demons before giving in and answering it. "Samantha, how the hell are ya?"

There was a moment's pause before she said, "Are you okay?"

"Perfectly fine, other than a few minor cuts and burns, a head that's spinning like a top, and a shoulder that's throbbing like hell." He left out the other shit for now, figuring that was enough already. *Nobody loves ya when you're down and out.*

"You don't sound that well. Are you drunk?" she said.

"A little."

"What have you been up to lately?"

"Cleaning the acreage. I want to sell it. I'm not such a big fan of Canada anymore."

"I got that impression from our last conversation."

"I know."

"Dare I ask, how's the novel?"

"Haven't touched it since the last time we talked."

"Sorry I mentioned it."

"Not a problem. How is *your* writing? And how are *you*?"

"Good and good."

"Good to hear."

"Listen, I'm not going to keep you. I just wanted to know if you want to meet for coffee tomorrow at around two at the usual spot. There's something I want to talk to you about."

Saul knew the usual spot. Starbucks, Queen Street, downtown Charlottetown. "Is it bad?"

"No, Saul, I just want to see you and talk about one of my publishing contacts. I won't say more until we can talk in person... I'm also a little worried about you. You didn't sound all that positive the last time we talked."

Saul thought about it. If he was going nuts, Samantha might be the only person who could help him. His other PEI friends were not of the inner-circle variety. He had a hard time relating to them and their damned domesticity. But Sam was different. Sam was an artist. Sam understood him better than most, had even been through a battle with alcoholism herself. He was getting dragged inextricably down a black hole, and maybe she was throwing him a lifeline.

"Okay," he said. "Tomorrow at two."

"And Saul?"

"Yeah."

"Please don't overdo it tonight."

"Okay Sam. Thanks."

"For what?"

"I don't know, for checking in on me."

"No problem. Tomorrow?"

"Tomorrow."

Chapter Seven

It was a black sky. Below, a few streetlights cast a suffused gray light on the quiet residential street. In the distance, the faint sound of a dog barking—*roop, roop, roop...roop roop.* Occasionally moving headlights lit up the street and then faded away. It must be late, Saul thought.

What was he doing on this balcony at this time of the night? Last thing Saul remembered, and this time he did remember, was going to bed at a respectable 10:36 pm, making good on his promise to Samantha not to overdo it. Nothing had led up to this point, except *boom*, here he was. Standing on the small third-floor balcony of a low-rise apartment complex in the middle of a city—what city?—and peering through some half-opened Venetian blinds... at what? A man and woman having sex on a bed. A small bedside table lamp illuminated them. The dark-skinned woman with long, flowing black hair was on top, cowgirl style, sweating, bucking, and moaning. The man moaned in unison.

Saul would be lying to himself if he said he didn't watch and enjoy the show for a few moments. But it wasn't long before that enjoyment turned to raw, cold fear. As his gaze swept across the room, a metal object near the foot of the bed caught a ray of light from a passing motorist's headlights and glinted.

A combat-style knife.

As cold goosebumps crawled up his spine and prickled the tiny hairs on the back of his neck, he realized something else. He recognized the woman.

Her—oh God, no.

It was Pearla, a well-known professional Costambar prostitute. Then he remembered his experience with Pearla. The sex was amazing, but that was where it ended. There was something unsavory about the rest that he just couldn't put his finger on. After a few seconds though, it came to him. Her reputation. It was bad. Bilking men for their money—or perhaps "milking" would be a better word, given that fellatio was her specialty. She was a pro at it. Saul didn't know what Pearla was capable of—but, after all the stories he'd heard, he wouldn't be surprised if murder was one of her many talents. And there was something else.

Pearla didn't like Saul much anymore. *Hate* was probably a better word.

It was the morning after an all-nighter with her. Saul had left his phone at his friend Marlon's apartment the night before. Marlon had Skype-called and said to make it quick if he wanted to retrieve it because he was still drunk and wanted to turn in for the night, or in that case, the morning.

Saul had quickly woken Pearla.

"I need to use your shower before we go," she'd said.

"You can shower in the ocean if you want," Saul said off-handedly before whisking her out of the apartment.

The next evening, Saul was at a beach bar with his friends when Pearla approached, taking a seat uninvited. After lecturing him for a few minutes about his rudeness, using profanities like "bastard" and "son of a bitch," she stormed off.

The last thing she said before leaving: "You'll get your comeuppance, Saul Climer."

Saul watched as Pearla reached back and grabbed the knife with her right hand. She raised it as the man's moaning intensified.

Saul broke into a cold sweat, darting his eyes around the neighborhood, looking for help. He saw no one, but suddenly realized where he was—Marpole, a community of Vancouver. It was unusually hot outside that evening. His heart beat faster and louder in his chest. He couldn't contain himself. "She's got a knife!"

Pearla's head turned toward the window. Her black eyes regarded him coldly. She swiftly tucked the knife under the mattress and pulled a white towel over her nude body. She pointed at Saul. "Mike, there's a peeping pervert. Do something."

Saul's legs did not obey brain commands. *You're dreaming. You must be. Jump off the balcony and you'll be fine.*

He looked down at the parking lot below and considered it. *What if I'm not dreaming?*

"What the fuck are you doing out there?" Mike said, rising and grabbing his underwear and a t-shirt.

"It's a sick peeping tom," Pearla said. "Get him, Mike."

Dream or not, Saul had no time to lose. He climbed over the metal railing and swung down onto the balcony below, his sore shoulder snapping and cracking in painful protestation. He still had the fingers of his left hand on the balcony above when Mike emerged, a towel-clad Pearla right behind him. Pearla stomped his outstretched fingers with the heel of her foot.

"Owww, you bitch… that hurt." Saul grabbed the sore fingers for a second, released them, and jumped down to the second floor. This wasn't exactly VIP treatment. He looked down at the parking lot, maybe ten or twelve feet below. It was time to leave. He looked up and that was when he saw it.

Mike was aiming a gun at him. "Try and break into my apartment, eh?" Mike fired. A loud blast echoed through the neighborhood.

The bullet hit a metal balcony railing, ricocheted into a streetlight and shattered the bulb, giving Saul cover of darkness in which to escape.

He wasted no time. He jumped from the balcony, hit the concrete below, and somersaulted a few times to break the momentum of his fall. A sharp bolt of pain shot through the injured shoulder. Wincing, he sprang to his feet running and climbed over the fence of a nearby residential backyard before another shot could be fired. Panting, he ducked down and waited, not knowing what he was waiting for. Maybe he'd wake up and this nightmare would be over. *Keep running, you fool.*

Dogs started barking. Lights came on. A man opened a window in Mike's building. "Who the fuck is shooting around here? Can't you see it's late and I'm trying to sleep? What the fuck's wrong with you people anyway?"

"Someone tried to break into our apartment and attack us," Pearla said.

"Fuck it," Mike said. "I'm going after him."

Saul heard the words and decided it was time. He ran through the backyard, heading for the street in front of the house. A back porch light came on and an overweight woman with curlers in her blonde hair stepped out, waving a broom. "Get out of my yard."

The words startled Saul. He lost his footing in the dewy grass and fell, a kind of sliding belly flop. He glanced back.

The woman was coming after him with the broom and Mike, armed with the gun, was already climbing her fence.

Saul got to his feet, the shoulder now screaming bloody murder. There were grass stains on the knees of his jeans.

The woman turned to Mike. "Hey, you can't come in here with a gun."

"It's an intruder," Mike said. "Stop him."

"Never mind," the woman said. "Get out of here before I call the cops."

Inside her backyard, Mike stopped, evidently re-thinking things.

The diversion gave Saul the chance he needed. He sprinted out into the street, turned right, and kept going. A half block later, he glanced back. They weren't coming after him. He kept running.

Suddenly he heard sirens. The sound was faint at first but quickly grew louder. Cops. Nearing. Almost out of breath, he slowed and glanced back.

A loudspeaker mounted on the roof of the cop car screeched static before an audible voice sounded: "Stop, or we'll shoot. Stop and get on the ground with your arms and legs spread."

Saul thought about it. This was real. Too real. How could he stop now? And be arrested for peeping? Have a permanent black mark on an otherwise clean record? No. He drew in a deep breath and picked up his pace.

The cop car stopped. An officer got out. "I said stop or I'll shoot!"

Saul closed his eyes. A gunshot blast echoed through the neighborhood. *This is it. You're dead.*

Chapter Eight

"You look like death warmed over," Samantha said.

It was the following afternoon. It was a bright, sunny summer day as they sat at the downtown Charlottetown Starbucks with their coffees.

The last thing Saul remembered from the dream was the sound of the gunshot. When he woke up he was in his bed in his house on PEI. His shoulder was damn sore and when he got up and examined his jeans, he saw they were carefully folded on the futon couch beside his bed. Grass stains on both knees. He wanted to tell Samantha the story, needed to tell someone. Either he was completely losing his mind, or something really dark and sinister was happening. As much as he almost believed it, he didn't want to believe he was nuts. Even though he now talked to the animals and himself regularly, and typically suffered alcohol-induced blackouts.

"Thanks," he said. "I feel like death warmed over."

Samantha sipped her coffee and absently pushed a lock of curly blonde hair away from her blue eyes. In contrast, she looked alert, happy—even glowing. And why shouldn't she? She successfully juggled a writing career, a teenage son and daughter still living at home, and a marriage.

"What did you do after I talked to you last night anyway? Did you carry on drinking?" she said.

"No, I was in bed before eleven."

"Well, what happened?"

This was a tricky one, Saul thought. To answer honestly would probably render him clinically insane in her mind.

But how many close friends did he have on the Island, really? Just her, actually. The rest were garden-variety acquaintances. Maybe slowly moving past that title, but certainly not anywhere close to the category of Samantha—a trusted, loyal, and true friend. Like family, really. *So tell her, then. You think you can solve this yourself? In your condition?*

"We'll get to it, okay?" Saul said. He needed time to process how he was going to word it. "Tell me about the novel-writing business. How goes the romance writing?"

"Very well. I'm near completion of *Chastity's Belt,* a steamy romance about a nineteenth-century puritanically repressed women who does a one-eighty degree turn. Penguin is excited about it and has already started pre-release promotion."

"So, what, she goes from virgin to slut?"

"Something like that."

"Sounds interesting. I'll have to read it."

"I'll give you a copy." Samantha shifted slightly in her chair and her expression turned serious, the little dimple on her right cheek becoming more pronounced. It always did that when she had something serious to say. Saul knew the signs. They had known each other for three years. "I'm not here to talk about my writing. I want to talk about *your* writing."

"What writing? I haven't done anything for months."

"Yeah, but you knocked out *The Final Hour* in four months. That's a pretty good clip. Even I don't write that fast."

"Yeah, but it's shit. It's quality, not quantity that matters."

"Why don't you let me be the judge of that? Let me read it. Do you still have it on computer?"

"No, I deleted it."

"What?"

"I deleted it, but I still have a paper copy somewhere."

"Why don't you let me read it, Saul?"

"We'll see."

Samantha offered her most charming smile. "Pretty-please, with sugar on top?"

Saul held up a hand. "Okay, I'll find it and bring it next time we meet."

"You promise?"

"Cross my heart, hope to die."

"Good, because if I like it, I want to submit it to my publisher on your behalf. Gail and I have been friends for a long time. I can put you way ahead of the line. Penguin is not even taking submissions for the next year, but I can bypass all that."

"Thanks, Sam."

"I want to help you. I read some stuff you wrote when you worked in PR. You *do* have talent, you just don't accept it. But, if I don't like the novel, or think it needs developmental editing, I'll tell you. I'll say it as gently as possible, but I'll tell you."

Saul had heard the term before. Developmental editing was a euphemism for garbage in the literary world. Back to the drawing board, buddy. "Don't sugarcoat anything."

Saul noticed a passing motorist ogling Samantha. There were many pedestrians on the street. A cruise ship had docked at the city's waterfront for the day. Droves of tourists wandered around, spending their money on trinkets and whatever else. The nearby street-side patio bars were full. Saul thought Charlottetown had a certain historic charm, but an old-city-now-modernized kind of juxtaposition; a personality complex of sorts. Beautiful turn-of-the century architecture in the downtown core with an invasion of nondescript big-box stores and super strip malls as you moved down University Drive and out of downtown proper.

As he returned his gaze to Samantha, thoughts of last night's horror flashed though his mind. She was staring at him intently, the dimple more pronounced than ever. "Why don't you tell me what's wrong?"

Women's intuition. No point in questioning it.

A long pause. Saul clasped his hands and brought them to his chin in a pose that resembled praying. "If I do, you'll think I'm crazy."

"Maybe you don't know me as well as you think. People think I'm crazy. And all artists are a little weird, eccentric—whatever you want to call it. We just process information differently than others. Simple as that. It's a left-brain right-brain thing."

"Which side is supposed to be the creative side?"

"Right."

"Right."

"So tell me."

"Okay." Saul told the story. The mysterious claw marks at the bonfire. The dream involving Joella. The nightmare involving Monica. The latest nightmare with Mike and Pearla. And the physical evidence indicating he had actually teleported back in time in at least two cases and, he somehow knew, to another location in the present in last night's nightmare.

He pulled up his pant leg, revealing scabby scratch marks. "Look at this. It all started after I got attacked."

"Have you told anyone else about this?" Samantha said, looking at him as if he had a weekend pass from an insane asylum.

Saul rolled his pant leg down, furrowed his brow, and shook his head.

"Good. Because they would probably have you committed. Those claw marks could be a coyote—maybe a raccoon or fox?"

"No. I found tracks in the bush where the noise came from. Nothing like any of those animals."

"That doesn't mean what attacked you came from the bush. You were passed out and wouldn't know the difference."

"Fair enough," Saul said. "But how do you explain the physical evidence from the nightmares?"

Samantha scratched her head and the dimple danced. "Are you sure the grass stains or that coffee stain didn't happen before you went to bed?"

"I wasn't that drunk. I did laundry before I went to bed. I didn't have any grass-stained jeans in the house. And they were neatly folded beside my bed when I woke up this morning. There was even a small tear in them that wasn't there before."

A long pause. "I want to believe you, Saul. I really do. But, given your mental condition lately—you've been hitting the booze pretty heavy—I just don't know. I'm not saying

I don't believe you. I'm not saying I do. I'm somewhere in the middle, and need some time to process all this. You know me, I've always been honest with you. If I think you're fucking up I tell you. And that's what I've been telling you lately."

"Well, I appreciate your honesty."

"This teleportation thing, I'd have a hard time buying that even if my husband said it. And he, thank God, has been mentally stable lately. You see where I'm coming from?"

Saul knew. What did he expect? That she would jump on board and help him solve this mystery? He couldn't shake the disturbing feeling that this Mike was real and was in real danger. *Who cares? The fuck shot at you and chased you with a gun down the streets of Vancouver.*

"Vancouver. That's it. I was in Vancouver last night. I even remember the neighborhood. Marpole. I've been there before."

"What does that prove?" Samantha asked.

But Saul could see her wheels turning. He knew what she was thinking. He pulled out his smartphone to Google it. He noticed a text message from Joella, which he read before going on the internet: *I exist only in your life.*

Holy shit, she really is waxing poetic lately. Of course, the consummate con.

He scanned news stories in the Vancouver Sun, not knowing what to expect. Then he found it, hidden in the bottom right hand corner of the page.

He showed the story to Samantha. "Pull this up and read it."

She showed him her phone: she'd already found it.

They simultaneously read their phones:

POLICE SEARCH FOR PEEPING TOM SUSPECT

A man has been charged with possession of an illegal firearm after chasing a suspected peeping tom away from his bedroom window in the Marpole district last night.

According to police, Michael Simmons, 59, was in bed with his yet unidentified girlfriend around 2:26 am when he noticed a man on his third-floor balcony peering through his bedroom window. Apparently afraid for his life, Simmons dressed and pursued the man, brandishing a loaded Glock 26 nine-millimeter pistol.

Simmons has been charged with possession of an illegal firearm. He has no prior criminal record.

When reached by telephone, Simmons said, "I only have one thing to say. There is a pervert on the loose who's prowling around looking in people's bedroom windows. Who knows what he's capable of? And I'm the one who gets charged for trying to protect myself and my girlfriend? This is ridiculous."

A witness, who refused to be identified, claims Simmons actually shot at the suspect, who later escaped, but police detective Bill Paxton refused to confirm or deny this. "This is an ongoing investigation and I can't compromise it by revealing sensitive details."

Police are searching for a Caucasian male, about 200 pounds, six feet tall with a medium build, possibly in his 60s, with medium-length gray-black hair and a small scar above his right eye. He was wearing a dark-colored, long-sleeved shirt, blue jeans, and dark-colored shoes.

Anyone with information is asked to call Crimestoppers at 1-866 577-3945. A reward is being offered.

Saul turned white, with just a hint of jaundice. His stomach lurched and he suddenly felt dizzy. He was dressed in blue jeans, black shoes, and a long-sleeved black shirt. He swallowed the acidy puke streaming up his esophagus.

Samantha stood and touched his shoulder gently. "Are you okay?"

"No."

Other patrons were beginning to stare.

"Come on," she said. "We need to go."

Silently, they walked for a few minutes. They located Saul's pickup and climbed in. Saul's stomach had settled a little. And he felt slightly less dizzy. He rolled down the driver window, found his smokes, and turned to Samantha. "You don't mind, do you?"

"Go ahead."

With an unsteady hand, he removed a cigarette, lit it, and took a long drag. He exhaled out the window and looked at Samantha. "Now do you believe me? How would I know all this?"

"This is strange indeed. I have to admit I have a hard time calling it a coincidence."

"That guy *did* shoot at me. And so did the cops, but that'll probably be covered up."

There was a long silence before Samantha answered. "You say that woman in the bedroom was trying to kill him?"

"Yeah, that's why I blew my cover, if you want to call it that. I told you she had a knife."

Samantha looked around the truck, saw a black baseball cap, and handed it to Saul. "Here, put this on."

Saul did. "Fuck, now I'm a wanted man."

"Yeah, but you've got a damn good alibi. It's physically impossible—at least as far as the cops are concerned—for you to be in two places at once. Sounds to me like you're a hero. You probably saved his life."

"For now. But maybe she'll finish the job. Wait and see. And something tells me this is only the beginning."

"What do you mean?"

"I think she'll come after me."

"What makes you think that?"

Saul told her how he had paid Pearla for sex and then ushered her out, filling in some previously omitted details. "So you see, she's pissed off at me for basically telling her to go jump in the ocean, and not wanting her to sit down uninvited at a table with me and some friends."

"Well, I can't see that you mistreated her enough for her to want to kill you."

"Yeah, but she doesn't see things that way. She's nuts." *The pot calling the kettle black.*

"Just take it easy, Saul."

"That's not an easy thing for me right now, Sam."

"I know, but if you're going to figure this shit out it doesn't help to worry or drink yourself to death. I know you're low on cash. So get your property sorted out and get it on the market. I don't think you're cut out for this rural living anyway. You're too much of a social animal."

"What about all this other shit?"

"I'll tell you what. I'll do some poking around to see if I can find out about what kind of animal experiments have been going on around here lately. I've heard about some animal tests on behavior modification, but it's all rumors. If we know what infected you, if you're actually infected, that will help." She slid a few inches away from Saul. "And if we can learn what you're infected with, maybe there's some way of reversing it. This is just a wild theory, don't forget, and I could be way off base. But I'd like to look into it to help you and satisfy my own curiosity. We both know that truth is often stranger than fiction. I don't think you or I could have invented this in our wildest imagination. Think about the story possibilities."

That was Samantha. Always finding an artistic angle. Or maybe she was just trying to stay positive. Either way, Saul felt lost and vulnerable. "What do you want *me* to do, besides getting my property ready to sell?"

Samantha looked at him like a mother about to impart some profound pearls of wisdom to her son. "Stay off the booze, get yourself some sleeping pills if you need a deep sleep. Maybe that will prevent you from teleporting. Get your tooth fixed. Get your shoulder examined. Maybe find out what you can about teleporting, and find out what you can about this Pearla woman. You have connections in the DR. Use them. Remember, knowledge is power."

Samantha looked down at her phone. She was getting ready to leave. She had writing deadlines, appointments with publishing people, research to do for upcoming novels.

She had a life, where Saul did not.

She looked up. "Why are you looking at me like that?"

"Like what?"

"Like I just pissed in your cornflakes."

"Sorry, I know you have to go. I won't hold you up."

"Hey, don't get the wrong impression. My friends and family are far more important than any novel will ever be. I don't have my priorities screwed up. Life's too short. You have to appreciate the little things, because one day you realize they *are* the big things... I'm not calling you a little thing or anything, maybe I didn't say..."

"I get it, Samantha. And thanks."

"For what?"

"For being there. For being you." He gave her a hug.

She tried a smile that wasn't quite her normal room illuminator. No wonder, after what she'd just heard.

She opened the door to leave, then closed it again. "Oh, I almost forgot. How are things going with Joella?"

"Long story short, not so good. I'm beginning to think she has a money agenda. I'll tell you another time."

"I'm sorry to hear that. I have five minutes if you want to tell me about it."

"This could take longer."

"Okay, another time." She kissed him on the cheek. "Don't worry about it, Saul. These things work themselves out over time."

Saul went to open his door, with the intention of getting out and opening her door.

"Don't. You're an injured man." She opened the door and stepped out. "Let me know what you find out. And, if you need to talk, about anything, please call. And answer your phone when I call."

"Okay."

"One more thing. I still want to see your manuscript. Give it to me next time we meet, okay?"

Chapter Nine

It was a quarter to midnight.

Pearla took a swig of rum from the half-full bottle. Then she lit candles and positioned them in a pentagram on the floor of her Ramada Hotel suite. She realized she hadn't planned for the possibility that Saul would appear out of nowhere and ruin her plans to murder Mike Simpleton. But then, how could she have predicted it? According to her information, relayed to her by DR associate Monica, Saul was still on Prince Edward Island. Yet he'd showed up mysteriously on Simpleton's balcony at the wrong time. How could he be in two places at once? Was he too confiding in the Voodoo spirits for guidance? She didn't know, but planned on finding out.

She lit the last of the candles, sat in the middle of the pentagram, and thought about her incantation. But there were other details to work through first before beginning. Troubling details. Because of Saul's interference, she had left Simpleton's apartment the following morning. And for two days now she had been laying low in the hotel, planning. Luckily, Simpleton had acquiesced to her suggestion to deal with the police outside of his apartment and keep her out of it. There was too much heat on her already after The Cockroach's murder, and she couldn't take any chances. So she rose early that morning, applied her oral talents to Simpleton's member, and told him she had to visit a troubled friend for a few days before returning. Pleased with her skills, he hadn't asked many questions. And he was probably too troubled by the weapons charge and Detective Paxton's suggestion that there may be more charges pending—something to do with trespassing and firing a gun illegally.

Unfortunately, what she'd thought was a finely tuned plan would have to be readjusted. If she wanted to do with Simpleton what she'd planned, she'd have to find time for it. Initially, upon arriving at his apartment, she'd almost thought he wasn't worth killing. He'd behaved so nicely; so damned courteous, well-mannered, and respectful. He had a bottle of red wine waiting on a candle-lit table, a lovely spaghetti bolognaise dinner, and a Caesar salad prepared.

But it didn't take long for him to show his true colors.

"Why don't you take your clothes off and lay spread-eagle on the bed and wait for me?" he said soon after dinner. "I'm sure you're used to that."

She gave him a look. Maybe she was, but she didn't want to hear it.

"What's wrong, honey, do you think I'm stupid or something?" he said. "I've been to the DR before. I know what it's all about. This is a business deal, nothing more. You fuck my brains out, and I pay you. If you're real good, I keep you around for a few days—maybe a few weeks if you're lucky. I might've been born in a day, my little angel, but it sure as fuck wasn't yesterday. Now be a good girl and go lay down for me."

So she did, stripping down and lying spread-eagle on the bed as per his instructions. That was when she'd made her final decision. This fuck was going to die. And painfully.

But she wasn't expecting him to return with four short lengths of rope and begin tying her to the bedposts. It was her fellatio talent that had had gotten her out of that one. She'd grabbed his erect member, stuffed it deep into her mouth, and expelled it with a cough. "Have you ever had deep-throat like that? You can tie me later."

And that was all it took. Simpleton dropped the ropes and Pearla took over, control and domination once again hers. Until Saul had come along.

Damn. Put it out of your mind. Concentrate.

She closed her eyes, took a few deep breaths, and waited for her breathing to slow. To invoke Kalfu, for the incantation to work, she needed to be in a deep state of meditation. Her Voodoo practices were far from traditional. She was beyond plunging needles into dolls or sacrificing animals to win the favor of the Voodoo spirits. Why use animals or dolls when you had people to sacrifice? The animals didn't deserve it. Neither did the dolls. But the scumbags who'd exploited her sisters did.

A few minutes later, she started a slow humming sound, which gradually became louder.

Then the phone rang. Bad timing. "Who the hell is that?" she said, realizing she'd forgotten to turn it off. That wouldn't please her master, Kalfu.

She stood up, walked to the windowsill, and checked the number. Monica.

"What the fuck does she want?"

But as Pearla glanced out the window into the darkness of night, lit only by a sliver of moon sliding out from black cloud cover, an idea occurred to her. Maybe Monica's call was a sort of divine intervention.

It gave her an idea. A small smile pursed her lips. She answered the ringing phone.

"We have a problem," Monica said.

"What's that?"

"Saul."

"What about him?"

"He was here last night."

"What?"

"I saw him at a bar on the malecón. Drinking with Spencer. I was gonna call you right away, but he disappeared. I went to the bathroom, came back, and he was gone."

Pearla's smile faded. "You should've called me right away. If that happens again, you call me right away."

"Sorry. I should've known, but I was so shocked to see him."

"Did he see you?"

"I don't think so."

"You don't think so?"

"I'm pretty sure."

Pearla rubbed the crinkle in her temple. Monica would need a lot more schooling if she was to become a star pupil. "I don't want you to be pretty sure. I want you to be absolutely sure."

"I'm sure."

Only because I'm saying it. But it didn't matter now. Focus on the task at hand. "How's it going with Joella?"

"Slow—she's pretty set in her ways. She's different."

"I don't care. I want you to step it up a bit."

"What do you want me to do?"

"Why don't we try a little extortion? Why don't we have our cop friend Anwar Gonzalez trump up some charges and throw her in jail for a while? That might wake her loser boyfriend up and get him scrambling over there with money. At least it will get him distracted so I can execute my plan."

"That will be expensive. Gonzalez is drinking a lot lately and demanding more money for favors."

"Don't worry about that. We still have a contingency fund, right?" Pearla knew her sisters spent money like it grew on trees, but she hoped Monica had benefitted somewhat from her financial guidance.

"Most of it is in the account, as you instructed."

"Good. Call Gonzalez and get him in motion. Tell him we'll give him ten thousand pesos. If he asks for more, you call me and I'll talk to him. Now let me finish my work. The plan has changed. I need to fix it."

"Okay."

Pearla ended the call and closed all the window blinds. She returned to the pentagram and sat down cross-legged, staring at the bottle of rum for a few moments. She took another swill, closed her eyes, and began humming a tune that would, with divine intervention, see Saul possessed by one of the most malevolent spirits in the spirit world.

He wouldn't know what'd hit him. He'd get sideswiped by Joella's cop story, careening him into a tail-spinning mind-funk; the perfect frame of mind she needed for Kalfu to work his magic, possess him, and push him over that precarious precipice of sanity that he'd been clinging to for far too long.

Her humming lasted ten minutes before she spoke: "All-powerful Kalfu, hear me. I know you have been guiding me and I call on your guidance once more. Possess this lost soul, Saul. Work your magic. Turn his pathetic and self-serving life into a living nightmare. Judge him and you will find him not worthy. And I beg you, I will be your faithful servant forever if you speed up his demise... mmmm... mmmmm... mmmmm..."

A small, cold current of air made Pearla open her eyes. She saw the candles flicker and suddenly felt cold. She was tempted to hug herself for warmth. But she left her hands where they were, outstretched in front of her, palms flat on the carpet. She knew she couldn't stop. She closed her eyes and resumed. "I know you hear me, dear Kalfu, and I call on your influence and power to end the miserable existence of this wretched soul. You, the protector of our people, know more than anyone the reckless debauchery Saul has wreaked on the very fabric of our culture. I beg and plead with you... end his miserable existence..."

Now it was more than a small draft that made her open her eyes a second time. The draft turned into a cold wind. The candles went out. The curtains fluttered. A bedside lamp tipped over. Pearla's heart began thumping spasmodically. She didn't know if it was more from adrenaline—would she finally meet the master?—or fear, but she closed her eyes again and began humming. The room went from cold to uncomfortably hot. She stopped humming, beads of sweat forming on her brow.

A voice spoke, demanding: "Open your eyes."

She did.

A fiery red form stood in front of her, with chiseled features and a black top hat. He grinned and a black, serpent-like tongue darted out, licking his pointy chin. It retracted in a flash. He had tiny red slits for eyes, framed by hollow black sockets. He was nude and his horse-sized member stood erect, pointing directly at her mouth.

He took a drag of a cigar and blew a perfect smoke ring into the air, illuminated by his fiery form. "You dare summon the forces of debauchery and lasciviousness to solve your issues of the same variety? What makes you think I have any interest in that?"

Pearla wiped the sweat from her brow and lifted her hands, supplicating. Here, standing in front of her, was the powerful spirit she had worshipped and adored since childhood. All her life's work, right here, right now. She wasn't about to blow it. Him, maybe, but not it. Never in her entire life's worship had she encountered Kalfu's physical presence.

"What would you have me do to win your favor, master? Tell me. I'll do anything."

Kalfu grinned. "You can start with some rum," he said, pointing to the bottle. "Pass that over."

She did. He drank, finishing the bottle, and tossed it on the floor.

"What makes you think I've had anything to do with your plans?" he said, inching closer, the spear-like member leading the charge.

Doubts flashed through Pearla's mind. Had she been mistaken all this time? He was the one who tampered with debauchery. Didn't he encourage it? He certainly had a history of engaging in alcohol-laced sexual orgies.

"Wasn't that you, master? Weren't you helping me rid our country of the nasty exploiters of women?"

Kalfu blew another smoke ring and grinned. A full bottle of rum magically appeared in his hand. He popped the top and took a long swig. "You might have me confused with someone else, my dear."

Pearla was getting more confused. "I do?"

"Do you want me to tell you?"

"Please, Kalfu."

"You'll have to do something for me first."

"What's that?"

"Take your clothes off, lay on the bed, and spread your legs. I'm going to tie you up and fuck the living shit out of you. I know you're used to that."

Chapter Ten

Joella's daughter Evelyn approached her mother that evening and touched her arm gently. "Are you okay, Mom?"

Joella forced a smile. "Everything will be fine, my love." She took Evelyn on her knee and hugged her tightly. Joella would never fully admit it to herself, but Evelyn was her favorite child.

Evelyn beamed and kissed her mother on the cheek. Then the smile turned into a frown. "Have you been crying, Mom?"

Joella wiped a tear from her left eye. "No sweetie," she lied. "My eyes are watery from the dust."

The beaming smile slowly returned to Evelyn's face. "You sure, Mom?"

Joella nodded and tried on the smile again. It didn't entirely fit.

"Can I go outside and play?" Evelyn said.

Joella checked the time: 8:38 pm. "Sure honey, but don't go too far."

Evelyn left.

Joella sat in her house on the couch, now alone, a rare moment in such a busy household.

Outside the unscreened and un-paned windows, motos roared by and some locals danced in the streets. The drink-accompanied conversations and laughter were loud and gregarious. Speakers mounted on the outside walls of a nearby calmado thumped out La Materialista's *La Chapa*

Que Vibran. It was Saturday night, and San Marcos was in full party mode.

But Joella didn't feel much like partying that night. She felt the tears coming again and fought to hold them back. She lost the battle. The tears flowed. She grabbed a roll of toilet paper, peeled off a few squares, and dabbed at her eyes.

How could everything that felt so right go so wrong? Saul still wasn't returning her calls or texts. To add insult to injury, one of her friends had said she'd seen him last night drinking in a bar on the malecón with his friend Spencer. He was here and still refusing to talk to her. How could that be? In better days, he'd told her he wanted to sell his house, finish a novel, and move to the DR permanently. But these things take time. Why would he just pick up and leave like that?

At one time, Joella had envisioned herself in the house with Saul, living with him happily ever after; maybe a few months in Canada, a few more in the DR during the cold winters. When he'd first returned to Prince Edward Island, he'd emailed her many photos: the raging beachfront bonfires; views of the ocean at sunset with magical blues, pinks, purples, and fiery oranges; the two-story 19th-century character house with wraparound deck; the manicured two-acre lawn surrounding it; the old cedar-sided barn and three other outbuildings. He'd also sent bedroom pictures: the luxurious king-sized bed and coffee-colored walls; his rabbit friends; the lush forest. There were even a few funny shots with the trusty chainsaw, Señor Stihl, perched atop a cut pile of wood, surrounded by empty Alpine beer cans. If people didn't think chain-sawing and drinking went hand-in-hand, they hadn't met Saul yet. He'd even included a few selfies of him drinking outside an outbuilding, standing beside an antique floor lamp. Who would've thought an indoor lamp would look so perfect outdoors. But it worked, positioned beside the peeling paint of the old chainsaw building, a droopy table-mounted umbrella nearby. In its imperfection, it was perfect.

But things were far from perfect now. The alcohol had gotten the better of Saul. And she was sure his life was still in danger.

Joella had asked for money and he'd taken it the wrong way, even misinterpreted her text message (*If you are sure you love me, then show me*) which to Joella meant be in touch more often and reinforce verbally that he loved her. Now she realized how he'd probably interpreted it. *If you love me, show me the money*.

She felt stupid for succumbing to her sister Gisella's urgings—"Get it from your boyfriend. He's got money. If he loves you, he'll send it to you." Gisella thought differently than Joella. When Gisella saw gringos, she saw dollar signs. At one time, she'd had an American boyfriend. Sure, she'd loved him. She'd probably loved his money more, though, because when they split after a two-year union, Gisella ended up with a new car and about ten thousand dollars. But that was two years ago. The money and the vehicle were long gone now. After living off the money, and contributing to the household with it, she'd been forced to sell the vehicle to pay bills. At least now Gisella was working in a clothing store and could contribute to the household with her own money.

This was part of Joella's misery. Gisella had been pressuring her to pay some of the household bills. "Me and my sister and brother are feeding and housing you and your family," she'd told Joella. "If you can't get it from Saul, then get a job."

Joella thought it was only a matter of time before her sister kicked her out on the street. At one time, she hadn't thought Gisella was capable of that. But now she wasn't sure.

Earlier that day, she'd pounded the pavement looking for work. She went to four restaurants and four bars looking for work as a waitress, then to six apartment buildings trying to secure work as a cleaning lady. When the boss was in, about half of the time, she was met with unfavorable responses: "We don't have any work right now." "If I had a position available I'd be offering it to my family before you." "Sorry, nothing right now. Try back next month. We might be firing someone." "No, and why don't you get lost? I don't have anything. Times are tough right now."

Times are tough. I don't have money for books to finish my education, I can't feed my kids, I can't find a job, we might be on the streets soon, and I lost the only man I thought I could spend the rest of my life with. I've hit rock bottom. She put both hands to her face, put her head on the arm of the couch, and let the tears flow. No point in holding them back now. Maybe she would feel better after a good cry. Soon the slow whimpers turned into wracking sobs. Not wanting to be seen by her family, she put her phone in her pocket and went into the bathroom.

As she was about to turn on the tap to splash some water on her face, she heard the scuffle of heavy boots entering the house. An intruder had arrived. She quickly towel-tried her tears and peered through the sheer blind covering the bathroom entrance. She heard his booming baritone voice, but could only see a black silhouette in the darkness. There was another man behind him.

Evelyn stood between them, scared and bewildered.

"Where is she?" Lieutenant Anwar Gonzalez said.

"Where is who?" Evelyn said.

"I told you. Joella."

"She's not here. Why do you want her?"

"None of your business, kid. Tell me where she is."

"She's not here, but I'll tell you where she is if you tell me what she did."

"She robbed a tourist. Tell me which room she's in."

Someone's setting me up. What's going on? Who's doing this? Joella wasted no time climbing through the bathroom window. When she was halfway out, she felt a vice-like grip on her ankle.

"Get back here," Gonzalez said. "You're going to jail."

Joella kicked the cop hard in the face. He released her and groaned in pain. She shimmied out the window and landed in the dirt on her shoulder, somersaulting and then getting up quickly.

She saw another cop coming toward her from the side of the house. Barney, a neighborhood dog that her family had befriended and fed infrequently, barked and attacked the cop, biting his ankle. He stopped and turned around, reaching for his gun.

Gonzalez had tried to climb through the bathroom window after Joella, but his formidable gut got wedged in it. "Kill that damned dog, Juan," Gonzalez shouted. "And get me out of here!"

Juan aimed the pistol. Barney looked up, saw the danger, and chomped down hard on the ankle. Then he released it and ran.

Juan fired.

Joella, fleeing down the street, looked back and saw Barney disappear into a neighbor's house. She heard the bullet ricochet off a tin roof. *Thank God he's safe.* She kept going, wondering if Juan would immediately give chase or stay back to help his fat partner.

Juan turned to run after Joella. Neighborhood partiers began gathering around Gonzalez, pointing fingers and laughing as he puffed and twisted in the window.

"Get me out of here," Gonzalez demanded. "She won't get far."

Joella ran on pure adrenaline. Reaching the bottom of the hill, she glanced back again and saw a white police pickup closing the distance, siren wailing, lights flashing.

Joella knew where to go. She spotted the raucous bar, ran across the street in front of the approaching pickup, and entered. The outside tables were packed with patrons who were listening to loud music, dancing, and drinking.

A man stood up, grinning, and waved her inside. She went in and he followed her. She recognized his scraggly hair instantly. It was Fernando Rodriguez, the leech classmate. "Get in here quick," he said, pointing behind the bar. "There's a hidden door that leads to the basement. Go hide in there."

"Thanks," she said, thinking that maybe her first impression of him had been wrong. Maybe he was a nice guy after all. But she didn't have time to give it much thought.

She didn't want to wind up in jail and get extorted, beaten, and raped by sadistic, opportunistic cops.

The bartender slid away a large table, revealing the door. He unlocked it and waved Joella inside.

She went down.

He locked it, slid the table back in place, and sat on it.

Fernando had already opened the back door to the bar. It was swaying and creaking in the breeze by the time the two cops arrived. He pointed outside. "She went that way, over the fence."

A beefy, mustached cop looked at his smaller partner. "Look around." Then he turned to Fernando. "You helped her escape?"

"I did not—"

The cop pulled out a black baton and struck Fernando once on the top of the head—*thwack*—and once in the forehead for good measure—*thwack!*

In another world, in another time, that might've been the end of it. The guys might've calmed down and ratted Joella out. But this was San Marcos. Cops weren't well-liked in San Marcos. They were known for being corrupt extortionists and thieves. In many cases, they were murderers as well. They often abused their rank and power.

So Fernando, fearing for his life, pulled out his switchblade, extending the razor-sharp blade lightning-fast, and plunged it into the eye of the attacking cop.

In the same instant, the bartender grabbed a full 40-ounce bottle of Brugal rum and smashed it over the head of the searching cop.

"Such a waste of good rum," a drunk man said, standing up, then falling flat on his face as the rum-struck cop also dropped to the floor, unconscious.

The stabbed cop screamed and toppled back, knocking over two chairs. Spewing blood like a lawn sprinkler, he landed on his back, both hands gripping the blood-soaked blade, trying to pry it loose. Twitching spasmodically, he pried it halfway out of his eye. Then the twitching stopped and he lay still, quite dead.

Fernando wiped the blood from his head wound, retrieved his blade, and plunged it into the throat of the unconscious, rum-struck cop. A small geyser of blood squirted out, covering the cop's mouth, chin, and starched khaki-colored uniform. Some splashed onto Fernando's face and white t-shirt.

The bartender threw Fernando a dishtowel. He caught it and wiped his face, hands, and the blade, then tossed it to the bartender, who tucked it under the sink. The bartender quickly slid the table away from the basement hatch and unlocked the door.

Fernando went in. The bartender locked the hatch, repositioned the table, sat down on it, and poured himself about four ounces of straight Brugal.

Some patrons gawked. A few toasted and drank. Others actually laughed. A few rushed out of the bar.

Toasting the toasters, the bartender drained the entire glass and slapped it down on the table. *All in a day's work*, he thought, trying unsuccessfully to wipe the grin off his face.

By the time Joella reached the bottom of the rickety stairs, she knew she *had* reached rock bottom. From here there was nowhere to go but up. She heard the screams and commotion upstairs and felt a dread certainty in her rapidly beating heart that people were dead. She had no idea who had been killed. Maybe there were rats upstairs who would, for a price, disclose her whereabouts.

The basement was pitch-black and reeked of mold and urine, and something else, unidentifiable to her quivering nostrils, but equally foul. As the battle upstairs erupted, she felt her way around, almost tripping twice over empty bottles. She stepped on a rat and screamed. The rat squealed and disappeared somewhere in the blackness.

Finally she felt a switch on a slime-coated wall and flicked it on. A small incandescent light bulb dangling in the center of the basement buzzed twice, then lit up, providing dim light.

She let her eyes adjust, clenching her fists to try and contain the fear. Its tendrils were spreading inside her like an electric shock, the voltage getting higher. Panic was taking hold. *Hold on. Find the door.*

She looked around the basement. Wooden shelves in one corner contained bottles, some full, some empty. Another wall was piled high with debris and something else—clothing. The voltage on the fear-meter ratcheted up a couple of notches. *Clothing? What are they doing throwing clothes down here?*

But she didn't have time to process the thought. Either that, or she didn't want to. She had to find a door. She had to leave. *Maybe I should wait until the cops leave.* Another wall was bare, except for a leaky pipe that steadily plunked large drops of water into an expanding, smelly pool. *Drip... drip... drip... drip.* It was maddening.

Noticing a small spear of light, she moved toward the leaky pipe. Then she saw it: a narrow hallway. She followed it to the end. It led to three doors. She tried the first one. Locked. So was the second one. But the third, where the spear of light was coming through, opened. She went inside.

That was when she heard footsteps descending the basement stairs. Her heart almost leaped clean out of her throat. With trembling hands, she closed the door. She turned quickly and spotted an assortment of wooden crates piled in the corner. Shifting them as delicately as she could, she crawled underneath and hid.

A rat scurried across her face in the darkness and she had to bite her tongue—so hard she drew blood—to prevent herself from screaming.

The footsteps grew louder. She heard a bottle break, crunching under a boot.

She trembled and waited.

A door opened, creaking long and loud. He was in the hallway now, Joella knew. It was only a matter of time. She held her breath. The thoughts tumbled like an avalanche. *Who is it? Who did this to me? Who set me up? And why? Was it Saul? No, it couldn't be Saul. Then who?*

Without realizing it, Joella began to pray: *Please God, if you're up there, get me out of this alive. I beg you, I beg you. Please.*

A voice interrupted the prayer: "Joella... Joella... where are you? It's me, Fernando. The cops are gone. You're safe now."

Her breath came in short gasps. She realized only now she had been holding it. *Thank God... thank you, God.* She pushed a crate away. "I'm in here."

Fernando opened the door and stepped inside. A sliver of light poking in from a loose board illuminated his face. Wide, crazy grin. Wide eyes. Blood-spattered face and shirt. Seeing him, the last thing Joella wanted to do was thank God.

Wiping blood from his lips, he said, "Thank God I found you, darling. I don't think you'll be ignoring me now."

Chapter Eleven

"Beam me up, Scotty. There's no intelligent life down here," Saul said.

"Ha-ha, very funny," Samantha said. "Now, tell me. What did you find out?"

"You might be surprised. There's more legitimacy to teleportation than I thought."

His desk was sprawling with notes and lists late that Saturday evening. He had spent the better part of two days doing research, trying to prove to himself as much as to Samantha that he wasn't quite ready for the men in white coats to put him in a straitjacket and haul him off to the nuthouse. He'd moderated the booze, and he'd gotten his tooth fixed on a teleportation trip to the Dominican Republic the night before. That was a story Samantha might not buy right away. He might have to save it for another time.

"Well, tell me," she said.

He removed the phone from his ear and put it on speaker. He might have to consult his notes. "Apparently, teleportation has been used as far back as the late 1960s on behalf of the United States government by DARPA, the Defense Advanced Research Projects Agency. A guy by the name of Andrew Basiago claims to have been involved in a highly classified research project called Project Pegasus as a young boy."

"What happened to him?"

"He says he was teleported all over the place—through some teleporter apparently invented by Nicola Tesla."

"You sure this guy isn't a nutcase?"

"Which one?"

"Basiago?"

"He has his critics, but I don't think so. He's a practicing lawyer, plans on running for US president, and is on a massive campaign to get the US government to declassify its teleportation and time travel secrets. Wants to have teleporters at all airports. Claims it's a more efficient, safer, and more environmentally friendly way to travel. Even has a book in the works, supposedly."

"It doesn't surprise me that the US government would want to keep this stuff secret. If they could teleport troops into enemy lines, the enemy, with this technology, could do the same thing."

"Not too hard to figure that out. Anyway, Basiago claims to have been teleported to Mars and even back in time. Says he's met George Washington and instructed him to withdraw troops. Also claims to have witnessed Abraham Lincoln's Gettysburg Address."

"Did he say anything about dream teleportation?"

"He might have, but I didn't find it. He talked about a woman who got in an accident and injured her head badly. Some adrenaline or something must have kicked in and she teleported to her mother's house from the accident scene, allowing her to get medical attention a lot quicker. And during Pegasus, some nine-year-old child was teleported, landed in a fountain of water and, because his feet hit the water at a slightly different time than the rest of his body, he sheered them off at the ankles."

"Yikes, that's not good."

"Well, these children were apparently used by DARPA as guinea pigs."

"What about dream teleportation? You're getting off topic."

"I got lost in the research, but I did find something on dream teleportation."

"I'm waiting with baited breath."

"Doctor Bruce Goldberg is a clinical hypnotherapist. He's written many self-help books, some bestsellers supposedly. He's been on *Oprah, Regis & Kelly*, CBS News, even CNN. Anyway, he claims you can teleport—physically relocate the body from one place to another site without touching it in any way—in a dream state. He differentiates between regular dreams and lucid dreams, claiming, and these are his words, 'your body physically leaves the bed and travels to another location on a different dimension.'"

"Interesting, carry on."

"He says if you watch someone teleporting, you'd 'see their body slowly fade away and disappear. Here are his words: 'Nothing else in the environment would be altered. The person teleporting would experience an increase in energy vibrating at high speed, accompanied by a tingling, buzzing sensation and/or the feeling of spiraling upward. Often a pop sound emanates from the top of their head...'"

"Did you experience any of that?"

"Well, I did notice I was highly charged with energy. I was also scared shitless, so that could have been just adrenaline. But one thing he said seems to fit."

"What's that?"

"When I wake from—may as well call it what it is—teleportation, my memory is clear. I can distinctly recall and feel physical sensations, like a sore shoulder from jumping off a balcony, that sort of thing. In regular dreams, most times my memory is hazy when I wake up and there are no physical sensations, other than maybe a hard-on if it's a sexual dream, or sweat-soaked if it's a nightmare. If I don't document a regular dream right away, it's gone. Not the case with teleportation. I remember everything vividly when I wake up, providing I wasn't halfway in the bag when I went to bed. And the memory stays with me, clear as a bell."

"Well, fair enough. But this Goldberg guy is talking about natural teleportation. What if yours is chemically induced? Then we don't know what the long-term effects might be."

Saul could envision a dozen scenarios, including the men in white coats coming with the straitjacket. "That's where you come in. What did you find out on your end?"

"It seems like you ran across lots of stories of teleportation, but no actual proof. I'm naturally a skeptic and was looking for proof. And I knew that would start with animal experimentation, especially given what you said about the claw marks."

"Did you find any proof?"

"Not conclusive. Saw a YouTube video where a guy seemingly teleports a dead bird. Bunch of comments at the bottom about why it's a fake. Another story about quantum teleportation where scientists were trying to teleport information to rats. A Dutch scientist who has his findings published in a respected science journal claims to have 'teleported an atom three meters with a hundred per cent accuracy.'"

"What about animal experiments?"

"Well, I thought it was nothing at first, and maybe it is nothing. In my random searching, I ran across a scientist, fired and disgraced as a quack by the Canadian defense department, called Nicholas Fry. He claims to have been carrying out teleportation animal experiments for a long time now—many that've ended in death or deformities for the animals. But he says he's finally successfully teleported a dog halfway around the world and back. Some blog post on a website that was followed by lots of comments calling him a fake, fraud, and nutcase."

"What do you think?"

"I didn't know what to think, so I kept digging. And then I came across some information that really shocked me."

"Just a minute."

It was damp in the old house that night, and Saul's shoulder and back had been acting up all afternoon. The pissing rain outside didn't help. Probably arthritis, aggravated by the moisture. He had made a point to limit his alcohol intake to three beers. But, after hearing what Samantha said and feeling the hairs on the back of his neck stiffen, he couldn't help it. He brought the phone into the kitchen and poured himself a four-ounce shot of Brugal rum. He swallowed half of it. Something told him he was an unwilling human guinea pig in an experiment gone horribly wrong. A macabre image of Jeff Goldblum as a half-fly, half-man popped into his head, and he squeezed his eyes shut, trying to suppress it.

He opened them and took another pull on the rum. "Okay, go ahead."

"Are you drinking?"

"I needed one. Just tell me already." Saul returned to the office with the drink and sat down at his desk.

"What's the name of the street that you live on again?"

"Howe Point Road, in Howe Bay."

There was a moment's pause.

"What are you doing, Samantha?"

"I'm checking something. Hang on... Here it is. Nicholas also lives in King's County, on the southeast part of the Island, maybe twenty-two minutes from *you*. He's on Christian Road in Cardigan Bay."

"What the fuck?"

"I wish I was joking."

"I wish you were too. And he's experimenting with animals?"

"Supposedly. Wanna drop by his house? I have his address."

"Let me think about it overnight. I'm hitting the wall here with fatigue. I need sleep. I haven't done this much research in months."

"Okay, but I think I'm going to try calling him tomorrow to see if we can visit him. I mean, I don't wanna see you turning into *The Fly*. We have to reverse whatever happened to you. There may be dangerous consequences if we don't."

She was right, even though there was something appealing about his condition. Hadn't he saved a life the other night? And he'd saved some money on the tooth repair in the DR. Five hundred bucks to be precise. But at what cost? The horrible fly image returned and he almost spilled his drink. *Tooth repair, five hundred bucks. The Fly, priceless.*

"All right, go ahead and call him. I'll call you in the morning. I'm done in."

"Okay. By the way, how's the tooth?"

Should he or shouldn't he? May as well come clean. "I got it fixed in the DR yesterday."

"You what?"

"I think you heard me perfectly well, Samantha."

"Holy shit, we got a lot to talk about."

"Tomorrow morning. Have a good night." Saul ended the call and checked the time: 10:38 pm. Time for bed. Carrying his drink, he went out to the back porch, sat down and lit a smoke, and thought. He hadn't done much about the shoulder, and he had done little to prepare his property for resale ever since the animal attack. He sipped his rum and absently rolled a tongue across the upper molar that had been repaired. A little sore still, but the good dentist had said that was normal. He wondered what Spencer would be thinking now, after Saul had spent three hours drinking with him last night before claiming he had a date and disappearing. He couldn't tell Spencer about the teleportation. Not yet, anyway. Spencer was a no-nonsense guy who would flat-out declare bullshit. And he didn't want to open that can of worms yet.

"Where are you staying anyway?" Spencer had asked just before Saul left.

"Blue Bay Hotel," Saul said. "Playa Dorada. I'm only here for a short time."

A tree branch suddenly crashed to the forest floor. Saul started, spilling some of his drink. In his mind's eye, Pearla's evil grin materialized. With an unsteady hand, he drained the drink. *She's coming to get you, soldier. You have more problems than you think.*

A few minutes later, he was in bed, and there was only one thought in his mind: Joella. The calls had stopped, but the text messages had not: *I know what you're thinking. That I only want your money. But that's not true. I love you. I wish you would return my messages. Love Joella.* And: *If you don't have the money, don't give it to me. I just thought since we were together I could ask you for help. I thought you loved me. I had no one else to turn to. I'm sorry if that makes you think I'm just after your money. I can understand that because most of the women down here are like that. But not me, I'm different. You have to believe me. I love you. Please call me.*

Still wearing jeans and a t-shirt, Saul checked his pockets. The three hundred dollars was there. Just in case.

A few minutes later, he succumbed to fatigue and started to drift off. Just before sleep took hold, the last thought that entered his mind was, *Maybe love and money are connected in a way I don't yet understand. Just give it to her, you moron. Give her the money...*

Chapter Twelve

"Help me, please!"

Saul recognized Joella's voice as soon as he heard it. But he couldn't see her. It was pitch-black. He got his bearings and felt around in the darkness. *Where am I?* Yet on some unrecognized level, he knew. He was here because Joella was in danger and needed him. This new teleporting ability delivered him to areas of trouble. That was the way it worked. His life would probably never be the same.

"Help me."

Fuck, where is she? I can't see shit. He continued moving toward the voice, using the wall for support. His finger touched a light switch and he turned it on. As his eyes adjusted to the light, he surveyed the mess. Glowing red eyes peered up at him from below, squeaked, and vanished. A rat.

He found the hallway and proceeded. He stopped when he heard a man's voice say, "You were once a cock-tease, bitch. But I'm gonna turn you into a cock-please. Now suck it."

"No!"

A loud slap. "I said suck it or I'll kill you, bitch."

"You're gonna kill me anyway."

Another slap.

Saul felt his heart begin to pound in his chest, like the fists of a man buried alive pounding on the inside of a coffin lid. Blood flowed through his body, pushed by the rush of adrenaline. He felt the veins in his neck bulge and pulsate, as if some newfound strength was coursing through his body. In an instant, he saw red.

He charged for the door and crashed into it with his good shoulder. It swung open, and in the gray suffused light from the small bulb down the hallway, he saw the horrifying spectacle.

Joella was crouched in a corner beside some wooden crates. Fernando stood in front of her, his erect member perched a few inches from her face.

Blood dripped from a cut on her lip and her face glistened with tears. Saul thought he could see handprints on her cheeks where Fernando had slapped her. Her blouse and bra had been torn and blood dripped from the left nipple. Saul charged forward. "I'll kill you..."

Fernando easily sidestepped the charge and Saul crashed into the pile of wooden crates, landing on his back.

"Saul, is that you?" Joella said. "That's you."

Fernando flashed his switchblade and lunged forward, thrusting the blade toward Saul's chest. Saul moved to the right and slipped on some crates.

Joella picked up a crate and thrust it forward, just in time. The blade struck the wood and penetrated it an inch or so. Fernando backhanded her in the head. She screamed and careened back.

Saul got to his feet. Fernando held the crate with one hand, trying to dislodge the blade with the other. Saul charged forward, hit the crate, and pushed Fernando back. Fernando hit the corner of the open door with his spine and moaned. The crate splintered and Fernando extracted the blade. Wooden pieces fell to the floor.

Fernando swiped the blade toward Saul's throat. Seeing the glint of metal, Saul stepped back. Swinging sharp metal missed his throat by inches.

"I don't know where you came from, gringo. But you're gonna wish you never got your stupid white ass down here by the time I'm through with you," Fernando said, inching closer. His eyes glowed red.

"Just leave her alone and go," Saul said. "If you know what's good for you."

"Are you kidding me, white man?" He pointed to Joella, who was trying to button up her tattered blue blouse. "I've had my eyes on this bitch for a long time now. And I'm not gonna let things end this easily. Besides, I've just killed two cops. They'll be coming for me. They're gonna want to kill me. I've got nothing to lose anymore."

"I've got cop connections. I can get you off."

Fernando stepped closer. "Too late for that." He lunged at Saul, aiming the blade at his throat. Saul stepped back and hit the moist wall. He saw the blade coming and tried to duck, but received a knee in the head for his effort. The room spun as his head jerked up. The blade was closer now. He was going to get it. He tried a knee of his own that glanced off the side of Fernando's groin, just enough to smart a little, and change the knife's trajectory. It sliced through the side of Saul's neck as Fernando landed on top of him.

Saul felt warm blood flow down his neck, onto his shirt.

Fernando thrust the bloody blade forward. Saul grabbed his wrists and they struggled for control of the knife.

"You're gonna die, stupid gringo," Fernando said. "Take our women? I'll teach you. You're gonna die."

"No, you're gonna die, you sick pervert," Joella said. She stood behind Fernando.

With almost superhuman strength, Fernando yanked his wrists free from Saul's grasp and turned his head, a little too late.

Joella held a chunk of wood from the splintered crate. It had a three-inch rusty nail protruding from the offending end. With both hands she swung it at Fernando, embedding the nail through his ear and into his head. Blood gushed out, soaking Saul.

Saul slid out from under the dying heap, crawling, gripping his bleeding neck.

Fernando removed the improvised weapon from his ear, looked at it disgustedly, and threw it at Saul. The nail-less end cracked Saul in the head and ricocheted into the wall. Then Fernando stood up and, waving the blade, staggered toward Joella. She ran down the hallway.

Before Fernando could reach the door, Saul was already on him, piggyback style, wrapping his arms around his neck. They swayed like drunken sailors for a moment before crashing onto crates.

Saul tightened his left arm around Fernando's neck and squeezed. Fernando stabbed Saul in the leg.

Saul winced—"You motherfucker!"—but continued choking him.

Fernando extracted the blade and, with draining strength, plunged it toward Saul's leg.

Saul moved and the blade tore through his pants. "Help me, Joella. Help me. This fuck won't die."

Fernando continued thrusting the knife at Saul's leg.

Joella ran into the room. Saul pointed to the wooden plank with the big nail.

She picked it up, ran over to them, and swung the weapon hammer-style, stabbing Fernando repeatedly—in the eye, nose, ear, and mouth. "Die, you fucking pervert... die!"

"Watch my arm," Saul said.

Joella continued stabbing Fernando, enraged, mesmerized by vengeance. "I said die, you son of a bitch. Die means die."

Saul, while strangling Fernando, counted the stab wounds—eight, nine, ten, eleven, twelve. Finally one blow through the ear and deep into his brain ended it. Fernando muttered something incomprehensible, spewed forth a fountain of blood, and went limp. His hand opened and the knife clattered out onto the floor.

It was a bloody mess.

Saul pushed the late Fernando Rodriguez off him and got up. He looked at his jeans and noticed three puncture wounds just above the knee. They didn't look that deep, but they would need a tourniquet. And so would his neck wound.

Joella stood, eyes wide open, mouth agape, still holding the spiked wooden plank. It dribbled blood and brain matter. She had buttoned her blouse haphazardly and her left breast poked out, dotted with red drops.

She ran into his arms. "You saved my life," she said. "I'm so glad you're back."

"I think it's the other way around."

"Thank God you're here."

Saul was about to kiss her, but she suddenly withdrew. "You think I want your money. You should know better. I love you."

He moved toward her. "I'm sorry. I haven't been thinking clearly lately."

"I know. I had a dream. You're in danger." They hugged again and he kissed her gently on the lips. In spite of himself, he couldn't help the stirring in his loins. He released her.

"We need to get out of here."

"Saul?"

"What?"

"Do you still love me?"

Before he had time to think about the words, they spilled out. "Of course I do." He didn't know if they were true, but now certainly wasn't the time or place to debate matters of the heart.

"What happened?" he said. "How did you get here?"

"You're bleeding. We need to fix you."

"So are you."

"Mine's just a cut lip. I'll be fine."

"Out here," Saul said, taking her hand. At the doorway to the killing room, he stopped and looked back at Fernando. He was an unrecognizable mess of blood, flesh, and brain matter.

They went into the center of the basement and stood underneath the small bulb. Adrenaline coursed through their bodies. For a moment they were speechless, panting and trembling. In shock. Their heart rates finally returned to something approximating normal.

Joella relayed the story of how she'd gotten there. As she talked, she tore the sleeves from Saul's t-shirt, fashioned a tourniquet, and wrapped one around his neck. Saul interrupted her. "Is it deep? The cut?"

"I don't think so."

"Good."

Still talking, she wrapped the other sleeve around Saul's leg wounds. "And these puncture wounds don't look too bad either."

"That's good."

She finished bandaging Saul as she told him of her ordeal. "I don't know who would do this to me. There. You look a bloody mess, but at least you're not dying."

"Thanks," Saul said. The handprints on her face had turned a purplish color. He touched the small cut on her lip, already crusted over with dried blood. "You sure you're okay?"

Her intense eyes penetrated Saul's soul as she nodded.

He looked down at the exposed breast and, without thinking, gently tucked it back in the torn blouse. His finger glanced over the erect nipple. She moaned slightly.

He gave her a knowing look. Then his expression changed. "So that guy in there, Fernando, he's a classmate?"

Joella nodded, adjusting her blouse to expose less cleavage. "He's been hitting on me for some time now, but I never gave him the time of day. I never thought he was this crazy."

"And you say two cops chased you?"

Joella nodded. "But Fernando killed them. Remember? Their bodies might still be upstairs."

Saul scratched his chin stubble. It didn't look good. He could hear shuffling around and mute voices upstairs; the frenetically thumping bachata music had suddenly stopped as well. The people upstairs might blame Joella for the cop killings. They could add two murder charges to the trumped up—*was it trumped up?*—gringo-robbing charge.

He couldn't take Joella to her house until this mess had been straightened out. The cops would be back, no doubt about that. Saul looked at the rickety stairs leading up to the bar. How could they get out of there? Not that way, that was for sure. Probably crawling with live cops by now, not to mention what other aberrations of humankind might be stalking around.

She interrupted his thoughts. "Who do you think would do this to me?"

"I have a theory. I'll tell you later. We need to get out of here."

"Any ideas?"

"Do you have your phone?"

"Yes." She pulled it out.

He lowered his voice. "Do you have any minutes?"

"A few." She handed it to him. He punched in Spencer's number. If anyone could get him out of this, Spencer could. He paid cops for protection and was actually friends with the one per cent of them who were honest. After five rings, it went to voicemail. No point leaving a message. Spencer didn't even know how to access voicemail.

"Where are we anyway?" Saul asked.

"San Marcos. The Jailhouse Bar."

Saul nodded. *That's fitting*. He knew the place. He'd even had drinks here before. And so had Spencer.

He sent a text: *It's Saul on Joella's phone. Call me. I'm in serious shit. At Jailhouse Bar.*

He noticed a stab of light coming from the room containing Fernando's dead body. "Come on, maybe it's a way out."

They went into the room and pushed a few crates away. Haphazardly nailed boards framing the wall. The one permitting light to enter was cracked and splintered. Saul peered out and could barely make out a streetlight in the distance. He tugged at the board. It sprang loose and dirt flowed in. He dug with his hands.

Joella helped.

In five minutes, they'd removed five or six boards and dug through dirt and rock with chunks of wood. More light flowed in, along with more street noise. The room was tiny and they couldn't help spraying some falling dirt particles on Fernando's bloodied corpse.

Saul stopped, wiped his brow, and looked at Fernando's dirt-covered body. *At least he's getting a proper burial*, he thought, biting his lip to prevent himself from laughing. *Maybe I am going nuts... and this is all in my head.*

Fifteen minutes later, they'd dug a small escape tunnel. There was barely enough room to shimmy to the surface due to some large, unmovable boulders. Saul pushed Joella in first and watched as she shimmied up.

Down the hall, the basement hatch creaked open. A voice called out, "Fernando, you down there, brother? I want sloppy seconds."

Stairs creaked as the man came down. Reaching the basement, he flashed a beam down the hall. Saul closed and locked the door.

"Hey, brother, don't keep her all to yourself," the man said. "The cops took the dead bodies and left. Let me have a piece of that pussy."

Footsteps came closer.

"Hurry," Saul whispered to Joella. "Someone's coming."

But she was stuck, and she was as skinny as a rail. How would Saul get out?

A knock on the door. "Fernando, what in God's name are you doing in there?"

Saul looked around, found Fernando's bloody switchblade, and picked it up.

"Hey, buddy, open up. It's my turn. Did that bitch fuck you to death or something?"

Saul felt a surge of rage. Some blood-boiling inner demon was giving him courage he'd never had before. How dare this clown insult Joella? She was clearly one of the finest women in the Puerto Plata area, both in character and in looks.

As Joella struggled and squirmed, Saul stepped forward and unlocked the door. He swung it open and thrust the blade forward. It grazed and cut the man's hand. Pulling his arm back, the man stepped aside and pointed the flashlight beam in Saul's eyes.

Momentarily blinded, Saul stepped forward anyway. Even though the man towered above Saul and had a lean, muscular build, Saul was angry and offended enough that he didn't give a fuck. His own appearance was slightly less than black-tie affair; disheveled hair matted with dirt and blood, a ragged, bloody t-shirt, and his face, hands, arms, and legs were blood-soaked. In a contest for most menacing appearance, the judges would have given it to Saul hands-down.

Jaw dropping and eyes widening, the man stepped back.

Saul raised the blade: "You better watch your fucking mouth when it comes to my girlfriend."

On cue, Joella said, "I'm out... let's go."

The man shone the flashlight on the floor for a split-second, bent down, and reached for an empty bottle.

Stepping forward, Saul swung the blade. "Don't try that unless you want to die trying."

The man retreated. "Hang on there, partner. I didn't mean any disrespect."

Saul could see it in the man's dark eyes. Fear was getting the better of him. Now was his chance to use that to his advantage. But another part, the rage demon, was saying don't take any chances, kill him, and don't leave any witnesses. It was more than that, actually; he felt a raw urge to kill for the thrill of it. *This isn't me anymore, is it?*

Saul narrowed his eyes, tightened his grip on the knife, and lunged forward. And a sound came out of his mouth that he'd never heard before. It was a low growl.

Trembling, the man began backing up quickly.

"I'm going to kill you just for the fuck of it," Saul said. "Teach you a little respect and enjoy every minute of it." *This is definitely not me talking. Something is wrong here. Terribly wrong. Get a grip.*

Yeah, grip the knife and kill this fucker.

He would have done just that if it wasn't for the interruption, again as if on cue.

"Come on, I'm out," Joella said. "What's going on in there?"

Growling like an angry wolf, Saul shouted, "GET THE FUCK OUT OF HERE! NOW!"

Whatever courage the man might have had vanished. He dropped the flashlight, turned, and ran.

Saul picked up the flashlight. He closed the switchblade, tucked it in his pocket, and headed for the hole in the wall.

Joella was standing outside, frantic.

"I'm coming, sweetie," he said. "Or at least breathing hard."

"What?"

"Nothing."

He crawled in. But his belly got stuck near the end of the short tunnel. Joella grabbed his outstretched hand and tugged. It was no use. He wasn't budging. The opening was just barely large enough for her, but Saul's beer belly girth was too thick.

He had an idea. "Hang on. Let go of me."

She released his hand.

With strength he'd never known he possessed, he gripped a large boulder and loosened it. He picked it up and threw it to the surface—well away from the object of his desire.

"Wow," Joella said. "You're strong."

"Well, smell isn't everything," he said, wondering how he could be so glib at a time like this.

"What?"

He pushed himself to the surface and stood up. "Just a bad joke, baby."

They were in a large, debris-strewn backyard of sorts, enclosed by a barbed-wire fence.

The thumping music had resumed inside the bar and neighborhood dogs barked. A few motoconchos were parked outside the fence, the drivers watching them escape. Saul shone the flashlight around. Perhaps fifteen feet away, a man leaned against a beaten vehicle and a woman knelt in front of him, performing fellatio. He moaned as she slurped and sucked. They were oblivious.

Saul couldn't help a small smile.

Neither could Joella. She pointed to a large hole in the fence. "Over there."

As they started moving, a man—Saul recognized him as the same man from the basement—opened the back door, exited, aimed a gun at them, and fired. The blast echoed through the neighborhood. The bullet ricocheted off the beaten vehicle and the conjoined couple ducked and rolled, the woman's mouth still attached to his swollen member.

It gave new meaning to the term joined at the hip, Saul thought, turning and running for the fence. Never bring a knife to a gunfight. He wasn't that stupid. Not yet, anyway.

As they arrived at the fence hole, two more bullets whizzed past them. Some motoconchos scattered. This really was a bad neighborhood.

Joella recognized a parked moto and approached. The driver waved them over. Then a black Chevy Trailblazer spun around the corner and stopped abruptly. A passenger door swung open. A grizzled man with long black hair and a full black beard said, "Get in." It was Spencer.

The man with the gun ran toward Spencer's vehicle.

They got in and Spencer sped away. A bullet shattered his right rear passenger window as he rounded a corner.

Saul turned to Joella. "You okay? You hit?"

"I'm okay," she said.

"Fucking cocksucker," Spencer said. "I know that guy. It's Ruddy Rodriguez. Fernando's brother. I'm gonna have that fucker killed."

An hour later, Joella and Saul sat in Spencer's two-bedroom oceanfront condo in Costambar, drinking rum and Coke. Spencer was out in the parking lot, vacuuming shattered glass from his vehicle.

Joella's cut turned out to be minor. She had a small bandage just below her lip. The red slap prints on her cheeks had turned a burnt burgundy.

She had sterilized Saul's wounds, applied bandages to the small puncture marks above the knee, and wrapped the two-inch cut on his neck with cotton batten and gauze. The knife had narrowly missed his jugular vein. One inch closer and he'd be dead. That was life and death in many ways. A game of inches. Prior to this medical treatment, they'd availed themselves of Spencer's shower and borrowed some clothing.

Joella wore a black t-shirt that said IF YOU DON'T LIKE ME, FUCK OFF. Saul wore an oversized gray t-shirt with a picture of a moose in the crosshairs of a rifle. BORN TO PARTY, it proclaimed.

In spite of the alcohol, the mood was quiet and somber. Saul had explained to Spencer and Joella that he actually wasn't staying in a hotel suite in Puerto Plata. He had teleported from his home on Prince Edward Island. He'd explained how it all began and where it had taken him, minus a few details. He told them he would be disappearing soon to straighten out some problems on PEI before returning.

They'd looked at him like he was nuts.

However, Joella couldn't explain how he'd shown up in the dingy basement of the Jailhouse Bar just when she needed him. And Spencer couldn't logically explain that either, nor could he figure out why Saul hadn't called him prior to his arrival for an airport pickup. That had always been protocol in the past. Why was he breaching it? And why would he stay in Puerto Plata proper? He'd always stayed in Costambar.

But, although disbelieving, Spencer had agreed to allow Joella to stay with him for a few days until the heat died down and they figured a way out. Spencer understood one thing. She was wanted by the cops for robbing a gringo, and possibly for two murder charges as well.

Joella said, "You said you have a theory about who's behind this. I'd like to hear it."

Delicate indeed, Saul thought. But he would have to talk the talk if he was going to walk the walk. "You know I had a bit of a history before we met?"

"Puerto Plata isn't that big. Word travels fast."

"Okay, I'm just going to say it. A woman I slept with before I met you, Pearla—the one I saw the other night when I teleported to Vancouver—has a little problem with me right now. I didn't do anything to her, but I suspect she feels slighted because I didn't fall for her game. I think she might be using you to get to me."

Joella winced as if she'd been slapped. "Do you know a woman named Monica Morales?"

"Before I met you I had a crazy stalker named Monica, but I never knew her last name. I slept with her once and she wouldn't leave me alone. Completely nuts."

Joella flinched, feeling a stab wound lance her heart. *Calm down, girl. He slept with her before he met you. That's not a reason for jealousy. Everyone has a past, stupid.* But it took a minute or so to compose herself.

She proceeded to describe Monica and list some of her hangouts. "She's also a classmate of mine."

Saul's face flushed. *What's there to be embarrassed about? You did her before you met Joella. Period. You've got nothing to hide.* "That sounds like her. She's a classmate of yours?"

Joella nodded.

"Stay away from her."

"I plan to. Anyway, my theory is that Monica set me up. Now it even makes more sense. Maybe she set me up to get to you."

A light went on in Saul's head. He knew Pearla and Monica were friends. Recent friends. "I think they're both in on it—Monica and Pearla."

Joella nodded, considering this.

Spencer returned, holding a vacuum cleaner and looking annoyed. "I tell you, I'm gonna have that Ruddy guy killed, especially after what he tried to do to you guys. Never mind the window. I don't see any other way. He knows your faces now. You killed his brother. He'll kill both of you."

Saul knew Spencer Arius was not the kind of man to make idle death threats. Sixty-five years old and living in the DR for the last ten years, he was a retired Canadian military soldier with a death wish. He'd been diagnosed with bladder cancer three years earlier and stubbornly refused treatment. He believed he only had a few years left to live and had vowed to make the best of them. Never mind work-hard-play-hard, his motto was play-hard-and-play-harder. He lived his life with reckless abandon. If it ever had been, fear was no longer a part of his DNA.

Sitting across from Saul, Joella sipped her drink, looking scared and bewildered.

Saul's legs suddenly felt itchy. He scratched them and rolled up his pant leg. Eyes widening, he quickly rolled the pant leg down again, hoping the others hadn't noticed.

"What's wrong with you?" Spencer said, pouring himself a drink. "You look like you've seen a ghost."

Shouldn't he? He'd just committed his first murder with the help of an able-bodied accomplice. To make matters worse, he'd seen something deeply disturbing on his legs.

He stood and approached Joella, reaching into his pocket and pulling out the three hundred dollars. "Here, honey, once we settle this shit, go buy your school books. And there's a little extra for your kids, food and whatever. Buy them some treats, and something special for Evelyn."

Joella took the money and smiled. "Thanks, honey. I appreciate this a lot."

Saul kissed her on the cheek and turned to Spencer. "Take care of her, will you? I'll be in touch. I have to go now."

"Where you going?"

But Saul was already heading into the bedroom. He closed the door behind him and went to the window to check the metal bars protecting it. They were padlocked as they should be. He tugged on the bars. *Not going anywhere. Now they'll believe me.*

He lay down on the bed, undid his jeans, and stared at his legs in shock. He saw them clearly now, and they terrified the hell out of him. Little black hairs protruded out of the scars from the beast attack. They were nothing like human hairs. They were thick, with little spear-like tips.

My God, what's happening to me? What am I turning into?

He closed his eyes and envisioned the bed in his home.

And like magic, he vanished.

Chapter Thirteen

To look at Nicholas Fry, you wouldn't think he was seventy-seven years old. His neatly cropped black hair had only a few silver strands. He had few wrinkles and all his own straight, white teeth. His blue eyes were clear and alert. At five-foot-nine, he was lean and even what some would consider muscular. He walked with the energy and gait of a man half his age.

His personal hygiene and appearance were impeccable. And he kept his turn-of-the-century two-story house and surrounding outbuildings in immaculate shape. Even his laboratory was the picture of organization and sterile perfection.

On a superficial level, it was hard to find fault with him. He was pleasant and amicable. Quick to help a neighbor in need, first to donate to various charities on the Island.

But once you stripped away that thin and polished veneer, you might find something perhaps a little unsavory. Maybe even a little sinister. Maybe you would find the reason Nicholas's neighbors considered him an oddball unfit for human conversation.

It was Nicholas's obsession with perfection and achievement that ultimately cost him his marriage with Maggie. That same obsession led to his disgrace and dismissal from the research department of the Canadian military. Being blackballed from the scientific community as a quack wasn't something an electrical engineer, mechanical engineer, physicist, chemical biologist, and futurist took lightly—especially one as obsessed as Nicholas Fry.

He had fierce Scottish pride. He had his credentials. And he had numerous successes and accolades proving his worth. His patented induction motor, to name only one, had been licensed by General Electric. The company still paid him handsome royalties.

But times had changed. He had been discredited. Five years earlier, the Canadian military research department, on behalf of the Canadian government, had destroyed his teleportation prototype, along with his research diagrams and schematics, claiming, "This type of machine could cause world chaos if it ever got into enemy hands."

They had crushed his vision. They had destroyed his career. But they hadn't destroyed his mind or determination. After a long period of depression and drug abuse, Nicholas woke up one day and decided to make it his life's mission to get back his stellar reputation and prove everyone wrong. He wanted to show the whole world that teleportation was not only possible, it was a much more economical and environmental way to travel, and in the process restore his reputation and become an international hero.

Kill two birds with one stone, he thought now, looking at the caged and nervous raccoon in the harsh fluorescent lights of his laboratory. He put down his schematic, went over to a metal container beside the cage, picked up a handful of peanuts, and set them down gently inside. His new test subject, Robbie, looked at him with sad eyes, then began eating the peanuts.

Some of the animals hadn't done so well. Some returned with deformities, others dead. One named Bill returned extremely violent, aggressive, and supernaturally strong. Another called Rex had returned with a paw growing out of his head and, more troubling to Nicholas, the latest test subject, Bob, hadn't returned at all.

But that was the sacrifice of science. Someone had to make a small sacrifice for the greater good of mankind. Nicholas couldn't find any human subjects, and he wasn't yet satisfied enough with the teleporter to put himself in it. Sitting at his desk, Nicholas eyed Robbie, hoping he would be the successful one. That he *would* return intact and normal. "Don't worry, you'll also be a hero," he told Robbie. "The teleporter is almost perfected."

Robbie looked at him with what Nicholas took to be a smile, then returned to his food.

Nicolas went back to work. For a moment, he thought about Bob. His efforts scouring the nearby forest to find him had been unsuccessful. *Where is he? What's he doing?* He closed his eyes and calmed his mind. It took a few minutes. *Forget about Bob for now.* He knew to find the right formula he needed a clear head. There was something in the original chemical injection he was giving the animals to calm them down, in some cases even knock them out, prior to teleportation, that was causing the problems. He had to perfect the formula. That was all. He was oh-so close.

******

Samantha and Saul were parked on Christian Road that sunny Sunday afternoon. They were in front of his house. Oh-so close. The irony wasn't missed on Saul when he saw the street sign. *God save the king,* he thought.

They were discussing whether or not to just drive up the driveway and knock on his door. Nicholas hadn't returned phone calls, texts, or emails.

Saul was smoking and struggling to hide his growing agitation. He'd woken up that morning at 11:36, with vivid memories of the night before. He'd redressed his wounds, analyzed the burns, which he'd thought had healed remarkably fast, given the approximate eleven-day time frame in which they'd occurred, and focused his attention on the nasty hairs. They were so sharp they pricked his index finger on contact. This made him angry, and he'd taken a razor to uninjured parts of his leg, shaving the hairs down to the bare skin in the hope they wouldn't return.

But something told him it was futile, like trying to change this new aggression that was manifesting itself in Saul's temperament; like trying to change this new strength he was starting to feel; or like trying to change the miraculous improvement in his sore shoulder. It just didn't hurt anymore. Period. Yet he knew that whatever was happening to him had led him to this very address at this very point in time. If he was going to be cured, if there was any chance whatsoever of making that happen, this was the place.

Saul had filled Samantha in on the night's traumatic events involving Joella, the death of two cops, and the self-defense killing of Fernando. He'd said nothing to her about the new beastly development. But it didn't matter. On some level, he knew she knew. Twice she'd caught him scratching at his legs, and asked, "What's wrong?" And twice he'd said, "Nothing."

She also noticed something different in his demeanor. He wasn't quite himself anymore. Driving to Nicholas's house, another vehicle had passed them on the highway, and then slowed to sixty kilometers an hour in an eighty zone. It took some time for Samantha to pass in her blue Toyota Camry. And when she did, Saul flipped the bird out the window, yelling, "Learn how to drive, you old fucking bag."

And, although she'd said nothing, Samantha had given Saul that look: *Something is wrong with you, my dear boy*.

Saul looked at the driveway, gated and bordered by thick forest. NO TRESPASSING - PRIVATE PROPERTY, a red-lettered sign warned. "Shit, we can't get in," he said.

Samantha got out of the car and approached the metal gate. She tried the latch. "It's unlocked." She swung it open and returned to the car. "Are you ready?"

"Are you sure you want to do this?"

"Do we have a choice?"

She started the engine and drove in. At the end of the long, winding driveway, she arrived at a manicured clearing and parked in front of the house. There was a newer model gold Ford Explorer parked in the driveway.

"Someone's home," she said, getting out of the car. "Come on."

Saul followed.

Samantha rang the doorbell a few times to no response. Then they walked around the property and finally arrived at a large steel gray outbuilding. DANGER - HIGH VOLTAGE - KEEP AWAY, a sign on the door said.

"This is it," Samantha said. "Where he does his experiments."

Saul put his ear to the door. He could hear a faint mechanical humming sound. He knocked. No response. He knocked again. Nothing. He tried the door. It was unlocked.

He looked at Samantha.

She nodded.

He opened the door and stepped inside. The humming was much louder.

Samantha followed, closing the door behind her.

Nothing in the world could have prepared them for what they saw. It's one thing to hear about teleportation, and quite another to actually witness it. A raccoon sat on a stage of sorts. An intense beam of light projected from a large black tubular pipe cast a perfect circle around it. The animal appeared to be sleeping.

Wearing a white lab coat, Nicholas sat behind a bank of computer monitors and a wall of control knobs and buttons. His right hand turned a large control dial while his right hand pressed buttons.

Suddenly there was a sizzling sound, followed by a large pop, and the raccoon vanished. Nicholas turned the dial down, pressed a few more buttons, and checked his watch. "I want you back in exactly two hours, Robbie. You're going to be a hero."

"Excuse me," Saul said.

Nicholas spun around so fast his chair rolled back and crashed into a counter of test tubes and meticulously arranged syringes. A beaker filled with a pink liquid tipped over and rolled to the edge. With a white-gloved hand, Nicholas caught it and set it upright. He snatched a white cloth and began wiping the counter. He looked at the intruders with narrowing eyes, opened a drawer, and extracted a handgun. He aimed it at Saul's head. "What are you doing here? You're trespassing. Leave at once."

"I'm sorry," Samantha said. "We mean you no harm. We need your help."

Unable to control the rage, Saul stepped forward. "You did this to me, you fuck. Where's the beast?"

Nicholas removed the safety and cocked the gun. "Take another step and I blow your brains out."

Samantha grabbed Saul's shoulder. "No, don't."

Though he wanted to brush away her hand and continue his attack—*a little worse than bringing a knife to a gunfight, buddy, you've got fuck-all*—Saul forced himself to stop.

"We need to talk to you," Samantha said. "We're not from the government or anything like that." She pointed to Saul. "I think he's been infected by one of your... one of your experiments."

The tense stare-down between Nicholas and Saul lasted a few seconds. Saul looked away first, slumping his shoulders in defeat.

Nicholas lowered the gun. "You're not CIA?"

"No," Samantha said. "We live here. He's your neighbor."

A half hour later, drinking coffee inside Nicholas's house, Saul told him practically everything, including the parts where—as a result of teleportation—he'd saved a few lives.

When Saul pulled up his pant leg to reveal a fresh new growth of prickly hairs on the infected area of his leg, Nicholas's expression turned grave. "I think Bob did that."

"Who's Bob?" Saul asked.

"A test subject. A raccoon who never returned."

"You mean a raccoon did this to me?"

"I think so."

"But I saw tracks. They were much bigger than a raccoon's."

Nicolas's brow furrowed. "I think he's grown, become more powerful. And aggressive."

"Well, how can you fix me?"

"We have to find Bob. Capture him alive. If I can study his biochemistry, maybe I can reverse it, create an antidote."

"How long will that take?"

"Maybe a month if I'm lucky. Maybe two."

Sounded like a long-shot to Saul. "And what do I do in the meantime? Just sit back and watch myself turn into some kind of a monster?"

Nicholas pulled a notepad and pen out of his lab coat top pocket. He scribbled something on it and replaced it, twirling the pen in his fingers. "I can sedate you and keep you under quarantine. That way you'll be safe."

"No, no, no," Saul said. He was becoming agitated. "I'm not going for that. I'm not one of your lab raccoons."

"Just a thought. If you're worried about what you might do... what you might become."

Saul was about to fly off the handle and say something sarcastic, but bit his tongue. Better to stay on this guy's good side if he wanted his normal life back, however abnormal it actually was. And something else made him curb his tone. If it weren't for Nicholas's experiment, Joella might well be dead right now. Wasn't she worth giving his life for? Initially, he might have wondered, but now he was pretty sure the answer was yes.

Nicholas scratched his head. "You say this happened on your beachfront?"

Saul nodded.

"Just up the road?"

"Yes."

"Well, raccoons are territorial." Nicholas's face brightened. "Chances are, Bob is nearby. And I know just how to bait him in."

Chapter Fourteen

It was just an afternoon stroll, really. Or that was what it started out as. Every Monday Monica would walk the beach to see what unsuspecting foreigners were available to bait. It was the best time; the beach was typically dead on Mondays. Not much competition, and there was a good chance foreigners were there, recovering from a weekend of partying. Their defenses would be down. Hers would be up. Seeing the advantage and working within its perimeters. That was what she was good at. Usually it worked.

Usually, but not always. *Not with Saul*, she thought, as she strolled along in a pink dental floss bikini. With Saul she'd completely lost the advantage and started some stupid stalker role that she'd mistakenly thought would eventually win his affection. Big mistake, although she had to admit, she did have him thinking she was a mentally challenged victim and feeling sorry for her at one point. Yet it hadn't been enough. And it didn't last long. Soon, he'd become terrified of her—exactly the opposite of the emotion she'd been trying to evoke. *Stupid, stupid, stupid.*

She frowned, suddenly realizing that wasn't the whole story. It would be ignorant to think that it was. The truth was, she'd fallen in love with Saul and completely lost sight of her money agenda. With over ten years in the trade, it was the only time that had ever happened. Getting absorbed in her thoughts, and becoming more depressed, her gait slowed. She found the shade of a palm tree and sat down.

She needed to work this out in her head before she could continue.

Why had she fallen in love with Saul and not the others? She stared out at the ocean, hoping the slow rhythm and beat of the gently lapping waves would provide the answer—*sshhhh... shshsh... shshsh.*

After a few minutes of watching and listening, the answer did come. Saul was different. The way he smiled. The way he spoke. The way he touched her. The way he made love. And what he wanted was different from the others. All they wanted was a paid romp in the sack, but Saul wanted something more. He wanted a relationship. He'd gotten tired of the one-night stands and wanted something serious. Maybe on some level she did too, because she'd fallen for it. She was supposed to be the one setting the bait, but not in this case. She took the bait—hook, line, and sinker. And it had just about destroyed her.

Until Pearla had come along and shown her how to stand above this emotional servitude that most of these idiots expected of women. Pearla had saved her from a complete emotional breakdown. Pearla had guided her to a path that would allow her to exact revenge for the emotional injustices Saul had so insensitively wrought upon her. God, she hated Saul for that. Leading her on, setting the bait, sucking her in.

But was that really what he'd done?

On some level, Monica knew there was more to it than that. Lack of a father figure meant a need to be loved by men, but also a need to hate them. Monica's father had abandoned her when she was two years old. She barely remembered him.

And she no longer spoke to her mother, Elma. It was Elma who, in order to put bread on the table, had led Monica into prostitution. She'd exploited her one and only daughter out of desperation and hunger.

And now what have I become? A murderer and a thief and a whore. And who's responsible for that? The whole world. But Pearla is my savior. Yeah, like Mom. Never mind. Get Saul and get revenge. The rest will fall into place. "I'm sure of it." Monica looked around, startled by her own voice; she hadn't realized she'd spoken her thoughts aloud in an attempt to cheer herself up.

A white man strolled by and smiled at her. She returned the smile, but out of the corner of her eye saw something that wiped that smile clean off her face.

It was Joella, relaxing on a bed-style lawn chair on a beachfront condo main-floor balcony.

Monica had given Pearla's instructions to Lieutenant Gonzales, and he'd assured her everything would be taken care of. Later he'd informed her, with minimal details, that everything had gone wrong. But San Marcos had ears, eyes, and a voice that travelled faster than the fastest internet. Monica's street connections had filled her in on the rest.

Gonzales had assured her Joella would be apprehended soon. There was a wide-ranging search underway. It was only a matter of time.

Well, no time like the present, Monica thought, shimmying closer to the palm tree, out of Joella's sightline. She watched. And plotted. When Pearla heard about this, if she hadn't already, she would be furious. What to do? What to do? How had Joella escaped and ended up in... was that Spencer's apartment?

Monica's frown transformed into a grin. She had an idea.

The smiling white man mistook the grin for an invitation. He approached. "You wanna get fucked, baby?"

"Why don't you fuck off," Monica said.

The man did what he was told.

As soon as she'd said it, Monica realized that this was not her normal modus operandi when it concerned white male prey. *Never mind. Get Joella.*

But as she approached Joella, she could feel it. There was an unsettling change taking place inside her that she didn't much like anymore. But she could no longer help it, and a part of her had given up even caring.

******

Joella was lost in thought. She'd cleaned Spencer's apartment, cooked him bacon and eggs, called her sister Gisella to let her know she needed to lay low for a few days—"Feed the kids and tell them I love them"—and was now reliving the horror of Fernando's gruesome death.

Then she saw Monica and they made eye contact. Joella had been discovered, and she was tempted to run and hide.

As far as she knew, Spencer was in Puerto Plata now, talking to the colonel, the highest-ranking member of the police force. If anyone could straighten this mess out, Spencer was sure it was the colonel. "Don't worry," he'd told her, holding his rum and Coke road pop, "If I want someone dead, he'll arrange it."

What stopped her from running was that Monica had spotted her, and to run would be an admission of guilt. Joella was confused enough over what had transpired the night before, and she didn't need to add a suspicious Monica to the mess. Although she didn't trust Monica as far as she could throw her, it was easiest to play it cool. Maybe Monica knew nothing. As Monica neared, Joella concocted a cover story.

"Joella, what a surprise," Monica said. "Nice to see you."

Throw her off, Joella told herself. "Yeah, likewise. How'd your night go with the two gringos?"

A line creased Monica's forehead. It took a few seconds for her to respond. "Oh, them... well, we finished early and they picked up some other girls. Real horny guys, I can tell you that much."

"I hear they're both dead."

"You know, I heard that too. Unfortunate. I hope you don't think I had anything to do with it?"

"I didn't say that."

"Of course you didn't."

"But I'm glad I didn't come with you."

"Well, I'm not under any suspicion—not like some people I know—if that's where you're going."

"What do you mean by that?"

Monica was playing her. This little conversation was turning into a big problem. Joella knew she had to think of a way out.

"Never mind," Monica said. "What are you doing here, by the way? Shouldn't you be studying or looking after your kids or something?"

"I'm cleaning Spencer's apartment. He offered to help me out. I need the money."

"Isn't that sweet. Such a nice man, that Spencer. Speaking of nice men, how's Saul? You use any of my suggestions?"

"No, and I don't think I need them, but thanks anyway." Joella could feel beads of perspiration sprouting on her forehead. *There, that's the equivalent of telling her to fuck off. Let's see how it works.* "Anyway, we're talking now. Things are improving."

Monica moved closer and put a hand on the balcony railing. Her black eyes narrowed as she regarded Joella, who had risen from the chair and backed away, close to the sliding-glass door.

"Well, that's good to hear. Have I ever told you I fucked Saul?" Monica said, a small smile beginning to purse her lips.

Two beads of perspiration rolled down Joella's nose and she wiped them away. "It makes no sense to be jealous of what Saul did before he met me. Everyone has a past."

"Really? Well it might interest you to know that I fucked him while he was going out with you. Several times, actually."

Joella's hands tightened into fists. "Saul would never do that to me."

"Oh, but he did, my naïve little angel. Why don't you ask him the next time you talk to him? See what his reaction is. Or even the next time you see him. Then again, I don't think that's too likely. I don't think he's ever coming back, at least not to you."

Joella had to bite her tongue to prevent from flying off the handle. *Is it true?* She didn't know how much Monica knew. There was a good chance she knew close to everything. Pearla and Monica were friends. Saul had prevented Pearla from killing someone. One phone call was all it would have taken to inform Monica that Saul was teleporting around the world and saving lives. Why hadn't she seen it before? Well, that wasn't hard, either. Her mind had been too troubled: economic problems, a relationship gone sour, no food on the table, you name it.

Now it was becoming obvious. Monica was using her to get to Saul. Monica was probably behind the cops trying to incarcerate her on fictitious charges, and baiting Saul into a trap. Joella was now almost certain that Monica was also involved in the recent murder and robbery of the two foreigners. If she hadn't actually wielded the weapons, she certainly had a hand in orchestrating their demise.

No, it couldn't be true about Saul's infidelity, she decided, even though there were nagging doubts. She wanted to believe he hadn't cheated on her while they were together. She couldn't control what he'd done before he met her, nor did it necessarily matter, as long it was in the realm of decent behavior. But this was madness, pure concoction, created by a murderer and a thief with a self-serving revenge agenda. *Yeah, but didn't I help Saul kill Fernando? Am I not a murderer as well?* But that was different—self-defense.

"I think this conversation is over," Joella said. "I want you to leave." But she was losing her composure and was afraid at any second she would fly over the balcony and begin throttling this psychotic bitch. If she'd never known before, she knew now. She was quite capable of murder. *Yeah, but so is Monica.*

"Oh, and he's such a good fuck, isn't he, Joella? He even licked my pussy. Is that what keeps you coming back? You like his tongue gliding expertly inside your tight little dripping pussy? Or maybe his rock-hard cock ramming you like there's no tomorrow?"

"Enough," Joella said. "I'll—"

"You'll what, my dear? Kill me? Like you did to Fernando? Like you did to those two cops?"

******

Monica picked up a rock and aimed it at Joella, who quickly grabbed a plastic chair and held it up as an improvised shield. *No*, Monica thought, *not now*. The "You-wanna-get-fucked?" man was watching. He hadn't left after all. He'd even stood up from his perch on a nearby log.

Also, Spencer had cop connections, maybe even a little higher-ranking than Monica's. She had often heard him refer to a man simply as "the colonel"—a man he claimed to know personally, who'd been to his house for dinner on more than one occasion. A friend. She didn't know where Spencer was now, but there was a good chance he was trying to reach the colonel, maybe even having a drink with him, and trying to clear up this mess.

The last thing Monica needed was to get into a fight with Joella and be arrested. Or kill her, as she wanted to do now, and get arrested for murder.

And there were more people on the beach now: a couple was strolling past, a little toddler wearing water wings running aimlessly on the beach.

Another jogger appeared, giving her an appreciative look as he passed.

Fucking nutcase, she thought, glaring at him. *Probably a sick motherfucker.*

She tossed the rock on the sand. *There will be a time. And a place.*

Joella still held up the chair. "Get out of here!"

"It's okay, honey, you can put the chair down. I'm not going to hurt you. Not right now, anyway."

She turned and walked toward the foreigner, who was still watching. By the time she'd reached him, he'd taken a seat on the log.

"What's your name?" she said. *Quite handsome. He'll do.*

He smiled, exposing straight white teeth. "I thought you wanted me to fuck off?"

"I'm sorry," Monica said, pointing to the balcony where Joella had once stood. "That girl stole my boyfriend and when I saw her my temper got the better of me. But I'm okay now."

He introduced himself as Brent and offered a hand. "Maybe it's my fault. I didn't mean to insult you earlier. I have to start thinking different—that here are real nice girls around here."

She shook the extended hand and introduced herself. "That's okay, Brent. Nice name. I like that. Instead of fucking off, why don't we just fuck?"

"Sure."

"Do you like rough sex?"

******

Joella hurried inside the apartment, closed and locked the door, and sat down on the couch. Her hands were trembling, her heart pounding. She wiped her sweaty brow and tried to will her hands to stop shaking. She wasn't entirely successful. An awful image of Saul licking Monica between the legs popped into her head. It made her sick to her stomach. She coughed and cleared her throat. *Don't get sick. Think.* After a few minutes, the nausea passed, but the image remained vivid. She tried to compartmentalize it to clear her head. In her mind's eye, she carried it somewhere deep into the back of her mind and threw it into a black hole.

She didn't know what to do. She looked at her phone—3:36 pm—and wondered if she should call Saul for his advice. She even starting punching in the number, and at the last second changed her mind. She was upset right now and might say something stupid, even accusatory. He had enough on his own plate to deal with, and Joella was sure her knowledge of it was only the tip of the iceberg. She was still having a hard time believing that he'd vanished into thin air the other day. *No, don't bother him. Call Spencer instead.*

That was it. She was sure Monica was going to bring those two cops back immediately and she'd get hauled off to jail. Spencer would be able to tell her if she should stay or go.

But Spencer didn't answer the phone. And Joella started to panic.

She went over to the balcony door, slid the fabric blind aside, and peered out. Monica was sitting on a log with a man. She was looking right at Joella.

And she was talking on the phone.

That was that. She couldn't take any chances. She hurriedly scribbled a note for Spencer, called her moto—he said a five-minute pick-up—and locked the door behind her. Outside, she crouched behind some poolside chairs, still shaking while she waited.

Chapter Fifteen

Pearla was sore. Sore, but deeply satisfied. The experience had left her elated at finally having consummated her thus-far unrequited relationship with Kalfu. Second, it had made her goals that much clearer. Get the TO DO list crossed off, and proceed to Prince Edward Island.

Yet there was another feeling, one that had slowly crept up on her, that left a bad taste in her mouth. It was a sense of surrealism; the feeling that she was going through life as if she were merely an actor in a movie, without any real deep connection to the external world around her. Or like some pawn in a chess game of such complexity it was above her mortal comprehension. It was as if her passion and conviction for worldly pursuits were slowly being peeled away. Like she was under some spell and no longer in control of her game plan.

She got out of the taxi that evening, paid the man perfunctorily, closed the door, and walked across the street to Simpleton's apartment. She glanced up at the starlit sky, fused gray with the many streetlights, and tried a smile. It didn't work. Her surroundings were a movie set. And she was an actor playing a bit part. She had a script, and it didn't allow for a smile at this juncture of the movie. *Stay serious. Follow the script. Win an Oscar.*

As she approached the entrance, another man opened the door to leave and held it open. Good. She wouldn't even have to buzz the birdbrain. She thanked him, entered, and climbed the stairs. She thought about the Dominican

Republic and her instructions to Monica. She hadn't even checked in, she realized, and had not received a call from Monica. It had slipped Pearla's mind, so focused was she on finishing the job with Simpleton. Something told her she should have moved to other TO DO list tasks until the heat died down on Simpleton; but she'd ignored that warning because of Kalfu's words.

He'd made it clear after pounding her furiously that evening in the hotel. "Complete your tasks, and you will be judged. If you're found worthy, you'll be given the powers you've sought for so long. Powers of the spirits. Powers to heal. Powers to destroy."

But he hadn't said anything about ignoring common sense, had he? It didn't matter now, Pearla thought, as she knocked on Simpleton's door. She was here now. She may as well get it over with.

He opened the door wearing only a pair of red boxer shorts and a sexually suggestive grin. Pearla walked in and looked around. Dimly lit room, candles everywhere, an uncorked bottle of white wine in an ice bucket on the dining room table. She couldn't have scripted it any better. Yet she knew on some ineffable level this wasn't her show anymore, and she wasn't scripting it. Kalfu was. Better to keep him satisfied if she wanted to ascend the limitations of the material world.

"Nice to see you, Mike," she said, entering. She planted a wet kiss on his lips, set her purse down, and took off her black jacket, revealing a red bra and panties that left little to the imagination. She moved to the dining room, picked up a glass, poured, and offered it to Simpleton.

He took it. "Thanks...I'm kind of nervous about this. I'm still in a little trouble over that pervert, and my neighbors are trying to say I fired the gun. There may be other charges."

He seemed more subdued and less aggressive. She wondered if she would enjoy it, if it was even worth it anymore. She ignored the thought and poured herself a glass of wine. They toasted and drank.

"You *did* fire the gun," she said.

"I was trying to protect us."

"I know. Don't worry about it now." She set down her glass and stepped toward him. As she began kissing his neck, her hand moved down to his crotch. She slowly stroked an erect member.

"Oooooooohh," he said. "We're quite the couple. Both wearing red."

Five minutes later, the wine bottle sat empty. Pearla, nude from the waist up, lay on her back on a little throw rug on the living room floor. Simpleton pounded her heaving, sweat-soaked breasts; occasionally she would break the momentum and suck him, slowly teasing him to the point of orgasm and then stopping before he exploded.

"I have a surprise," she said.

He stopped. "What's that?"

"Go in the bedroom and lay spread-eagle on your back. I'll bring it to you."

""You gonna tie me up?"

"It's a surprise."

"I'm supposed to tie you up. Remember, we didn't get to it last time."

"Just be a good boy and get in the bedroom. I promise you won't be disappointed. Do you know when a person is tied up they get so turned on they can have an orgasm with just a little touch?"

"I know, I've done it."

"What, on the receiving end?"

"Not yet."

"Well, now's your chance. You let me do you, then you can do me. Deal?"

"I want to do you first."

"No. If you don't agree to my terms, I'm leaving."

"This is bullshit."

"Come on, Mike." She took his member in her mouth, deep-throating the entire length for a few seconds before coughing it up. "I'll make you cum like you never have before."

"Okay."

In a few minutes, he was blindfolded, his extremities tied to the bedposts. True to her word, Pearla didn't disappoint. Licking his body, some of the surrealism started to fade and she actually started enjoying herself. She started by lowering her breasts into his waiting mouth, moaning while he sucked and licked. Then she lowered her crotch slowly onto his tongue and bucked and moaned as he brought her to orgasm. Finally she licked him from head to toe before taking his member in her mouth and sucking him to a shuddering, screaming, exploding climax.

She stood up, licking her lips. "Hang on."

"Where are you going?"

"It's the final surprise."

"Hey, it's my turn. Take this blindfold off."

She returned with a carving knife from Simpleton's collection. He was beginning to panic, bucking and trying to free himself.

When she spoke, even her voice felt hoarse, detached and deeper than her own rasp. "Open your mouth and shut up."

"What are you putting in it?"

"My tit, you dumb fuck."

Simpleton struggled harder. "No need to get nasty, you fucking bitch."

She climbed on the bed and knelt beside him, raising the knife. "You're nothing more than a sick, perverted exploiter of women, and an ugly one at that. Men like you have caused all the problems in my country. Who do you think you are? You think you can exploit us? You think you can treat us like paid sluts? You think we need you, need your money?"

Simpleton bucked and squirmed. "No, no... don't do it!"

Pearla ignored him, continuing her soliloquy. "When you find a good one, what do you do? You give in to the whims of your little fucking head and cheat on us. You can cheat, but we can't because we need your money. Is that it?"

"When I get out of here I'm gonna kill you, bitch."

"Shut up and listen. What you do is a double standard and you're all a bunch of hypocrites. I'm gonna put a stop to all that. So I hope you enjoyed your orgasm—"

She gripped the knife tighter, preparing to thrust it down.

"—because it's the last one you're ever gonna have."

As she plunged the blade down, Pearla felt stinging in the back of her head before she realized what had happened. She glanced back and realized Simpleton had broken an ankle strap and kneed her hard in the back of the head. The blow changed the knife's trajectory, and it sliced through his ear, instead of going into his mouth, her target.

Still gripping the knife, she fell off the bed. A little dazed, she got up. As she approached, she noticed he had an arm loose—the sneaky bastard had a knife hidden under a pillow and had carved himself a modicum of freedom before his final calling. He cut his other arm free, cut the blindfold off, and pointed the knife at her. "Don't come any closer."

This was not exactly going to plan, Pearla thought. *Kalfu will be disappointed.* "Fuck you," she said, clenching the knife in both hands and diving on the bed. She tried to stab him in the chest, but he moved and it stuck in his shoulder.

"Oooowwww, you crazy bitch," he said, swinging his knife at her throat. She moved and it narrowly missed her. She pulled the knife from his shoulder and steadied her arms for another strike.

He swung his foot up and clipped her in the back of the head. She fell off the bed and rolled along the floor.

As she got up, she realized he'd cut himself completely free. He jumped up and charged—a panicked naked man with a knife and blood streaming down his chest.

Losing her will, she said, "Maybe we can talk this through."

"Let's see how you talk with your tongue cut out," he said, pointing the blade at her chest and leaping forward.

With reflexes she didn't know she possessed, she sidestepped the charge and tripped Simpleton. He flew headfirst into the wall, impaling his head in the drywall. The knife flew out of his hand and clattered along the floor.

Grunting, he struggled to free himself.

She picked up his fallen knife and attacked, stabbing him once in the back of the neck with one knife, and once in the back of the head with the other. Leaving the knives imbedded, she pulled him by the hair, yanking him loose from his drywall incarcereation. She looked into his eyes and he spit blood in her face, trying to speak but only accomplishing a gurgling sound as blood spewed from his mouth.

She wiped away the blood, wiped some along her tongue, and extracted the knife from his neck. Again, with strength she never knew she had—*Kalfu is here with me*—she threw him on the bed. He landed on his back, still frothing blood and gurgling.

By the time she'd knelt on his chest and cut his tongue from his mouth, he was already dead. She brought it to her nose, smelled it, and grinned. The surrealism was fading big-time now. She was enjoying this—in touch, in tune, in perfect harmony with all the delicious sensations of putting another loser out of his misery.

She brought the bloody tongue closer to her mouth, satisfied at what was left of Simpleton. "What's wrong, cat got your tongue?" She giggled with giddy satisfaction. This was euphoric and better than she'd ever remembered. Two drops of blood fell on her tongue and she savored the coppery taste before inserting the tongue in her mouth. She took two quick bites and swallowed it.

After a few minutes of basking in the sheer joy of ridding the world of sick predators, she realized she was covered in blood and dressed only in her red panties. She saw her bra on the floor and was about to get up off the bed to retrieve it. Then she changed her mind. *May as well enjoy this just a little longer.* She sat on the bed for another minute, massaging the warm blood into her breasts. She watched and felt her nipples grow erect and a small moan of pleasure escaped her lips.

She closed her eyes to savor the sensation for just a little longer. And when she opened them, he was standing in front of her.

She smiled and continued tweaking her nipples. "I knew you'd come." She closed her eyes and opened her mouth wide.

"You've done well, my child," Kalfu said, grinning. He loosened the fly of his black pants. With both hands, he pulled out his behemoth red snake and fed it into a waiting and wanting mouth.

Chapter Sixteen

Hiking through the forest in the middle of the night with a flashlight, Saul felt like he was the star in his own movie. Only problem was, it was a horror movie, and he was an unwilling laboratory rat slowly morphing into a monster. He was living a nightmare.

Samantha and Nicholas were searching together closer to the fire pit area of the beach. Nicholas had suggested that Saul wander off alone. Nicholas had set up caged live traps in various locations around his property, using blueberries (Bob's favorite food) as bait. Saul was also being used as bait. According to Nicholas, Bob might show an affinity for what he thought was one of his own, and might be reluctant to approach Saul if the others were around.

They'd been out two hours, and so far they'd spotted nothing resembling Bob.

Saul stepped on a pile of dry twigs. He stopped and listened. Snapping branches. But wait—something else. Howling in the distance. He knew the sound. Coyotes. The sound ebbed and flowed, ebbed again. Looking up at the starlit sky, he realized it was a full moon. Did that mean he would turn tonight? Into what? He wished it was a joke, but he wasn't laughing.

Once he'd arrived home from Nicholas's house earlier in the day, he'd made a list of the changes occurring in his body and mind. The hairs on his legs had emerged with a vengeance, covering most of both legs. Even his chin scrub seemed to be coming in thicker, and the hair on his head was becoming wiry and stiff.

But there were other, less unsavory changes. His shoulder felt like it had never been injured. The leg and neck cuts he'd suffered during the fight with Fernando had already scabbed over nicely. The burns had all but disappeared. The cut above his eyebrow was already a pink scar, with no sign of infection.

Then again, the infection might be elsewhere, he realized. This new aggression he was feeling was getting harder to contain; now he felt it was always there, bubbling just below the surface. And it was accompanied by an almost superhuman strength. While making a sandwich earlier, he'd accidentally dropped a knife on the floor after loading a dollop of peanut butter on it. He'd flown into a rage and thrown the peanut butter jar against the wall so hard it shattered, bits of peanut butter-encrusted glass sticking to the wall in a circular pattern. The remainder splattered all over the kitchen. After cleaning up the mess, he decided a four-ounce shot of Scotch was in order. That didn't work either. As soon as he'd drained the glass, he felt as sick as a dog—well, maybe as sick as a raccoon. He'd rushed to the bathroom and vomited the entire contents, along with a gooey yellowish substance.

Hearing a sound, he stopped suddenly and shone the beam. A chipmunk eyeballed him cheerily, chattered, and scurried up a tree. He carried on, only half paying attention to what was going on in the external world. Right now, he was more preoccupied with the internal. There were other frightening events that had occurred earlier in the day that were still playing a mind-cinema.

After talking with Nicholas in his house, they were invited back to the lab to see the return of his latest test subject, Robbie. If Robbie came back physically and mentally intact, Nicholas Fry would be an international celebrity and a hero, and maybe it would pave the way for a cure for Saul's condition. Maybe they wouldn't have such an urgency to find Bob, although for now it seemed like a good idea. If Bob had done this to Saul, what had he done to other Islanders? How many other dream teleporters were out there, slowly morphing into human-sized, powerful, aggressive raccoons?

He'd waited anxiously with both fingers crossed, praying for Robbie's safe return. The raccoon came back all right, popping right into the teleporter. But, the result, in light of recent events, was terrifying. Robbie lumbered around the teleporter pod lackadaisically for a few seconds before his legs gave out. He slumped onto his stomach, his eyes rolled in his head, and he puked out a gooey yellowish substance. Then he slipped into a coma. Now he was in an animal intensive care unit, a tube sticking in his nose and intravenous bags with needles poking into his two front legs. He was under observation in a quarantine unit, where Nicholas thought Saul ought to be.

Saul found an old moonshine distribution trail and decided to take it, wondering about Nicholas's sanity—or lack thereof. There was a fine line between genius and insanity, and Saul wondered where Nicholas fit into this equation. On the surface, the man was bright and amicable, but Saul sensed something sinister lying beneath that veneer. He wondered if Nicholas had the capacity to use human test subjects against their will, as he was doing with the animal test subjects. For starters, the animal experiments were unsanctioned by the government or any recognized research center, and Saul wondered what Health Canada or animal rights organizations would have to say about that. Yet he had to take a leap of faith here. Nicholas was his only way out of this horror movie—his only hope that it might have a happily-ever-after ending.

"Shit," Saul said, beginning to worry even more. *Happily ever after. I missed Joella's call earlier. I forgot to call her back.* "Fuck sakes."

But he didn't have time to worry about her safety. A pained yelping sound coming from just around a small bend in the trail gave him cause to worry about his own.

He moved quickly toward the sound and what he saw almost made him throw up what remained of his peanut butter sandwich lunch. A coyote writhed in pain beneath his feet. Its body had been badly gorged and entrails were spilling out on the trail. Its face was badly clawed and its lower jaw was hanging on by a thread. Blood was everywhere. Wincing, Saul watched it writhe. It yelped in agony for a few seconds before it stiffened and died. A fresh kill.

Robbie was near; he could sense it. He was about to shout for Samantha and Nicholas, but then realized it might frighten Robbie; besides, during his introspective journey, he'd wandered off farther than he intended. They might not even hear him.

He listened. In the distance, he heard it: more coyotes howling, a crescendo of sound slowly getting louder and—he could tell by the pitch—more fearful. They were afraid for their lives and had banded together, as they often did, for protection in numbers.

Suddenly the coyotes stopped howling.

Adrenaline coursing through his veins, Saul continued on. Three minutes later, he heard it—a low growl on the path, about ten feet ahead. He shone the beam and saw two large red eyes glowing in the dark. It was a raccoon all right, but had grown to twice the size of normal and morphed into some beast far more ferocious. It reared up on its hind legs and opened its mouth, revealing large fangs. Its growl was loud and menacing.

Saul heard another growl and was startled when he realized it was coming from his own mouth. He was growling back. He'd taken two steps toward Bob before becoming conscious of it. He stopped. He reached for his knife. Why didn't he have a tranquilizer rifle like Nicholas was packing? That was what he needed out here. What did he expect to do, anyway? Slice and dice his only ticket to Normalville?

Bob's eyes followed Saul's hand. The beast snarled, dropped to all fours, and inched forward, bearing bloody fangs.

Saul removed his hand from the knife sheath and stepped back. "Bob, I'm your friend. I'm not going to hurt you."

He was trying for diplomacy. Weren't they two peas in a pod?

Bob stopped.

So did Saul.

They stared at each other, four feet apart. Bob closed his mouth, the seething anger dissipating, and looked at Saul curiously.

Saul closed his mouth and slowly held out a hand. "I'm one of you, Bob. I need your help."

Bob seemed to smile, and inched closer.

"That's it, Bob. Come here. Come to papa." Saul had no idea how he was going to get Bob to follow him to the others and willingly undergo captivity and more experimentation. He was unprepared for this meeting, simple as that. Next time—if there *was* a next time—he'd be equipped with a walkie-talkie and a tranquilizer gun.

If he could lure the animal into the beachfront clearing, where Samantha and Nicholas were, maybe Nicholas could tranquilize him there. Then he remembered the blueberries, in a paper bag, in his pocket. As he reached for it, Bob backed away and hissed.

Saul removed his hand from the blueberry pocket and raised an open palm. "Okay, maybe you're not hungry. Come here, Bob. I won't hurt you."

Bob seemed to consider this. Motionless and soundless, they stared each other down for almost a full minute.

Then the coyotes howled, closer now and more aggressive. The precursor to a kill. Bob's eyes darted into the brush and returned to Saul briefly. Bob growled, low and guttural. Then he turned and ran down the trail.

Instinctively, Saul gave chase. He rounded a bend in the trail, and gained some distance on the retreating raccoon.

Behind him, he could hear the coyotes coming fast. The barking and howling behind him grew louder. A snarling sound followed, and Saul felt vice-like teeth biting into the back of his ankle. Hot pain shot through his leg.

A rush of blood suddenly pumped through his extremities. His clothes shredded. His arms and legs grew long and furry. Sharp claws extended from his hands and he dropped the flashlight. He turned around and lashed out at the coyote biting into his ankle. He sliced it across the nose. It released its grip, yelped, and backed off.

Saul glanced back quickly. Beady red eyes danced nearer, accompanied by howling and snarling. Saul turned quickly and ran. The pack of angry coyotes pursued him.

He reached a clearing lit by the rising full moon. There was Bob, standing in the middle, reared up on hind legs. Bob swung paws and claws into the air, growling. *Come and get me.*

By the time Saul reached the center of the clearing, he realized he'd gotten there on all fours. A survival instinct kicked in, overriding all attempts to try and analyze this transformation.

As Saul reared up on his hind legs and turned his back to Bob, the beady red eyes circled and moved in for the kill. One of the coyotes left the circle and charged forward. Nearing quickly, it leaped in the air at Saul. With a lightning quick flick of his clawed hand, he smashed the coyote out of the air. It howled in pain, flew about ten feet, and hit the ground rolling. Then it stood and retreated, squealing like a stuck pig.

Another coyote attacked Bob. He swatted it out of the air with little more effort than one would swat a fly. It squealed as it launched airborne and hit the ground running.

But the circle of coyotes inched forward, knowing their power in numbers. Simultaneously, Bob and Saul growled, even howled at the incoming predators. But they kept coming. With two-thirds human mind and a third biologically enhanced animal mind, Saul tried to think of a way out.

He remembered the documentaries he'd seen on television of young boys in Peru banding together and attacking tourists, slicing and dicing their clothing to rat shit, and robbing them. By themselves, these ten to twelve-year-old pricks were no threat to most adults, but they had power in numbers. They kept coming until they overwhelmed you. Then, expert with the knives, they shredded your clothes and robbed you, leaving you naked, embarrassed and penniless; but in most cases uncut and unmarked by the blades—they were that good.

Well, these weren't little boys and there were no knives involved. Saul had already lost most of his clothes, including the knife. But the general principal held true, Saul thought. What were his options? Probably the same as with the Peruvian juvenile pricks. Run like hell.

The circle was tightening. There was nowhere to go but right through it.

Bob went down on all fours, bearing his fangs and snarling.

Saul watched and did the same. Was Bob getting ready to bolt right through them? He thought so. It felt like it, communicated to him on some unspoken animal level.

Things were happening too fast; the coyotes' frenzied howling and snarling confused Saul. Before he could cement the plan with Bob—if they were indeed hatching a plan—the coyotes, en masse, issued a blood-curdling battle howl, and charged.

Kaplow... Kaplow!

The gunshot blasts echoed loudly through the forest. The coyotes disappeared into the woods one way, Bob the other. Saul looked down the trail that had led him here and saw Nicholas pointing a smoking handgun in the air. Samantha stood behind him, hands covering her ears.

Saul's extremities grew weak and he collapsed on the ground. Looking up at the full moon, he felt a black void of unconsciousness dragging him down. His eyes slowly closed and darkness enveloped him. *Am I dying? No, I will dream again and leave this hellhole forever.*

Nicholas holstered the handgun and removed his shoulder-strapped tranquilizer rifle. He aimed it at the tree line and fired. But it was too late. Bob was long gone.

Samantha rushed over to Saul. Shining a flashlight beam, she examined him. He was naked except for a pair of shredded blue boxer shorts. With widening eyes, she watched him transform. Hairs disappeared and his claws retracted slowly, replaced by human extremities. Large fangs shrank and morphed into human teeth. Even his face, which looked like some horrid half-raccoon, half-coyote mutant aberration, was normalizing.

Samantha stepped back, wondering if she should even touch him. *Will I end up like him?*

She bent down and brushed Saul's hair away from his face. "Saul, wake up. Are you okay? Saul, wake up!"

Nicholas stood at the tree line where Bob had exited, pointing his flashlight beam.

She waved to him. "Over here, he needs help."

He turned and pointed the beam at her. "Bob... we need to get Bob."

"Never mind him now."

Nicholas slung his rifle over his shoulder and approached her cautiously. "How is he?"

She felt his wrist for a pulse. "He's alive."

"I didn't think he'd be dead. If anything, he's going to come back better than before."

Samantha's eyes narrowed. "What? Better than before? He's been hunting like an animal, for God's sake. I just saw him transform from a beast. Better than before? You should choose your words carefully, Nick. He isn't one of your laboratory animals."

"It's Nicholas, by the way—and he is now."

Samantha stood up and faced Nicholas, her face tight and white. "What's that supposed to mean?"

He didn't budge. "I think we should take him to my lab. Put him under observation in the medical wing until we can capture Bob. He's not safe in his own house. You said yourself he's been on a drinking binge for months."

Samantha thought about it. It was true. Saul had become almost suicidal lately, nearly killing himself more than once in an alcoholic stupor. And with this new development, who knew when he might fly into a rage and become a threat to others—animals and people alike. Not to mention, he could be contagious.

"But what about Bob? He seems to have a connection with him. Maybe Saul's the only one who can capture him. Maybe *Saul* is Bob's only hope of becoming normal again."

"Well, I don't think Saul was ever normal in the first place. He has some serious problems."

"Yeah, but how many of them have been caused by *you*?"

"That doesn't negate my point. I say we take him to my lab, get him cleaned up, sedate him, and continue looking for Bob. If Saul stays on the right side of the normal line, we'll let him search for Bob. If he continues to deteriorate, well, that's another story."

Samantha brought her face to within a few inches of Nicholas's. "What story?" she said, spraying a drop of spittle in his face. "You gonna put him down like one of your lab animals?"

"Of course not." Nicholas's brow creased. "What do you take me for, some mad scientist or something? That just means different treatment options. Let's not get ahead of ourselves here. For me to develop an antidote, I need to study the changes taking place in him. I need blood samples from Saul and Bob."

Samantha felt hot anger coursing through her veins. Had she too become infected? It was possible, she thought. And if she had, she would also require the antidote. She bit her lip. There was no easy solution. "Well, when he wakes up, I doubt he'll be that happy about this. That's the other thing you have to deal with. His temper. Saul has a say in this."

"Let me handle that."

Samantha's faced flushed. "And how are you going to do that? You can't hold him against his will. That's kidnapping."

"Well, I think we have special circumstances here, like the health and welfare of Saul and the general population. But, no, I won't hold him against his will. I'll convince him that it's in his best interests—in everyone's best interests. If he doesn't agree, he can leave. That's all there is to it."

Samantha knew there was a lot more to it than that, but she'd lost her will to argue. They were in the middle of the forest, in the middle of the night, with a friend who had just morphed into a beast and back again and successfully defended himself and another of his kind against a pack of angry coyotes. It was just too much information to process. She looked down at Saul. His tongue was hanging out at an odd angle and his expression looked eerily peaceful.

In the distance, the coyotes howled, a synchronized crescendo growing louder.

Samantha shuddered and bent down to Saul. "All right. Help me get him to his feet. And if he wants to leave, we let him leave."

Nicholas nodded. Then he pointed his rifle at her.

Samantha started. "What are you doing?"

After a moment's pause, he said, "Here, take it. And hold my flashlight for a minute. I'll carry him."

She sighed heavily, obeying his instructions.

Nicholas bent down, lifted Saul, and slung him over his shoulder like a sack of potatoes.

Amazing strength for an old man, Samantha thought.

"Guide the way," he said.

She turned, shone the beam, and they started walking back to the fire pit area, where Saul's pickup and Nicholas's vehicle were parked. Samantha's car was parked at Nicholas's house.

The sound of the howling coyotes became fainter. And then it was no more. They silently walked the trail, the quiet broken only by the snapping of the odd twig.

******

Saul saw large fangs approaching. Monster-sized, blood-dripping fangs. Coming right for his throat. He tried to move but couldn't. The beast was closing in, coming to kill him. But for the fangs, strangely glowing, he was surrounded by blackness. Then a snapping jaw materialized, controlling the fangs. It bit into his jugular vein and blood sprayed out like an errant lawn sprinkler.

"Noooooooo, nooooooo," he shouted, swimming out of unconsciousness, flailing his arms.

"Calm down," Nicholas said. "You had a nightmare. Only a nightmare."

Saul opened his eyes. He felt weak. Dizzy. Disoriented. He looked at the man behind the wheel. Who was he?

"It's me," Nicholas said. "Remember?"

Slowly the memory of the man, the horrible memory of recent events, flooded back and he nodded. The fangs flashed in his mind, larger than life and snapping at his throat. He swung at the air with an open hand. "Get the fuck out of here. Leave me alone, for fuck sakes."

Nicholas looked at him with a raised eyebrow. "Easy."

Saul was having a hard time differentiating between reality and dreams. Lately they all seemed to meld together. The fangs might have been a dream, but this wasn't. This was his nightmare, his reality.

He shivered, realizing, he was clad only in a pair of shredded boxer shorts. He looked at Nicholas. "Where am I? How did I get here?"

"Here," Nicholas said, reaching in the back and grabbing a blanket. He tossed it on Saul's lap. "You're in my vehicle. You passed out in the woods."

Saul covered himself with the blanket, noticing the black prickly hairs on his legs were thickening. "Did we get Bob?"

"Not yet, but we will."

"Where's Sam?"

"She's right behind us, driving your truck. She's fine."

"What time is it?"

"It's five-sixty-six in the am. It's dawn."

Saul looked outside. A thick blanket of black clouds covered the rising sun. Tiny spears of yellow-red light poked through. "It's a black dawn."

"Things will get brighter. Don't worry."

"Where are we going?"

"To my lab. You need medical attention. You need my help."

"Oh no we don't. Joella's in trouble. She needs *my* help."

"There'll be time for that. Don't worry."

Saul grabbed the steering wheel and tugged. The vehicle swerved on the double-lane dirt road. "How the fuck do you know?"

Nicholas quickly pulled out a syringe and plunged it deep into Saul's neck. Saul released the steering wheel, withered, and fell unconscious.

Tossing the spent syringe into the back seat and regaining control of the SUV, Nicholas said, "Trust me, I just do."

Chapter Seventeen

It dawned on Joella just how desperate she was when she realized she was talking to her smartphone. Maybe not that unusual in some people's eyes. After all most smartphones could tell you the time, the weather, and answer any number of questions with Google's new speech recognition feature. But her Samsung wouldn't answer her questions: "Where is Saul? And why won't he answer the phone?"

After checking the time—11:36 am—she put the phone down on a makeshift wooden table, put her head in her hands, and tried to figure out her next steps. She had to leave here, that was for sure. She wasn't safe. Not safe at all.

After leaving Spencer's apartment the previous afternoon, she'd managed to reach her sister Gisella, who made an arrangement for her to stay at her boyfriend's one-bedroom wooden shack high atop a hill in San Marcos, where she still was. She felt nervous about the invitation, based on Emmanuel Perez's suspect reputation for womanizing. But in light of the unsettling developments with Monica, she didn't know what else to do or where else to go. So, with Gisella and Emmanuel sleeping in the adjacent bedroom, Joella had made a bed of blankets on the floor.

She'd tossed and turned most of the night, worrying about Saul and her own safety. When the bed had started creaking in the humble abode's only bedroom, she covered her ears, but was unable to block out the squeaking and moaning sounds.

To make matters worse, the sounds of carnal pleasure died down after about an hour and she heard Gisella's familiar snore, like a sputtering chainsaw, echoing through the corrugated metal shack. Then she felt something tugging on her blanket a little later. She switched on the light, and saw Emmanuel standing in front her. He was nude and erect, grinning from ear to ear.

"Suck me," he said. "Don't worry, she's dead to the world."

Joella covered her scantily clad body with the blanket. "I'm not sucking you. You're my sister's boyfriend." It was all she could think of to say, so traumatized and shocked was she by the unexpected assault.

"Don't worry, she'll never find out," Emmanuel said, grabbing his member and guiding it closer to her mouth. "You know I've always had a thing for you. The others, well they're easy. Takes the challenge out of it. But you're different. Not promiscuous like the rest. You give off a vibe of unavailability. That's what makes it exciting. We all want something we can't have. Now, Joella, come on. Just a little suck. A little suck for daddy."

Joella snatched up the small lamp and raised it high in the air. She also raised her voice. "Get that thing away from me or I'll smash it to shit!"

Emmanuel's shit-eating grin transformed into a frown. "Keep your voice down, you'll—"

"Honey... where are you?" It was Gisella, from the bedroom.

Emmanuel looked at Joella and raised an index finger to his lips. The silent communication of his eyes was sinister.

He turned around. "I'm just in the bathroom. I'll be right there."

Reliving the horror in her mind, Joella thought Gisella had inadvertently saved her from being raped, maybe even beaten.

She stood up from the small plastic chair in the living room and looked out the window. The sun shone brightly. A clucking rooster ambled across the street. A man in a nearby house sprayed his motorcycle with a water hose. A dog barked. Otherwise, it was a relatively quiet part of the barrio, a few miles removed from the music and mayhem below.

Get out of here. What if he comes back? That had been the overriding thought since 8:30 this morning, when Emmanuel and Gisella had both left for work—Gisella to a clothing store and Emmanuel to a mechanic shop. But it was getting close to lunchtime now, and his shop was only a couple of blocks away. What if he came home for lunch? He probably had *her* on the menu.

She returned to the living room and looked at her phone. She suppressed a bitter image of Saul tonging Monica's erogenous zones. With an unsteady hand, she picked up the phone and speed-dialed Saul, her fifth call now. It went to voicemail without ringing—*if he has it turned off, he must be in danger*—and she left another message: "Honey, call me as soon as you get this. I had to leave Spencer's and I can't reach him. I... I don't know where to go. I hope you're okay. I love you." Pressing the END CALL button, she wondered how many times she had repeated the same message, or something similar. Her mind racing like a caged rat on a treadmill, she couldn't remember. She felt trapped. Just like the rat.

She dialed Spencer's number. *How many times have I tried him today?* Again, she couldn't remember.

On the third ring, he finally answered. His voice sounded groggy and half-asleep. Probably out on a bender last night. What else was new?

"Where the fuck are you?" he asked in decent Spanish.

"I... I went to my sister's boyfriend's house. I didn't know where else to go. I couldn't reach you."

"Are you okay?"

"Yes, but I can't stay here. And I don't know where to go."

"Have you talked to Saul today?"

"Can't reach him."

"Why did you leave?"

"Didn't you get my note?"

"No."

"Monica stopped by your place."

"That bitch? Did you let her in?"

"No, no... but she made some threats. I think she's in on it."

"Wouldn't surprise me at all."

"Were you able to get things straightened out?"

"Not yet. But I'm working on it. These things take time. It would be a little easier if two cops weren't dead, but that's what I'm working with. I'm trying to get the rap pinned on that sleaze-ball Fernando, maybe his fucked up brother Ruddy as well."

"So, I can't go home and I can't return to your apartment?"

"Not right now. In a little while, maybe, but not right now. And I don't think you're safe where you are."

"You know Emmanuel's reputation. I don't trust him."

"I wouldn't trust that horny fuck as far as I can throw him." There was a momentary pause before Spencer continued. "I think I have an idea. I have a friend who lives in the country. I think I'll take you there."

"That would be goo—"

Joella started and dropped the phone as the door creaked open. Emmanuel poked his grease-stained head in and grinned. He was shirtless. His long black hair was matted to the side of his head like he'd greased it with engine oil.

"Now, you little cock-tease. We have an hour before I return to work."

Joella hurriedly picked up the phone. She could hear Spencer's faint voice echoing from the tiny speaker. "What's going on there? What the fuck is going on? Answer me! Are you okay?"

Joella backed up toward a window and said, "Help. He's here. Emmanuel's here." But that was all she had time to say.

As he grabbed her arm, she managed to stuff the phone in a pocket with her free hand. She hadn't hung up. She could still hear Spencer's frantic voice on the other end, now muffled and incomprehensible.

She reached for the windowsill. Emmanuel grabbed her other arm roughly. "Get down on your knees, bitch. And suck. Gobble the cob."

******

Saul felt an overriding sense of panic when he opened his eyes and looked at the bedside clock. It was one in the afternoon, exactly noon in the DR. But why was he converting to DR time? And why the panic? He hadn't dreamed, at least not that he could remember. *Joella, that's why. She needs you. She's in trouble.* He didn't know how he knew, but didn't bother questioning it anymore. It was just another gift from Nicholas Fry. Among his other recently acquired skills, he'd also become psychic. The gift that kept on giving.

He tried to move his arms, but couldn't. Leather restraining straps bound ankles and wrists. An intravenous needle was taped to the inside of his forearm. The IV line led to a bag that hung from a metal pole. The bag dripped a clear liquid. On one arm, he noticed a small piece of white tape holding a cotton ball. *Blood samples. He took blood samples.*

He surveyed his surroundings. A white, sterile-looking room. Two bedside chairs, a small white dresser in a corner, a table tray. A black television screen mounted on the wall. Beside it, the eye of a video camera, equipped with a small blinking red light.

Juxtaposed with this sterility and coldness, he saw a window, which appeared to be painted, on one wall. Hunter green cloth blinds, dark brown trim, and a peek-a-boo view of lush, manicured greenery and bright yellow rays of sunshine. The window was open a crack and a cool, gentle breeze blew in.

Saul blinked a few times, trying to clear the chemically induced grogginess from his head. *Chemically induced. That fuck drugged me. Where is he?*

A door opened and Nicholas entered with a tray of food. He set it on the tray table and lifted a metal lid. Underneath were scrambled eggs, two sausages, a toasted English muffin, a decorative bowl of diced fruit, and a glass of orange juice. "Good afternoon," he said, wheeling the food bedside. "You must be hungry."

"Why am I tied up?"

"Oh that," Nicholas said, as if it was no more than the minor annoyance of a slightly overdue utility bill. "That was for your own safety. You do remember what you turned into last night?"

Saul did have a vague memory of the night, although bits of it were still unclear. *He drugged me. He drugged me against my will.* "Can you untie me?"

"Of course." Nicholas began unstrapping Saul. "I didn't want you turning into a monster and running off into the woods. Who knows what could have happened."

When Saul was free, he sat up in bed, rubbing his wrists. "Where's Samantha?"

"She went home. She called earlier. I said you'd call her when you woke up."

"Why am I here?"

"In your condition, Samantha and I thought this was the best place for you."

Saul eyed the food. He was hungry. And thirsty. He grabbed the glass of orange juice and gulped it down in three swallows. He eyed the dripping IV bag.

"That's just fluid replacement," Nicholas said. "Electrolytes, minerals and vitamins, that sort of thing. You were extremely dehydrated. Still are, by the looks of things."

Saul tried to stand. Dizziness swept over him. The room started swaying. Nicholas grabbed his arm gently and sat him back down. "Not so fast. I don't know how you've been living lately, but you haven't been taking care of yourself. You're not in stellar condition."

And how much of that is your fault, asshole? Never mind, be nice. "Where's my phone?"

Nicholas retrieved it from the dresser drawer and handed it to Saul. As Nicholas studied his face, Saul listened to numerous voicemails from Joella and set the phone down grimly. "I knew it."

"Knew what?"

"It's Joella. She's in trouble."

"What kind of trouble?"

"I don't know, her life's in danger I think." Saul stood up. "I don't have time to explain."

He tore the IV out of his arm. Dressed in a white hospital gown, he staggered a few times but made it to the dresser. He opened a drawer. He had guessed right. Nicholas had laid out clean clothes for him, even a new pair of Nike running shoes. This man was prepared and methodical to a fault.

Saul started getting dressed.

"I wouldn't do that," Nicholas said, approaching.

"Do you mind?" Saul said.

Pleading for him to stay, Nicholas looked the other way. Saul finished dressing. "I'm done."

Nicholas turned around as Saul approached the door. "I'm leaving."

"Where are you going?"

"Joella needs help. I'm going to help her."

"What, in the Dominican Republic? How are you going to get there? You can't teleport unless you're in a deep sleep. And even then, you can't control it."

Saul stopped. Nicholas was right. What was he thinking? *About getting so drunk you pass out, that's what. Then if you're real lucky, you'll board the 12:55 pm Teleporter Airlines Flight 2207 to exactly where she is, precisely when she needs you. But what if you're too late?* "Do you have any better ideas?"

"Well, I don't think you want to be the first human test subject on my teleporter. At least not until I get all the bugs worked out."

******

Emmanuel forced Joella to her knees. Did this idiot actually think she would suck his dick? Bite it off maybe, but not suck it. Then she got an idea. She stopped resisting and released her hands from Emmanuel's arms.

"That's the spirit," he said, releasing her and unzipping his fly. "Just give me ten minutes of your time. I'm sure you're that good."

She watched him stroke his member erect, thinking how quickly his grin would disappear if she bit it off. When it was stiff, he shoved it in her face. Wincing, she moved her mouth closer. *Bite it off. Sick fuck deserves it.*

That was when the unexpected happened. He pulled out a knife from his back pocket and quickly pressed the blade to her neck. It pinched the skin, drawing a tiny drop of blood.

"You think I'm stupid?" he said. "Suck it gently. You try anything and it'll be the last thing you try."

Has everyone in the barrio gone crazy? Joella wondered. Everyone pulling knives out at the drop of a hat—or currently, at the drop of Emmanuel's drawers. What the hell was in the air?

But she didn't waste any time thinking about it. With her left hand, she grabbed the knife. Even as her right hand clenched his nuts and starting squeezing and twisting, she already felt the hot pain of the knife slicing her palm, warm droplets of her own blood dribbling down her arm. She ignored the pain and continued squeezing.

Emmanuel flushed red, yelping like a dog in heat, and doubled over in pain. She felt his grip loosening. She twisted hard, deepening the cut but gaining control of the knife. She continued squeezing his nuts as he lay on the dirt floor, whining like an injured puppy dog.

When he finally brought a hand down and grabbed her hair, she'd already adjusted her grip on the knife, palm firmly gripping the handle. She sliced at his hand. The blade missed, but opened a large gash in his wrist. He released her hair, took his nuts in both hands, and cried like a baby. "It hurts so much... Oh God... it hurts so much."

The door burst open and a voice Joella didn't recognize said, "What the fuck is going on here?"

******

"Is this going to hurt?" Saul asked, standing in Nicholas's teleporter.

Hunched over computer monitors and a wall of controls a short distance from Saul, Nicholas said, "I don't think so, but I've never tried it, so I don't really know. When you teleported in your dreams, did it hurt?"

"No," Saul said, not feeling too reassured.

"Well, probably not then. Are you sure you want to do this? It could be dangerous, until I work out the bugs."

But Nicholas's eyes said something different, Saul noticed. He was thrilled to death about finally finding a willing human test subject to prove his theories correct.

"Let's get it over with. I need to reach Joella. What do you want me to do?"

"You have to imagine a destination."

Saul could visualize a one-room shack somewhere on a hill, but he had no idea where it was. He would have to guess, no way around it. He thought about Joella's house, also on a hill in San Marcos. At least he knew the exact whereabouts of her house. If he could get close, maybe someone would tell him.

"Okay, I have it."

"Is it where she is?"

"No, but I think it's close."

"Is that all you can come up with?"

Saul nodded.

"Well, I guess it's going to have to do then. Now close your eyes and concentrate on the destination. I'm going to give you two hours there. I hope that's enough. Don't open your eyes unless I tell you to. You understand?"

"Yes, let's get going."

Nicholas turned dials, pressed buttons, and watched computer monitors. The room darkened and a circle of white laser-like beams surrounded Saul. He felt tingly and hot. He heard a siren-like wail, low at first, but slowly becoming louder.

This is it, he thought. *The point of no return.*

Then two things happened. A metallic thumping sound—someone or something was pounding on an exterior steel wall—and Saul's phone started ringing.

Nicholas frantically adjusted controls. "Shit. Don't open your eyes."

Saul felt his body temperature rise and his heart rate quicken. He kept his eyes shut. In his mind's eye, he saw an all-encompassing thick purple mist. There was a euphorically pleasing quality about the mist that suffused his senses, leaving him with an overwhelming feeling of calm and peace. He didn't even want to ask the question, but he did. "What's wrong?"

Nicholas turned off the controls, switched on the lights, and ran over to the phone. He picked it up. "Your phone. I thought I told you to turn it off. The radio waves could interfere with the teleporter and really mess things up."

"Can I open my eyes?"

"Yes."

Saul opened his eyes, stepped off the teleporter platform, and approached Nicholas.

As he did, the metallic banging on the wall resumed.

"Who is it?" Saul said.

"At the door?"

"No, the phone."

"The name says Spencer Drinker."

That's how Saul had entered him in his contacts. "Give it to me."

Nicholas handed over the phone. "Let me see what that racket is," Nicholas said. "Good God, we can't even conduct scientific experiments in peace in the middle of nowhere."

"Spencer," Saul said, as Nicholas approached the door.

"I'm with your girlfriend and she's out of danger," Spencer said. "But I can't say the same for that piece of shit she was with. He's unconscious and bleeding like a stuck pig. And I feel like giving him another fucking kick in the head just because I can."

"Who was she with? What are you talking about?"

Spencer brought Saul up to speed. "She'd already done a number on him by the time I showed up. Had the fuck cut up, bleeding, and buckled over in pain, holding his nuts and screaming bloody murder—the whole time he still had a fucking boner, can you believe it?"

"Is Joella hurt? Did he, you know, touch her?"

"She's got a small cut on her hand and neck. I bandaged them. But no, he didn't touch her in the way you're talking about. If he did, I would've killed the fuck. And I still might."

"What did you do to him?"

"Emmanuel's a sick fucking rapist, Saul. You know that, for fuck sakes."

"I know. I don't know what Joella's sister sees in him. What did you do to him?"

"I cracked him about seven times in the face. Broke a few bones, I'm sure. Then I kicked him in the head—I don't know how many times, I lost count—maybe six or seven. And the ribs, two or three times. What would you have me do to this useless piece of shit?"

"You did well. And thanks."

"Anything for a bro."

"Where do you plan on taking Joella?"

"To a buddy's place in Mamon. In the country. She'll be safe there until this shit blows over."

Saul thanked his friend and Spencer handed the phone to Joella. "Here, say hi to your boyfriend. And make it quick. We gotta go."

Nicholas returned, waving Saul over. He held a wicker basket, its contents concealed by a white cloth. His blue eyes showed concern. "I need you outside. You have to see this."

"Be right there," Saul said, as Joella said hello.

"Are you okay, baby?" he said.

"Yes, are you?"

"I'm fine, honey. Just fine. Listen, I can't talk right now. I'll call you later, okay?"

"Okay. Spencer wants to get going. I better go. I love you."

"I love you, too." Saul hung up.

"Can we save the soap opera for later?" Nicholas said. "You have a friend outside."

Saul followed him outside into the sunlight. Under an apple tree, about fifty feet from Nicholas's multi-winged research facility, Bob the raccoon sat comfortably on his rump, looking around like a lost dog who'd finally made it back home. He didn't look misshapen or deformed. He looked like a normal, healthy raccoon—even a happy one.

"What do you want me to do?" Saul said.

Nicholas lifted the white cloth from the basket, revealing blueberries. "Feed him, like I was doing. He ran under that tree and I didn't want to spook him." He handed Saul the basket. "Here, keep him distracted while I get my tranquilizer gun. This could be my breakthrough."

Chapter Eighteen

Pearla didn't care much about the list anymore, even though she'd reviewed it that evening in her hotel room. She'd knocked off three of the six names; with any luck, a fourth and a fifth would be dead soon enough. In her mind she went through the kills. The Cockroach, Rodney Balkwist, thrown under a bus; Simpleton, Mike Simmons, stabbed to death; The Loser, Ronnie Lossing, strangulation by rope. Three names remained: The Cocksucker, Stanley Rogers; the Scumsucker, Simon Socket; and lastly, the Cling-On, Saul Climer. *Little shit will get his, that's for sure.*

She set the phone down, rose, and headed for the bathroom. At the door, she stopped and glanced back at the bed. On white bedsheets, The Loser, Ronnie Lossing, lay naked and spread-eagle, his extremities still bound to bedposts. The rope was still cinched tightly around his neck. His face was bulbous and purple. His eyes bulged. His tongue hung out like a thirsty dog. His penis was still erect. He had shit himself. A blackish-brown stream flowed down the sheets and dripped on the plush carpet. At one time, Pearla had thought he vaguely resembled a younger Mickey Rourke. Not anymore. Not with the purple face, the black and blue eye sockets, and the trail of shit leaking from his asshole. Now he looked more like a macabre clown in a freak show.

She laughed. "Such a waste of space you are... Loser. You're full of shit. Or at least you were."

Inside the bathroom, she washed her hands. Three of her knuckles were cut from some hard fists she'd delivered to The Loser's eyes. Just another internet sexual predator preying on Dominican women. Now his predatory days were over, and it was time for her to leave. It was getting too hot to trot around the streets of Vancouver. Way too hot to trot. She dried her hands, looked in the mirror, and thought about how she'd abandoned strategic planning in favor of ascension into the spirit world.

As she applied fresh eyeliner, she realized some of it was Kalfu's fault. No, not fault—credit, she quickly reminded herself. *Don't disrespect the spirits*. Kalfu had promised her a higher calling during those heated carnal encounters that occurred after every kill. Pounding her senseless—her crotch and throat still ached a little after the most recent sexcapade—he'd said: "Obey my commands and you will be rewarded in the spirit world." To Pearla, this meant that she was destined to become a spirit. She even had a name for herself when that redemptive transformation was complete—Pearlita, spirit of love and lust.

In this new role, she imagined herself traveling between the physical reality of Earth and the spirit world at random, judging and ruling on who was in love and who was in lust. Of course, she wouldn't disrespect the existing spirits or usurp their powers. Kalfu would guide her and explain her job description. A large part of her role would be determining the difference between real love and exploitative carnal lust. Those in love would be spared; those in lust, well, they might run into a few problems.

But where was Kalfu now? On the last two kills, he'd appeared within minutes after the deed had been done. Now, almost an hour later, and no Kalfu.

She finished with the eyeliner, picked up a pair of scissors, and began cutting her long black hair off in clumps, watching the strands land on the vanity counter, on the floor. She became obsessed with changing her appearance and less concerned about Kalfu. The gods work in mysterious ways, she reasoned. Who am I to question his all-knowing authority and power?

There was a knock on the door. For a moment, Pearla was about to open it, still half-expecting Kalfu to show. But she regained control of her senses. "Who is it?"

"Did you order room service, ma'am?"

She turned on the hot and cold taps. "No, and I'm in bathroom."

"Sorry for the disturbance. Enjoy your evening."

She hurried to the door and listened. The sound of footsteps grew fainter. She sighed and returned to the bathroom.

She finished cutting her hair, applied some hair gel, and slicked it back. She removed a blonde wig from a cardboard box and put it on, grinning at the new look. Clad in a red bra and matching red panties, she couldn't resist admiring herself in the mirror for a moment before dressing, even doing a little pirouette to see her shapely ass. It was her best asset, next to her large breasts.

She dressed in a conservative mid-length black skirt, white blouse, and black jacket. She applied the last touches to her make-up, gathered her toiletries, and exited the bathroom. She wasn't even worried about wiping down fingerprints, knowing she was being guided by divine intervention. A religious calling of the highest order—ridding the world of its male pestilence.

She packed away all her things, approached the door, and listened. It was quiet and early, only 8:37 pm. She still had three hours before her flight to Toronto, and she would gain another three hours in Toronto due to the time-zone change. If she was lucky, and she could reach The Cocksucker, Stanley Rogers, at his Toronto home, she would have one last little tryst before boarding her connecting flight to Prince Edward Island. An overnight layover; just enough time to get laid and get it over with. Or get The Cocksucker over with.

Opening the door, she turned, scanning the room one last time. On a whim, she closed the door and approached The Loser. She brought her face to within inches of his and coughed, drawing up a large green snot ball, which she spit into his eye. Gooey mucous strands dangled on his eyebrow and eyelash briefly before a few gobs dribbled loose and snaked down his purple, swollen cheek.

"You're a piece-of-shit Loser and I hope you burn in hell," she said. Then she left.

Outside, she opened her purse, removed her passport, and tossed it into a nearby wastebasket. A male pedestrian glanced over and she cast him an approving smile. He returned it and continued on. She pulled out another passport and examined the likeness. *Pretty smile. Pretty good likeness.* She hoped it was good enough to finish her work and eventually return home. She was no longer traveling as Antonella Rosario. Now she was Rubina Diaz, a fake identity created by her contacts back home. She had no idea who Rubina Diaz was, but she was about to make her into a national hero.

She hailed a taxi. On the way to the airport, she made a call. She had talked to Monica earlier, but needed to make sure the new plan was in place. This Cling-On was more mysterious and powerful than she had initially suspected. Neutralizing him, she was sure, would be her biggest challenge yet, and the final task that would catapult her into celestial stardom with her mentor, Kalfu.

Monica answered on the first ring. "Are you on the way to the airport?"

"Yes. Is everything in place?"

"Yes."

"Good. You've done well and you'll be rewarded. I'll call you tomorrow." She ended the call without waiting for a response. Smalltalk wasn't necessary. If things went picture-perfect, she could kill two birds with one stone. Quite literally.

The cabbie eyeballed her in the rearview mirror. "Rubina, did you say your name was?"

"That's right."

"You some kind of a movie star or something?"

"Something like that. Something like that."

Pearla texted The Cocksucker: *I'll be arriving in Toronto tonight at about one am. I have an overnighter and would love to spend it with you. I'll suck you like you've never been sucked before.*

That should get his attention, she thought, gazing out at the distant setting sun. Out of nowhere, a robin swooped down and smashed into the passenger window, splattering blood and guts right in front of Pearla's face. She didn't even flinch. She smiled, appreciating the wild geometric pattern its entrails left.

"What was that?" the cabbie said.

Kill two birds with one stone. "A bird just smashed into your car window. Quite dead I believe."

"Is the window broken?"

"No."

"Are you okay?"

"Yes."

"What's it look like back there?"

"It looks like a little star pattern," she said, trying unsuccessfully to contain a spreading grin. "A star is born."

Chapter Nineteen

Spencer didn't even see it coming. He heard the crunch of metal and felt a stinging pain as his neck snapped back from the impact. His Chevy Trailblazer spun recklessly—two 360-degree circles on the two-lane highway leading to Mamon—after another vehicle crashed into the driver side door at high speed.

"What the fuck?" was all he had time to say as he wrestled with the steering wheel. He saw the ditch rushing toward him and realized there was little time. He was going to hit it and there was nothing he could do about it. He was able to angle the trajectory just enough so the vehicle hit the ditch, launched into the air, and landed roughly in a sugar cane field, clear on the other side of a barbed-wire fence.

The vehicle bounced twice, staying upright, and Spencer brought it to a slow stop, knowing a fast stop would likely flip his vehicle. Not what he wanted right now.

In the passenger seat beside him, Joella blinked repeatedly and rubbed a growing lump on the side of her head. On impact, her head had smashed into the window and bounced off. She was seeing stars but she pushed them away, glancing through the barbed-wire fence at headlights, luminous evil white eyes, parked on the shoulder and glaring at them.

In the dark blue light of dusk, she saw two men emerge from the vehicle, armed with machine guns. There wasn't time for social pleasantries. "Spencer, get going! They're coming."

"Fucking assholes," he said, reaching into the glove box and producing a handgun. He glanced back. A third man emerged from the vehicle, also packing a machine gun. Armed only with his little Colt-45 revolver, it was almost like bringing a knife to a gunfight.

He jammed the vehicle into Drive, spat a trail of dirt and sugar cane debris at the pursuers, and drove off, striking and slicing through sugar cane plants until he hit a service road that ran parallel to the highway.

No shots were fired, but the pursuers climbed into their vehicle and began chase.

In the headlight beams of Spencer's SUV, Joella saw another barbed-wire fence nearing, a farm house behind it with a light on and two utility tractors parked in front. There would be an entrance road, allowing the enemy access to capture or kill them.

She pointed to the middle of the field. "Over there," she said. "They can get in on that side."

"I can't go through the middle of the field. It's too rough."

Spencer looked back. Another vehicle was now behind the first. He could make out the models—newer black Ford Expeditions. Two of them, in hot pursuit.

"We don't have many options," Joella said.

"Fuck, now we have two." He turned into the field and sped up, bouncing over and snapping rows and rows of sugar cane. Some farmer wouldn't be too happy about this, but that was the least of his concerns right now.

Midway through the field, Joella looked back. Both Expeditions had entered the field through a service road and were hightailing it toward them. They were closing the gap. This didn't look good at all.

"The frame is twisted or something," Spencer said. "I can hardly control this fucking thing."

Up ahead, Joella saw a road that spiraled up—a ramp of sorts—but she couldn't see the other side, if it had one.

Spencer saw it too. He looked at her. "You ready?"

Joella didn't hesitate. Going to an unknown fate was better than winding up in the clutches of these gun-toting thugs. She nodded. "Go for it."

Spencer jerked the steering wheel toward the ramp and floored it. They bounced up and down as it picked up speed.

The enemy was right behind them—four bouncing headlight beams, gaining fast. And now they were firing shots. As Spencer hit the ramp, a bullet smashed through the back window, narrowly missing his head, and exiting the front windshield.

Joella bent down, hands protecting head. She closed her eyes.

"Not a-fucking-gain," Spencer said, as the SUV flew into the air a second time. Forty or so feet later, it crashed through the peaked roof of an old house. As part of it collapsed, the structure broke the fall somewhat. Spencer's vehicle landed in the living room of the home. On impact, shards of glass, chunks of metal, splintering wood, and dust flew everywhere.

A sleeping dog woke, barked twice and fled, his surprised male owner fleeing right behind him.

The enemy chose not to proceed with the ramp detail, instead crashing through the barbed-wire perimeter fence, stopping outside the house, and disembarking. The lead vehicle blew two front tires on impact, paving the way for the second to get through relatively unscathed.

Joella raised her head, brushing away chunks of wood and debris. She examined her extremities and decided she wasn't injured. But the front end of the vehicle had been crushed on impact and her leg was pinned.

She looked at Spencer, who was brushing off debris and opening his door. He didn't look too happy, not least of all because most of the glass was missing from his SUV.

They heard voices outside. Speaking English.

"The girl is priority one, okay?"

"Got it."

"Team one, the perimeter. Team two, in that way."

"Roger that, Commander."

"Yes sir."

Spencer looked at her. "Let's go."

Smoke rose from the hood of the vehicle. Joella could smell gas.

"I can't. I'm pinned. You go. Someone has to tell Saul what happened. Go on, you don't have much time."

He shoved the Colt in his pants. "I ain't leaving you here."

"Yes you are. Get out of here. Now!"

After a moment's hesitation, Spencer climbed out of the smoking vehicle and ran out of what remained of the back door.

A man on a horse rode up and Spencer aimed a gun at him. "I need your help. I need to get out of here. I'm not going to hurt you."

The man extended a hand, pulled Spencer onto the horse, and rode away in full gallop down a small serpentine path. Staccato bursts of machine gun fire trailed their exit.

"I think he got away," a man with a gun said.

"You think?" another man said. "Never mind. He's not important. Let's get the girl."

Chapter Twenty

It was strange indeed, Saul thought, looking into the cage at Bob the raccoon. The camaraderie he had with the animal was akin to a dog with its puppy. Following Nicholas's instructions earlier, he'd approached Bob with the blueberries. Sitting under the apple tree, Bob was a little nervous at first, but it didn't take long before Saul was hand-feeding him. They ate blueberries together, a couple of reunited brothers sharing a snack under the comfortable shade of an apple tree on a postcard-perfect sunny afternoon. Saul was even able to pat Bob affectionately. The animal seemed fully recovered from the deleterious effects of teleportation and chemical injections. Neither one of them resembled the ferocious beasts that had fought off coyotes in the woods earlier.

Who knew when they would turn again. But for now, they were back to something approximating normal.

The kinship was so fast and intense that Nicholas hadn't even bothered with the tranquilizer gun. With a trail of blueberries, Saul was able to lure Bob back into the lab and back into the cage. It was almost like Bob wanted to go, wanted to do his part to help Saul out of his conundrum. He displayed alertness, awareness, and intelligence that Saul had rarely seen in animals before.

Saul extended a hand to the cage. "Bob, I have to go to bed now. But I'll be back, okay?"

Bob looked up at his buddy affectionately. Saul squeezed his fingers in and scratched his head. Bob nodded, made a whistling sound, and curled up to go to sleep.

Saul turned to Nicholas, who was busy looking into a microscope. "Did you see that?"

Nicholas raised his eyes. "See what?"

"He nodded at me."

Nicholas left the microscope and approached Saul. "Raccoons are intelligent, you know. They have a vocabulary of over fifty-one different vocalizations."

"Yeah, but doesn't he seem smarter than the average bear?"

"I have to agree. He's changed."

"Like me?"

"I don't know if you've changed in that way. I'd have to run some tests. Do you feel smarter?"

"I don't know. When I got up this morning, I felt like shit. But after the sedative wore off I started to feel more alert and alive than ever. I felt my strength coming back. And my wounds are practically non-existent now. Wounds don't normally heal that fast."

Nicholas scratched his head. "No, they don't."

There was a brief silence. They'd been around this bend earlier in the day and there was no point repeating it. They'd talked about Saul's condition. The hairs were still growing thicker on his legs, but fortunately had not spread to his other extremities. He could teleport in his dreams, was physically stronger, and healed like some genetically altered super-soldier. He was also psychic. Only problem was, sometimes he felt sick to his stomach, had unexplainable, horrible nightmares, and had physically transformed into a half-raccoon, half-coyote beast. When in this state, he was obviously far from himself mentally. His behavior could be violent and unpredictable.

That was why Saul had agreed to stay in Nicholas's lab for a few days. Nicholas would continue monitoring him while working on the antidote. And now that Bob was back, safe and sound, that process had already begun. Nicholas had blood samples from both Bob and Saul, and was conducting a thorough DNA analysis that would, he hoped, lead to an injectable cure.

There were still other nagging questions. Had other people been infected? If so, what were they capable of? Had other animals, possibly coyotes, been infected by Bob?

And where was Pearla? Where was Monica? How many people had they killed? And the last one suddenly struck Saul like a freight train. Was Joella still in danger? Saul reached into his pocket for his cell phone before he even realized it.

"What's wrong?' Nicholas said.

Saul checked the time: 11:36 pm. Shit, the night had run away from him. He had texted Joella earlier in the day and everything was fine. She and Spencer were on their way to Mamon. He'd promised to call her back, but instead had taken a nap and forgotten all about it.

Now he sensed it. Something was wrong. This new psychic ability of his had been dead-on so far.

He noticed a voicemail from Spencer, but no texts or calls from Joella. He looked at Nicholas. "It's Joella. Something's wrong."

On speaker, they listened to Spencer's message. His voice was urgent, strained: "Call me as soon as you get this. Joella's been kidnapped or killed. I'm gonna have those fuckers killed, I'll tell ya. Anyway, call me."

Panicking, Saul called Joella and got her voicemail. He didn't leave a message. Instead, he hung up and sent a text message, asking where she was and if she was okay.

He tried Spencer. Straight to voicemail again. No doubt he was on another bender. He left a message asking Spencer to call him ASAP.

Then he made a decision. "I have to go."

"Go where?"

"Home. My only hope is to fall asleep and teleport to where she is."

"There's no guarantee that's going to happen. You didn't teleport last night."

"Yeah, but I was under sedation and strapped to the bed."

"Well, you've been severely intoxicated before and still teleported. And the straps shouldn't matter, based on my theories of a fifth dimension."

Saul wasn't prepared to listen to theories he probably wouldn't understand anyway. "I don't have time for this. Joella's been kidnapped. Your teleporter still needs tweaking. I might end up in the DR with a third arm or something."

Nicholas's brow furrowed. "I'm getting closer. I can feel it."

But Saul had already grabbed his keys and stood at the door. Nicholas didn't try to stop him.

Bob stirred from his slumber, eyed Saul, and made a "whoop-whoop" noise. Saul had no idea what it meant.

He opened the door. "I'll call you tomorrow." And, as an afterthought, added, "If I'm still alive."

******

Twenty minutes later, he sat on a plastic chair on his back porch, watching a full moon, drinking beer, and smoking. At least he didn't feel like a laboratory raccoon anymore, although he might be one, now that his DNA had been altered by Bob's scratches.

Although a self-confessed dipsomaniac, the first sip of beer had almost made him vomit; he didn't know if it was due to the changes taking place in his body or the recent laboratory detox. He forced another sip, then another, and his system finally started to grudgingly agree with his brain, which said he was drinking the nectar of the gods.

He polished off the beer and went inside for something stronger. He knew in his state of worry, he wouldn't be able to fall asleep without the aid of sleeping pills—even then it would be a challenge—and he didn't want to medicate for fear it would prevent teleportation. So, the plan was to put himself into pass-out—maybe even blackout—drunk mode. It had worked before. Maybe it would again.

He found a half-empty 26-ounce bottle of rum, brought it outside, and started tying into it. Straight. No mix. His stomach lurched a few times, but he held the vomit back, forcing the hooch down. After some time, his system began to fully embrace the comfortably numbing buzz.

Then the phone rang. It was Spencer.

Saul answered, dispensing with social niceties. "Do you know where she is?"

"No. We were maybe two-thirds of the way to Mamon when the Expedition hit me." Spencer filled Saul in on the details and finished by saying he was holed up at his friend's in Mamon until he was sure it was safe to return to Costambar.

"Let me get this straight—when you left, Joella was pinned in your vehicle?"

"Right, so I don't know if they kidnapped or killed her. I think they kidnapped her."

"What makes you think that? For all you know, they might've blown up the vehicle."

"No. These bastards are professionals—not just a bunch of low-life, hired thugs. They spoke English like it was their first language. One fuck said, 'The girl is priority one,' or something like that. They have an agenda with Joella. I think she's alive somewhere."

In his alcoholic fog and rising panic, Saul couldn't imagine what this agenda might be. But first things first. He needed to pass out, and with a little luck wind up where Joella was being kept—*if* she was being kept. Then what? Play superhero and disarm maybe six professionally trained and well-armed assassins?

"Do you have any ideas on how to solve this?" Saul said.

"I have the colonel looking into it. Luckily, he's a good friend. Oh, and I have some good news."

"Good news?"

"Yeah, the colonel assures me that Fernando will take the rap for the cop murders. Joella is no longer wanted for robbery or murder. Neither are you, for that matter. And Fernando's brother, Ruddy, the bastard that shot at us?"

"What about him?"

"I had him killed."

"You did?"

"I told you I was going to."

Saul should have known better than to doubt Spencer's word. He was nothing if he wasn't a man of his word. But he also realized none if it mattered if Joella was dead.

"How much is this gonna cost?" Saul asked.

"We can talk about that later, when everything is settled. When are you coming back?"

"That's what I'm trying to do right now."

"Okay. I'm gonna let you go. Don't go doing anything stupid."

Saul didn't know what that meant anymore. Seemed like almost everything he did lately was stupid to some degree. Probably just a part of his modus operandi, and always would be. "Okay."

Spencer hung up.

Saul finished the bottle. He returned to the kitchen and rummaged around in the cupboards. He still had beer in the fridge—gotta have the staples—but he wanted something stronger. He wanted to pass out. Right now.

He found it. A 26-ounce bottle of Absolut vodka. Full. Just what he needed. He cracked the seal, twisted off the cap, and took a long pull. By the time he wobbled out to the back porch, he was three-quarters of the way in the bag. Perfect.

But what he saw next was pretty far from perfect. Dimly lit by the soft yellow porch light, a pack of coyotes, maybe sixteen in all, had surrounded the house. They formed a perfect circle of glowing red eyes, backdropped by blackness.

Vodka bottle in hand, Saul froze. A part of him said, *Get inside and batten down the hatches.* Another part, the part that was now dictating his thoughts, said, *Stay and enjoy the show. Have a drink, pull up a front-row seat, and enjoy Mother Nature at her ever-loving finest.*

One coyote barked. Then it howled. Another did the same. Then another. And another. And another, until they were all howling.

Saul watched, struggling to make a decision, hoping some voice of reason would prevail. He had read that coyote attacks on people were rare and fatalities rarer still from an animal that averaged about thirty-five to fifty pounds fully grown.

Yet it had happened.

In 1981, a coyote attacked a three-year-old girl in California and ran off with her. Although she was rescued by her father, she later died in surgery from a broken neck and blood loss.

In 2009, a nineteen-year-old Canadian musician died from his injuries and blood loss sustained in an attack by two coyotes in Cape Breton Highlands National Park in Nova Scotia, Canada.

They had power in numbers. And he'd recently provoked them, fighting them off in the woods, defending his life and Bob's life. They'd attacked then. Wouldn't they now? Didn't they have a motive? Yes. Revenge.

Against his better judgment, Saul sat down and watched. He wanted to know how this would play out. The terrible nightmare in Nicholas's vehicle replayed in his mind. Bloody fangs snapping at his jugular vein. Was it a premonition dream? Would this be how he met his maker?

But the raw fear was being replaced by something else. An animal courage began coursing through his veins. He noticed hairs springing up on his forearms and took a swill of liquid courage. He felt the lip of the bottle click against two large fangs that now protruded from his mouth. Before he knew it, he'd set the bottle down and was growling, low and guttural. He was becoming *it*—half-raccoon and half-coyote.

He didn't know, but he crawled on all fours to the middle of the circle, stared up at the moon and began howling, joining the chorus of coyotes. Some semblance of reason entered his mind as the coyotes closed in on him. He closed his eyes. Was this actually happening, or was it some macabre, alcohol-induced hallucination? Or some yet-unrealized bizarre religious ritual? *It's happened before. It will happen again.*

He opened his eyes and gazed around at the circle of frenetic sound and motion. Moving closer, their blood-red eyes looked inside his soul.

Saul stopped howling and scanned the forest, looking for signs of other predators. At the tree line, he saw five raccoons curiously watching the ritual play out. They started a low whistling sound.

He scanned the treetops. Hundreds of birds flew in and perched on branches. They began chirping in harmony with the coyotes. Looking around, he saw the property fill up with other animals. Squirrels and chipmunks appeared and chattered. Even a few rabbits and a red-tailed fox had arrived.

He turned to the moon, admiring its fullness and relishing this rare moment of oneness with nature. He howled, low at first, but increasing in volume along with the forest congregants.

Whatever happened to him now, he didn't care anymore. If he had become part of nature's food chain, part of the pecking order, so be it. It was no longer his decision to make. Some higher power was now calling the shots. It was the dawn of a new era, an era incomprehensible and yet profoundly comprehensible—a once-in-a-lifetime oneness with nature.

Let them come.

And they did. And what they did when they did was the last thing that Saul expected.

Chapter Twenty-One

Joella was flabbergasted at the way she was being treated, considering the brazen manner in which she'd been pursued, captured, and kidnapped. These people who had her imprisoned in a fancy house somewhere in the mountains were laying out the red carpet treatment. Her well-appointed room was on the second floor, overlooking a panoramic lush green valley view backdropped by majestic green-carpeted mountain peaks. She could hear the hypnotically soothing sound of a babbling brook nearby.

It was just before midnight. Since arriving four hours earlier, she'd been given a fresh pair of clothes and permission to shower. A doctor had diagnosed the lump on her head as a minor concussion; the ankle injury, a minor sprain. After wrapping it in a tenser bandage, he'd given her a painkiller.

A shorthaired man in a black suit and sunglasses had just delivered a food tray. Fresh, diced fruit, an assortment of cheeses and crackers, breads and buns, a variety of cold cuts, a jug of orange juice, and a bottle of white wine in a bucket of ice. It even included a corkscrew and a decorative gold-rimmed wine glass.

She reclined on a plush red loveseat, sipping wine and gazing at the stars. She almost felt like she was on vacation—a brief respite from the drudgery and poverty of her life at home in San Marcos. Sure, there were steel bars on all the windows, probably a 24-hour guard outside the locked doors, and a video camera mounted in the room, but otherwise life could be worse. She could be dead right now, for starters. She still could end up dead. So her attitude was to enjoy it while it lasted, because happiness was fleeting and could disappear in an instant.

She tried to remember what they'd said to her when they rescued—*maybe the wrong word*—her from Spencer's burning vehicle. "Get in the car... Cooperate with us and we won't hurt you... This will all be over soon... I'm not at liberty to discuss what we want with you right now. But in time, you'll find out."

All further questions were related to her comfort, wellbeing, and food and wine preferences.

What was happening? She'd never been treated so well in her life—well, maybe a few times, but that was different. That was with Saul, her boyfriend.

Then she remembered something. She'd put her phone inside her shoe. Maybe she could retrieve it and call Saul. For as comfortable as it was here, she sensed the underlying agenda was something sinister. Comfortably buzzed on wine, she went to the bed and picked up her shoes. Out of camera range, she slipped her cell phone out and pocketed it while placing the shoes on a doormat.

She went over to a nearby desk, picked up *El Diario*, a Puerto Plata newspaper, and slid the chair over to the window. Then she retrieved her glass of wine from the coffee table next to the loveseat, returned to the chair and sat, back facing the camera, pretending to read the paper. She slowly slid her smartphone out and placed it inside the open newspaper.

She texted Saul that she was alive and well but had been kidnapped and needed his help. Five seconds later a text message came back saying the text could not be sent because she was out of phone minutes. Shit—the worst possible time to run out.

Not knowing what else to do, she began scrolling through all the text messages they'd sent back and forth over the past four months. She read them, reminiscing about how quickly, deeply, and passionately they'd fallen in love.

The day before he returned to Canada: *Yesterday with you was the most incredible time in my life. I have to tell you I love how you make love to me. You know how to please me so well in the bedroom and everywhere else, for that matter. I love you so much, Joella. I can't live without your love.*

A misunderstanding they'd had over money. A panicked series of messages she'd sent to Saul when he hadn't responded for a few days: *Hello, what's wrong with you today? Tell me... Hello, how are you? Tell me... I love you a lot. Don't forget it... I love you without your money. Your money is not important to me... You're important to me because I love you... Why don't you answer my call? I was joking with you... It's because I love you, and I'm so worried that I'm in the clinic with a fever... If you want to leave me, if you want to separate, that's fine... I'm not with you for your money... If you feel bad about what I said, I'm sorry I upset you... My love, please forgive me. I don't want you to feel bad for something I said... If you want to leave me, that's fine, but answer me, please. I need to hear your voice... Forgive me, my love, I was just joking with you, but our relationship is important to me... I'm sorry, my love, I'll love you forever. I'll never be able to forget you...*

Answer me, please, my love. I feel really bad... Please forgive me, my love. My life is not worth living without you. I need you now.

Then another misunderstanding about money. When Saul got pissed off at her, he tended to retreat into his own little world and punish her by not answering the phone. She'd written him: *Hi my love. I called you, but you don't answer... I know I bothered you yesterday but I still love you... I don't know what I did, but you don't need to be so far away from me... I know you are not that busy. You just don't want to talk, that's the truth... How come you don't answer? Don't you love me anymore? I need to know... My love, what I said to you yesterday was not the truth. You treat me really well. I'm not a bad person... Forgive me, I don't want to bother you but I have a headache because you are not talking to me.*

Saul's answer, seven hours and multiple texts later: *I will forgive you. I love you a lot.*

Joella's response: *You should be able to communicate with me and tell me what's wrong. I'm your girlfriend.*

The morning after the first night she'd slept over at his apartment, she wrote: *How did you feel with me in your bed last night? Tell me.*

On and on.

Reading through them, Joella started to realize how vulnerable she'd become when it came to Saul. When they'd first met in the second-floor cafeteria of La Serena supermarket in Puerto Plata, she didn't know what to think of him. He was bold, she had to give him that. He'd approached her while she was sitting alone, having lunch. After a short conversation, he'd asked for her phone number.

She'd been taken by surprise and given it to him, with no intention of really pursing a relationship. Her first impression: *he's just another gringo on holiday looking for a lustful adventure. Like many of the others, he'll eventually return to his country and forget all about me.*

And Joella didn't want that. So the first two times Saul had called, she hadn't answered. Two texts also went unanswered. On the third call, however, she answered, deciding to at least give him the benefit of the doubt. And that was how she'd ended up exactly where she was right now. *We have no idea how someone is going to change our lives until we decide to take that path.* She'd gone down the path and here she was. Did she regret it? No. Would she do it all over again? Yes.

Yet certain things still troubled her, not least of all her current predicament. Wanted for robbery and murder. Kidnapped by people with an unknown agenda. Had Spencer escaped? Had they killed him? How were her children? But somehow these problems seemed small in comparison with her relationship. Maybe she was having trouble prioritizing, because if she didn't have her health or wellbeing, how could she have a relationship?

She had more questions than answers. What exactly were the details of Saul's relationship with Monica? *Did he sleep with her while he was going out with me? While declaring his monogamous love for me? Was it true what Monica had said, or was she just trying to upset me? And if he did sleep with Monica, how many others were there?*

Thinking about it made her heart heavy with sadness. She finished off the glass of wine and set it on the floor.

What started as contemplation was transforming into wallowing in self-pity.

The way Saul handled their disagreements was also troubling. Lack of communication. Rejection. Why had he suddenly stopped returning her calls after arriving in Canada? Sure, her request for money had gone over like a lead balloon, and she couldn't blame him for that. There were countless foreign suckers sending Dominican women money regularly, believing foolishly they had a loyal, caring, and loving girlfriend. The lines halfway down the block outside the Western Union office in Puerto Plata spoke volumes.

She had the feeling there was something Saul wasn't telling her, and women's intuition suggested maybe it was because he was embarrassed. She started adding up the pieces and then it came to her. Most of their little disagreements were over money. Yet he'd said he was a successful novelist. Had she bothered to research any of these so-called novels or even ask him any questions about them? No. She'd taken it for granted that he was telling the truth. But maybe he was lying. And, if he'd lied about that, what else was he lying about?

Was this just a sex adventure for Saul? Was he a master of deception? Was she being played for a fool? On an emotionally intelligent level, she doubted it. But the seeds of doubt had been planted. And when seeds involving matters of the heart were planted, they often grew into heart-wrenching weeds of destruction—even relationship killers.

With a heavy heart, Joella folded the newspaper over the phone, rose, and refilled her wine glass. She set the newspaper on the coffee table and took a large swallow of wine. She'd thought herself into a state of sadness and depression; she could even visualize the seeds growing into nasty weeds.

The door opened. Black Suit entered and closed it behind him. At least he'd removed the shades. He had the look of a computer geek-turned-CIA agent—even the signature pen and white folds of a writing pad poking out of his top pocket.

"Do you like the wine?" he asked.

Joella nodded. "Do you have a name?"

"You can call me Koby. I'm sorry, but you're going to have to hand over the phone. You'll get it back later."

Joella didn't try and interfere as Koby picked up the newspaper, removed the phone, and placed it in the top pocket with his other fashion accessories.

"Are you going to kill me?" she asked.

"No."

"Did you kill Spencer?"

"No."

"Did one of your associates?"

"No."

"What do you want with me?"

"I can't discuss that. Is there anything else you need?"

She emptied the last of the wine into her glass and held up the bottle. "Can you get me another bottle of this?"

"It's getting late, ma'am. You should get some rest."

"One more bottle? For all I know, it might be my last."

"It won't be your last, but okay." He left.

Later, after finishing half the second bottle, Joella lay in bed and watched the room slowly spin. She wasn't a big drinker normally, but had become quite drunk. She closed her eyes and tried to blank her mind. After a few minutes, she opened them. The room had stopped spinning, thank God.

The weeds returned and she tried to mow them down. She wasn't entirely successful. They began sprouting and spreading, infesting and infecting. If Saul were here now, maybe he could make things right, transform the weeds into red roses.

Where are you, Saul? Where are you?

Chapter Twenty-Two

Saul didn't know where he was. He gazed at the cityscape of high-rise office and apartment buildings. Then he recognized the familiar shape of the concrete communications and observation tower, a signature icon of Toronto's skyline. It glowed neon green against the night sky, the unmistakable flying-saucer pod two-thirds of the way up. The CN Tower.

What am I doing here? The last thing he remembered was the animal orchestra and sort of being worshipped by the indigenous birds and wildlife of the forest. Now, here he was again, on another balcony, perhaps eighteen floors up. There was no jumping off point here. Not one that he could possibly survive, anyway.

The night was calm and still. The air, even at this altitude, was thick with humidity. Sweat beads popped up on his brow and he wiped them away. *You know what to do. Of course you do.*

He approached the sliding-glass door and peered in. It took a few seconds for his eyes to adjust. He saw a big-screen television in the corner, showing an orgy in progress. On the screen, multiple men and women paired off, getting it on in different positions and levels of intensity. Moaning and groaning.

The room was painted a dark red color and decorated with statues of Greek gods and goddesses. On the walls, colorful abstract art.

A naked, fat, bald man knelt on the floor in front of a black sofa, his back to the pornography on screen. He was gagged and his arms were tied behind his back. It appeared as if his legs were also bound, but Saul couldn't tell from his angle. Multiple lacerations across the man's chest oozed blood.

The man groaned every time the woman with the leather cat-o-nine-tails whip lashed him. And every time he groaned, the blonde woman, dressed only in red panties, cackled loudly.

Of course Saul had heard of sadomasochism before, but not this gory. Unless one participant was unwilling.

The woman flicked the whip and lashed him again, one whiptail slicing into his lip and splitting the gag loose. He howled in pain as blood squirted from the ensuing gash. "Please, Pearla, I beg you... no more. Take my money, take anything you want, but please leave me alone."

"I'll leave you alone in hell, you fucking Cocksucker," she said, lashing him again across the face, chest, and exposed groin.

"Ooowwww... ooowwww... ooooww... no, no, please."

Saul felt the metamorphosis before he knew what hit him. His arms grew bigger, hands morphing claw-like. Hairs sprouted across his forearms and face. Then he felt an adrenaline-like surge of energy course through his body. At first the low growling startled him, but then he realized it was rising from the pit of his stomach.

Pearla swung around and saw him. She was different, Saul thought. More than just the wig. She was bigger, more muscular. Her eyes were larger and blood-red. Her nose had grown longer and pointier, her teeth more prominent. Horse teeth.

Grinning, she said, "Kalfu, is that you?"

Saul had no idea who Kalfu was. He considered crashing through the window, but decided to try the door instead. It was open. He entered and charged her.

Lashing at him with the whip, she stepped aside. "I should have known better."

Saul crashed into the couch, narrowly missing The Cocksucker. The momentum catapulted him over it. He landed on his back in front of the porn show. To erotic oohs and aahs, he stood.

Then Pearla did something unexpected. Dropping the whip, she plucked a dagger off the coffee table and plunged it into The Cocksucker's heart. She looked into his horrified eyes and said, "Did I break your heart, you filthy pig?"

As Saul moved toward her, she withdrew the knife and plunged it into the dying man's throat for good measure. Blood spurted out and his head lolled to one side. A small groan escaped his lips before he died.

She extracted the blade and waved it threateningly at Saul. He stopped just out of striking range and growled, circling, looking for an opening.

"You come for him?" she said, pointing to the deceased. "Looks like you're a little too late."

"What's wrong with you?"

She took a step closer. "No, Saul, the question is, what's wrong with you? You look like a freak show."

"I don't know if you've looked in the mirror lately, but you're not looking so hot yourself."

Pearla swung the blade at Saul's neck. Still circling, he dodged it.

"You made the mistake of disrespecting me, not once, but three times." She charged forward, thrusting the blade at him. "And three strikes, you're out, you fucking Cling-On."

Saul dodged the blade again, and stuck a leg out. Pearla tripped and face-planted into the wall, the blade tearing into an abstract painting of a full moon with a macabre smiley face. Growling, he leaped on her back and sunk his fangs into her neck. She spun him around while stabbing at his arms with the blade. Saul managed to grab the blade and twisted her wrist.

"Oww." The knife flew out of her hand and dropped to the floor. As she spun around, Saul wrapped his arms around her neck and tightened.

"No you don't," she said, pushing him toward the television screen. Saul slipped and fell headfirst on the TV, Pearla landing on top of him. The screen popped, sparked, and sizzled. Dazed, Saul released her. She leaped to her feet, retrieved the knife, and advanced.

Saul scrambled to his feet and dove for her knees. She brought one up and kneed him square in the head. He dropped face-first on the carpet, the room spinning as he turned his head. He'd thought he was strong, but it appeared whatever beast or demon Pearla had turned into was a little stronger and quicker.

He saw the knife advancing and rolled quickly along the floor.

Pearla stabbed it into the floor and wrestled for a split-second, trying to free the blade.

It was all the time Saul needed. He sprang up and kicked her hard, square in the side of the jaw. "Tit for tat," he said.

"Uuuff," she said, rolling over, blade in hand.

Saul advanced. He wasn't expecting what happened next. She whipped the knife at him and he had to duck quickly to avoid getting stabbed right between the eyes.

She stood and landed an uppercut to his jaw, the force of the blow so hard it sent him flying into the wall. He hit it back-first and crumpled down onto his butt. Stars danced in front of him, multiplied, and grew. *This is not good. Not good at all.*

He tried to stand. He got part way up and his legs gave out. He fell on his ass again. Pearla leaped in front of him, kicking him square in the jaw. His head lolled to one side and the room flickered black and white, black and white. He was losing consciousness. He saw another foot moving swiftly toward his face and it was all he could do to move his head.

Pearla kicked so hard her high-heeled foot penetrated the wall.

As she struggled to dislodge it, Saul, dizzy and with draining strength, got up and delivered a straight right to her jaw. It landed flush but had little effect.

"Is that all you got?" She freed her foot and advanced on him.

Saul staggered back. In a flash, she was on him. She tackled him to the floor and started pounding fists into his face.

Black and white, black and white, black and gray, black and gray. He was on the precipice of unconsciousness. Soon it would be black and black.

Desperately, Saul flailed his arms, trying to block the blows. His arms became weak, then limp. He was getting pummeled to death. Somehow Pearla's strength had increased as the battle waged. Saul's, on the other hand, was draining mercilessly.

Something was wrong with Nicholas's formula, he decided as the dark fog thickened. *Have to do something about that if I ever get out of here.*

Satisfied with her work thus far, Pearla stood, leaving Saul lying there like a limp ragdoll, nearly unconscious. One eye had been punched closed and the other was barely open. Blood oozed from facial gashes.

He saw three black Pearla silhouettes and white twinkling stars. He wondered grimly if it was a full moon.

He watched the fearsome three locate and pick up three knives. In his haze, he couldn't tell which one was real. He struggled to stay conscious. But his arms and legs no longer obeyed brain commands.

Pearla stepped forward. "You've saved me a trip to Prince Edward Island. You're nothing more than a twisted predator and exploiter of women. You insulted me... you insult and abuse the female population of my country. And for that, you will pay with your life. You fucking Cling-On."

She knelt down beside him and with both hands raised the knife high in the air.

Saul tried to move but couldn't. He tried to clear the cobwebs but couldn't. He tried to convert the three Pearlas into one but couldn't. His world was turning black. He tried to convert black to white but couldn't. Nothing is black and white, he thought stupidly. There are always gray areas. And he was seeing a hell of a lot of gray right now.

The knife began its downward thrust.

Saul saw a glint of white light as the blade caught the moon's reflection outside. Must be a full moon, he thought. *The stupid things you think about when you're about to die. No rhyme nor reason. Just utter nonsense. Shit, I need to control this. I had strength and it's gone. Please, if there is a God, grant me the courage and strength to change the things I can.*

It was as if someone had answered his prayer. Just as the knife pricked his jugular vein, a lightning bolt of incredible strength shot through his body.

With incredible speed, he brought a forearm up, deflected it, and leaped to his feet. This time he wasn't going to wait around to test how long the strength would last. At one time—when he had a death wish—he would have. Now, though, with Joella in his life, he wanted to preserve his life and his relationship. If it weren't for Joella, he'd have time-tested this new strength. But he'd promised himself he wouldn't let her down this time, wouldn't slip into the silent, non-responsive pattern that came so naturally.

Saul ran for the door. By the time he reached it, Pearla had retrieved the knife and now stood glaring at him. He opened it and bolted down the hallway.

Instead of immediately pursuing, Pearla began dressing. Even in her madness, she still had a sense of decorum. She didn't want to go gallivanting around downtown Toronto buck-naked, especially at this hour.

That little pause gave Saul a head start. He reached a red EXIT sign and swung the door open. He glanced back before fleeing down the stairs, and saw no one. Three floors down, he realized the new power was holding; he wasn't wheezing like a terminally ill lung cancer patient.

Halfway down, he saw a middle-aged man sprawled out in a stairwell landing, remorsefully pouring his heart out to a half-full bottle of Captain Morgan spiced rum. The man clutched the bottle with both hands, staring into it forlornly like it represented the key to his salvation. "I didn't mean to do it, Mona... please come back to me... come back... pleeeeease!"

Saul stopped and looked down at him. The man put the bottle to his lips, sucking on it like a baby bottle. Finishing a large swill, he wiped his mouth and stared at Saul, jaw open, eyes widening. "I'm sorry, I didn't mean it. Are you the grim reaper, coming to get me?"

Saul had to fight the urge to ask the drunk for a drink. "No... but the woman chasing me might be. I'd get out of here if I were you. Go home."

"I don't have a home anymore. I have nothing."

"You have your life. Make the best of it." Saul stepped over the man and continued his descent. He heard the sound of a bottle breaking above. He didn't know if the man had smashed it over his head or thrown it against the wall. No time to find out.

He arrived at the main floor and swung open the door.

Pearla was standing in the lobby, pointing a handgun at his head. She squeezed the trigger.

Saul ducked. The blast thundered though the contained quarters and the bullet ricocheted off marble walls.

Behind Pearla, an elevator door opened. A beefy security guard stepped out and clutched Pearla's gun hand. "No, you don't. Drop the gun."

She squeezed the trigger again and a bullet shattered a glass chandelier above. A woman helping a drunk man through the main doors froze and screamed.

Saul ran for the open door, the fear-frozen woman eyeballing him like he was some kind of monster as he passed. He heard three gunshot blasts and a terrifying scream as he fled. *Why didn't you help the people in the lobby?* he asked himself. *You're super-human now. You're a monster. Yeah, and a chicken-shit one at that.*

He ran across the busy street, leaping out of the way at the last second to avoid getting run over by a large black van that had appeared out of nowhere. Narrowly missing Saul, the van swerved and stopped, tires screeching. The driver window lowered and an angry motorist flipped the bird at Saul. "What the fuck is wrong with you? You fucking nutcase." Then the window closed and the vehicle sped away, tires squealing.

As other motorists passed, Saul looked across the street. He saw her coming, expertly weaving around and leaping over oncoming cars like an Olympic Gold medal track-and-field athlete.

He cut down a dark alley and sprinted for about a block. He saw a decrepit old warehouse building and ducked inside.

At first it was pitch-black, then his vision adjusted and he saw where he was going. *Maybe I have an advantage in the dark?* There were puddles everywhere, leaking pipes, debris piles, spent syringes, and soiled condoms littering the dank interior. Some ceiling panels were missing entirely and others clung on by one or two edges.

He found a stairwell and went up. One floor, two floors, three floors, four. The roof. Had he walked right into a trap?

There was a small building in the middle of the roof. A place to hide. He approached it and tried the door. Solid steel. Padlocked. He pulled on the door handle with his newly discovered strength. The padlock snapped. The door squeaked open. Closing it behind him, he went inside and sat down in a puddle of water next to rows of piping and large, rusted air conditioning units.

A mouse squeaked and skittered away.

Saul steadied his breathing and waited. He thought about how he would defend himself if she found him. With the ebb and flow of his power, he had no idea if he would be at his best or worst if and when that scenario presented itself. He needed an advantage, at least a chance. A weapon.

He stood up and examined the wall. Feeling along it, he spotted a cast-iron pipe about five feet long that had rusted at the connecting end. The other end protruded from the wall and expelled dirty, smelly water. Saul reefed on the pipe. With some effort, he snapped it free with a metallic crunch.

The door opened and a deafening gunshot blast rang in his ears. The speeding bullet struck the iron pipe in his hands, zinged around the tiny cubicle, and exited the small mechanical building.

Saul swung the pipe. It connected hard with Pearla's wrist. She cried out in pain. The gun snapped out of her hand.

She grabbed one end and pulled Saul, still holding it, outside. They did the cast-iron shuffle—one step, two step, three step, four—before Pearla yanked it loose.

It took her some effort, Saul noticed. She was having trouble with his growing strength. Was he getting stronger, she weaker?

She lunged forward, swinging the pipe. Saul backed up, dodging blows. She advanced, still swinging. Saul felt rushes of wind as it narrowly missed his head. She swiftly changed the trajectory of the arc and delivered a hard blow to his wrist.

"Fucking bitch," he said, grabbing the injured wrist and grimacing.

"You *can* feel pain. You're only human, after all. You're not like me."

"I wouldn't want to be," he said, ducking another blow. "You're a fucking psycho."

Pearla's eyes narrowed and she stopped swinging, glaring spears of hatred.

Saul looked back. He was almost at the roof's edge. He looked down. Concrete sidewalk, asphalt road. Passing cars. Nothing to break his fall. Everything to break.

Pearla stepped forward and swung the pipe. Saul stepped aside and gripped it with both hands. She thrust it forward and let go.

The momentum sent him falling back. As he teetered on the edge of the roof, she moved in and shoved his chest hard with both hands. He released the pipe, clutched her wrist, and pulled, hoping to use her as an impromptu rope to rescue himself and send her to her death.

But it didn't work that way.

He fell, dragging her down with him. As they plummeted to their deaths, twirling through the air, they locked in an embrace. *An embrace of death*, Saul thought. *How ironic that I would bring my enemy in life with me to my death*. The thought brought him a macabre sort of inner peace.

It was fleeting. *I can't die now, not with Joella's life in jeopardy*. He had to make things right with himself, with her, and with the creator, if there was one. Wasn't there a happily-ever-after written into this script?

"Noooooooo," he shouted.

Pearla clutched him tighter as they closed in on concrete. "Yes... it's time."

Saul saw flashing white lights. He heard a loud splat and a shrill scream, snipped short by the hand of death.

Then he succumbed to a world of abrupt blackness.

Chapter Twenty-Three

Waking up, Saul thought he was dead. He pinched his arm three times before realizing it wasn't so. But he knew it wasn't a dream. He knew he'd teleported, knew he'd come razor-close to death. What a horrific experience.

It wasn't his time to die. He was alive, with a second chance to make things right. This was an epiphany. "Thank you, God. Thank you."

Energized, he rose, noticing it was already a quarter past noon. When had he returned home? Why was he still fully clothed? Why weren't his clothes ripped and tattered? How long had he slept? What had happened to the animals? Was Pearla dead? Was Joella dead? Questions tumbled through his confused mind like a swelling tidal wave.

In the bathroom, he examined his face. Black sockets around his eyes, which he ignored. Two-day stubble, which he also ignored. No bruises. No cuts. *What? This is some kind of miracle. I'm getting stronger, healing faster.* He pulled up his jeans. Hair covered his legs. He touched it. The hairs were a little softer, but thicker, almost like a coat of fur. He unbuttoned his shirt, ignoring the beer belly, and looked. Nothing out of place there.

He made some coffee and brought a cup outside on the back porch. He stopped to put on his shoes. Picking one up, he saw it—mud-stained and still wet from the slimy warehouse puddles. He smelled it and turned his nose—urine, vomit, and alcohol.

Fighting an urge to puke, he stepped off the porch and wandered around. It was windy, but sunny and warm. The nausea passed. He sipped his coffee and lit a smoke. A few birds chirped from treetop branches. A rabbit, startled by his arrival, stopped nibbling grass and bolted into the bush. Otherwise, nothing was out of place; not a sign of a frenzied animal ritual.

He returned to the house and checked his phone. Nothing from Joella. Two voicemails from Samantha requesting a call ASAP. Another call from Nicholas, also requesting an urgent callback.

He dialed Nicholas first.

"Did you teleport to Joella?" Nicholas said.

"No. I went somewhere else."

"Are you okay?"

"Yes."

"Where did you go?"

"Toronto. I was fighting with Pearla. Saw someone get murdered. I almost died. Tell you about it later. What's so urgent?"

"I think I've made a breakthrough. I need you in my lab immediately."

"Did you find a cure?"

"I'll tell you about it later. Get over here. Now!"

A half hour later, Saul was en route to Nicholas's lab. As he drove, he ate a ham and cheese sandwich he'd hastily prepared. It was the third one. He'd woken up ravenous, hungrier than he remembered being in a long time. *That's because you were on a liquid diet and didn't want to ruin your buzz.*

Before leaving, he'd called Spencer and Joella and left messages. He'd also talked to Samantha and learned the reason for her panicked call. She'd been worried about him and felt guilty for not offering to spend the night monitoring his wellbeing. After she'd calmed down, she'd agreed to meet him at Nicholas's that afternoon.

Inside the lab, they watched. Nicholas was crouched over computer monitors, control switches, and dials. Samantha and Saul stood a safe distance back.

Bob sat in the teleporter, looking ready, willing, and able for his next sacrifice for science.

Nicholas had explained that last night he'd safely teleported Bob to Nicholas's beachfront. He'd strapped a video camera, something he'd been reluctant to use in the past for safety reasons, to Bob's head, and had recorded the teleportation. "One small step for Bob, one giant leap for mankind," Nicholas concluded. The video footage showed Bob doing what raccoons often do: digging for clams on the sandy shoreline. At one point the video footage turned black and fuzzy, but Nicholas attributed that to a minor technical malfunction.

Nicholas turned on some switches and turned up a dial. A white, laser-like beam surrounded Bob. He made a "whoop-whoop" sound, and seemed to be smiling.

Saul watched, wondering if the so-called "minor technical malfunction" was actually something major. He'd described his life-and-death battle with Pearla to Nicholas and Samantha, but had yet to detail his communion with the creatures of the forest. He was starting to think the whole thing was a hallucination, as he had nothing concrete to substantiate it. His mind was far from concrete, and likely—in the eyes of Samantha and Nicholas—capable of all manner of hallucinations and concoctions. One reliable sixth sense Saul possessed was the ability to read what people really thought about him. And with his reckless disregard for his own life, coupled with alcohol abuse, he had given them every reason to think he was a certifiable wacko.

His mind wandered. Had Bob's presence last night caused the animal ritual? Had he been there? Genetically modified, was he now capable of creating a new forest order, one with more harmony and brotherhood? *Ridiculous. There is now, and always will be, nature's pecking order.* Yet he wasn't convinced.

Samantha nudged him and whispered, "Your hands are shaking."

"Alcohol withdrawal."

"Don't space out. Bob's about to disappear."

Saul nodded, returning his attention to the teleporter. The lights dimmed, and a siren-like wail gradually intensified. There was a pop, and Bob vanished. Through the eye of the video camera lens, they saw him appear on Nicholas's beachfront and glance around, momentarily confused, then proceed to the beach. Bob waded a few inches into the water and started digging for clams.

For a few minutes, they watched him dig them out, crack them open, and eat, tossing the empty shells onto the sand. Everything seemed normal.

Then birds began chirping. Startled, Bob looked high up into the treetops, the camera eye documenting the objects of his attention. Hundreds of birds—swallows, humming birds, blue jays, robins, seagulls, even an eagle—were perched high atop the trees. They squawked and chirped, and watched Bob.

He watched them briefly, then returned to filling his stomach, as if sensing he now had some natural immunity from nature's predators.

A bark suddenly startled him. His eyes scanned the tree line. About fifty feet away, he saw a pack of coyotes. A low growl began. The others joined in and soon it was a chorus of growls.

"Get him out of there," Samantha said.

"I can't," Nicholas said. "He's programmed for an hour."

"Well, change it," Saul said.

"I can't," Nicholas said. "It's too dangerous."

Watching the predators, Bob reared up on his hind legs. He snarled and growled. Then he began to whistle.

In a few minutes, the coyotes grew quiet. So did the birds. Bob returned to foraging for food. Then more sounds: the flapping of wings, the rustling of brush. Bob looked into the treetops. The birds had vanished. Some circled high above. He scanned the tree line where the coyotes were. They too had disappeared.

A loud splash. Then another. And another and another. Bob looked out to sea. A school of sea lions danced in the water about thirty feet away, leaping into the air and plunging nose-first into the water. One sprang up and did a comical belly flop before submerging into the ocean.

Bob watched them for a few minutes, then returned to his lunch. After a while, the ocean grew quiet.

"He's got some weird new affinity with nature," Saul said. "Like me."

"It's pretty obvious something is going on," Nicholas said. "But I don't understand why."

"Well, I hope you figure it out," Saul said. "Because I've got the same problem."

"I don't know if I'd call that a problem," Nicholas said.

"What about these?" Saul said, pulling up his pant leg.

Nicholas's eyes widened at the fresh crop of hair. "As you know, I'm working on that. And I think I may have found something. But, please, no talking right now. Let's watch Bob in peace. This is perhaps the largest scientific discovery in the world. At least give me the opportunity to observe the fruits of a lifetime of hard work and dedication."

The rest of the video was uneventful. Bob ate for a while, lumbered up on shore, found a comfortable spot by the fire pit, curled up in the sea grass, and went to sleep. Right in the open, exposed and apparently unafraid of any predators.

A few moments later, after a loud popping sound, Bob reappeared in the teleporter. Briefly, he looked confused. Then his eyes found Saul. "Whoop, whoop, whoop," Bob said, a mischievous grin playing across his face.

While Nicholas fiddled with controls, Saul, with Nicholas's permission, approached the teleporter. "You did well, Bob," Saul said, extending a hand. Bob smiled and stuck his head out, exposing a furry chin. Saul scratched it and Bob responded amicably, jumping right into Saul's arms. Carrying him over to the cage, Saul scratched Bob's chin.

"He likes you," Samantha said, keeping her distance.

Nicholas was beaming. "How is he?"

"He's wet and muddy from the water, but otherwise seems okay."

"Teleportation," Nicholas said, after Saul had safely put Bob into his cage. "A resounding success. A new era for mankind."

"Congratulations," Samantha offered.

"Thank you."

"I'll offer cautionary congrats," Saul said. "But don't get ahead of yourself. I'm still turning into some kind of freaking monster, and my girlfriend is still in a world of shit. You have yet to safely teleport humans, at least with that machine. Mine was unintentional, and not exactly what I'd call a resounding success. One small step for Bob, and one giant leap for the planet of the apes."

Later, after a long discussion, Saul wasn't sure they'd made the right decision. But both Samantha and Nicholas had assured him it was "the only decision."

Samantha sat in the teleporter while Nicholas played with controls. Saul watched from a distance. Nicholas had to operate the teleporter since he was the only one who knew how. And Saul needed to remain behind, because his behavior when he teleported could turn unpredictably violent and aggressive. What if he hurt himself or the woman he loved once he arrived?

Nicholas said a teleportation trip should only be attempted by someone of sound mind and body. That discounted Saul on multiple levels, but didn't stop him from wondering why he'd already been in the teleporter once, and the meticulous scientist hadn't been in disagreement then. *That was different. You were in panic mode. And Samantha wasn't here. Why wouldn't he want a better human subject if one was available?*

And there was something else. Saul had explained his strange communion with nature to them. Digesting the new information, Nicholas thought there was no time like the present to inject Saul with his creation, a chemical and DNA concoction called TSC-1—Transform Saul Climer One. While Saul didn't understand the biochemistry of the antidote, he understood what it was supposed to do: rid him of his beastly metamorphosis characteristics. And while cautioning Saul about possible irreversible, unpleasant side effects, Nicholas also said he wasn't sure if TSC-1would curtail Saul's growing strength and acumen, or his dream teleportation abilities.

However, Saul still believed it was worth a shot. He was already an unwitting guinea pig—no point in stopping now, especially since he didn't relish being a monster for the rest of his life. Joella might not find him physically attractive anymore, for one thing.

With the TSC-1 coursing through his veins and making him feel giddy, he watched Samantha as Nicholas fidgeted with the controls.

"Are you sure you want to go through with this?" Saul asked.

The lights dimmed.

In the corner, Bob said, "Whoop-whoop."

"Let's get this over with," Samantha said.

"You're sure?" Nicholas said. "I don't want to be accused of using human test subjects against their will. If you want to back out, now's the time to do it."

"Just turn on the damn machine," she said. "I won't blame you."

He did. After the usual cinematic sights and sounds, Samantha disappeared, scheduled to return in exactly two hours.

Saul stood in front of a sink in a corner of the lab, running the cold water tap. The lights came on. He realized he'd made it through the maze of equipment in near total blackness without bumping into anything.

"Oh, there you are," Nicholas said. "I didn't see or hear you leave. How do you feel?"

"Thirsty." He filled a glass with cold water. As he put it to his lips, it shattered, evidently because of the increasing strength he'd not yet learned how to control. "But otherwise better than ever."

Chapter Twenty-Four

Based on Saul's description, Samantha recognized the woman curled up in bed having an afternoon nap. It had to be Joella.

Samantha remembered watching Saul's bug-eyes as she'd teleported away from the lab. Then she was whirling though some sort of portal or wormhole in the fifth dimension, according to Nicholas. It was black, then white, then flashing black, white, and gray like a high-tech disco light. Then a popping sound left a faint ringing in her ears, and boom, here she was in an unknown bedroom in an unknown location, watching Joella nap.

She scanned the room, looking for any signs of trouble. Other than the flashing red light below the camera mounted on the wall, she found none. Her heart rate increased and her palms grew moist. They could see her. They could hear her. What would they do when they caught her?

She tried the bedroom door. Locked. She went to the bay window, pulled aside a curtain, and surveyed the scenery. The sun shone over the mountainous horizon, yellow and pink against a gray cloudy background. *In the middle of nowhere. Fuck.* She tried the window. Locked, and fortified with steel bars.

Joella stirred, woke, and looked at Samantha.

"Who are you?" Joella said in understandable English. She wiped her eyes. It looked like she'd been crying.

"I'm a friend of Saul's. Samantha."

Joella sat up in bed, putting her feet on the plush green carpet. She wiped tired eyes. An empty wine bottle was on the bedside table. "You're his girlfriend?"

"No, I'm married. *You're* his girlfriend. We're just good friends. He told me about you, Joella."

"Where is Saul?"

"He's on Prince Edward Island. He's safe. He's working on coming here."

"How did you get here?"

"We can talk about that later. Are you okay? Did they hurt you or anything?"

"No, they've been treating me well."

"Did they say what they want?"

"No. But I think it concerns Saul."

"I need to get you out of here."

"How are you going to do that?"

It was a good question, Samantha thought. There was no easy way out, if there was a way out at all. Their so-called plan was badly organized from the get-go. She'd teleported right into the lion's den. What did she think she was going to do, turn into some superhero, smash the windows, and fly Joella to safety? Or smash through the door and, weaponless, fight off multiple attackers before stealing their car and escaping?

Before she'd left, Saul had told her, "Just find Joella, make sure she's safe, determine a location, and fuck off. Don't go playing Wonder Woman."

"Do you know where you are?" Samantha said.

Joella shook her head.

That confirms it. A brain-dead plan born of desperation. "No idea whatsoever?"

"We're in the mountains somewhere. Three or four hours north of Puerto Plata, maybe."

"We have to do something," Samantha said, searching the room frantically for a weapon. She tipped over the coffee table, and with some effort broke a leg free. She picked up the wooden table leg and approached the window. She raised it high in the air.

"Are you sure that's a good idea?" Joella said.

The door burst open and Koby rushed in. Leveling a gun at Samantha's head, he stopped. "No, I don't think that's a good idea. Would you mind dropping that coffee table leg, ma'am? I don't want to have to use this."

Chapter Twenty-Five

The epiphany resulting from the near-death experience with Pearla had faded from Saul's consciousness. "What do you mean, you forgot to set the timer?" he said. "I thought you said exactly two hours?"

"I did say that," Nicholas said. "But I forgot to do it."

Samantha was due back five minutes ago. When she hadn't returned, Nicholas had busied himself analyzing his equipment. It took him the full five minutes to realize what had happened.

For the past couple of hours while they'd been waiting for her, Nicholas had examined Saul, doing reflex tests, strength tests, symbol recognition, and puzzle-solving, along with a physical check-up and a series of questions. In the end, Nicholas said Saul was a changed man. He had an uncanny and rapidly developing psychic ability that Nicholas maintained he could learn to control with patience and the proper training. He was stronger and more alert, and his cardiovascular system had improved. Even the nasty fur coat on his legs was thinning. He was shedding. "Remarkable," Nicholas had said, "I never imagined results like this. I'm not only perfecting teleportation, I'm also creating super-soldiers, perhaps even extending human life."

The mood during the exam had started off serious, but by the end turned almost jocular, with both men thrilled at the improvements.

But now that Samantha hadn't returned, the mood had changed. They were serious, somber, and stressed out.

Even Bob was unusually quiet, eyeing the two men intently from his cage.

"How can you forget something like that?" Saul said. "She put her life in your hands."

"Well, I'm not perfect. I've been stressed lately. So many things on my mind. I guess I got distracted thinking about all the possibilities with TSC-1, and lost track of what really mattered... err, what really matters."

"Can you bring her back?"

"I don't know. I don't think so."

They couldn't even call Samantha, as her phone had been left behind for safety reasons. Some safety, Saul thought. *Bad to worse..*

The phone rang and Saul hurried to answer it.

Nicholas looked cross. "I told you, no phones in the lab during experiments."

"I brought it in *after* she teleported. I didn't think it mattered—" He saw Spencer's number appear and held up an open palm.

Nicholas narrowed his eyes as Saul answered. "Spencer."

"We've got more fucking problems now," Spencer said.

"What?"

"Remember I said Joella was off the hook for murder and robbery?"

"Yeah."

"Well, that's not necessarily the case anymore."

"What?"

"Someone's been paying off the cops to continue the hunt. Someone with deeper pockets than mine."

Saul could not even begin to comprehend this now, in light of his certainty that Joella was being held against her will. He had bigger problems to deal with. He started to speak, but Spencer interrupted him.

"I'll let you go, don't worry. But there's something else you should know."

Saul sighed deeply. He'd reached the end of his rope. *Now what?* "What's that?"

"I'm being told that they may try and implicate you in this. Charge you for fucking murder."

After ending the call, Saul felt hot blood boil in his veins. "Fucking son of a bitch," he said, turning to Nicholas. "Can things get any worse? Now I'm wanted for fucking murder in the DR, and for all I know Canadian cops are looking for someone fitting my description."

He suddenly felt faint.

"You don't look good," Nicholas said, rushing over and steadying him. "You're going white."

Saul's face turned white and his world went black.

******

He spun head-over-heels down a black vortex and thought it was the end. His alcoholism, combined with the teleporter experiment and the latest—maybe lethal—injection of TSC-1, was finally killing him.

But the blackness was fleeting. A tiny white light appeared, distant, but expanding rapidly. He heard a whistling sound, then a pop not unlike the sound of a cold can of beer opening. He opened his eyes to a blinding white light.

"We've been expecting you," Koby said, turning off the flashlight. "I'm Koby Cyber."

"Expecting me?" Saul said, clearing the cobwebs, realizing he was sprawled out on a floor. *Not a very good landing. I'll have to work on that.*

"Yes."

This man who called himself Koby Cyber sat on a chair beside him. Saul sat up and looked around. He was in a tastefully decorated bedroom. Plush couches, armchairs, a round table with four red leather-bound chairs near the sliding-glass doors to the balcony. Samantha and Joella were seated calmly at the table.

Saul did a double-take. "Joella?"

As he stood up, she rushed over and embraced him, kissing him repeatedly on the cheeks, neck, and lips.

"Honey, you're here?" he asked, amazed.

"I'll always be here."

"I hope so, baby. I sure hope so. I can't go too many days without you."

Samantha joined in and soon it was a group hug, a happily-ever-after ending, Saul thought. Just like in books and movies.

Koby allowed them a few moments before he said, "I know you're wondering what you're doing here. And I'm going to tell you." He turned to Saul. "I need you to come with me. The others can stay here."

He led Saul to a small white room with a video camera mounted in the corner, and what Saul presumed was two-way glass covering one wall. Koby and Saul sat across from one another at a small table table. A glass ashtray sat on the middle of the table. Vents on the ceiling hummed; otherwise it was quiet.

Koby reached into his jacket pocket and pulled out a pack of Marlboro Lights and a red BIC lighter. "Would you like one?"

Saul lit up.

Koby did as well. "Congratulations," he said. "You're a teleporting super-soldier. How does it feel?"

Saul took a long drag. He exhaled a large cloud of blue smoke, watching the vent fans suck it up. "Where am I?"

"You're in Jarabacoa, about three hours north of Puerto Plata. In the mountains."

"What do you want?"

"I'm not going to waste your time. I'll get right to the point. I'm a senior-level CIA agent. We've been watching Nicholas Fry's experiments for some time now. Frankly, we didn't think he'd pull it off, but it looks like he has. You're living proof. What we want is Nicholas Fry's technology. We don't want to steal it from him. We want him on board."

"Why don't you just ask him?"

"We've tried that. He hates us and wants nothing to do with us. Ever since he was humiliated and discredited—fired and blackballed—he blames us. But it wasn't us. It was DARPA, the Defense Advanced Research Projects Agency."

"If you want it so bad, why don't you just steal it? I doubt that's out of the realm of possibility for the CIA. I hear one of your thugs got a little trigger-happy on my buddy Spencer when you kidnapped Joella."

"Those two agents should never have been assigned to that operation. They've been fired. And stealing the technology is not as easy as you think. When DARPA ruined Nicholas years back, they thought they had all his formulas and schematics. But they could never perfect teleportation or super-soldiers. We can't do anything with the technology without Nicholas's mind. He's a little nuts, but he's a genius. We need him."

"Why did you kidnap Joella?"

"It was an experiment. We didn't hurt her and don't plan to. We wanted to see if the teleportation could be channeled without a specific destination in mind. And it worked. You're here."

Saul stubbed out his cigarette and blew a cloud of smoke in Koby's face. "You're experimenting with my life, with my sanity."

"Well, I apologize for that, but it had to be done. We had to be sure Nicholas was on the right track before investing in his technology."

"You're worse than him. You use unwilling test subjects."

Koby stubbed out his cigarette and blew a cloud of smoke in Saul's face. Saul coughed and waved it away.

Koby's eyes narrowed. He pulled out a pen and paper, scribbled something, then began twirling the pen between his thumb and forefinger. "I'm not here to discuss morals or ethics with you. Let me finish. Hear me out before you start jumping to conclusions."

Saul reached for another cigarette. "You have the stage."

"You can understand why we want to get our hands on this technology and develop it. We wouldn't want it getting into the wrong hands. Basically, we want two things. We want you and Nicholas on board, and you'll both be rewarded handsomely. You may get the odd assignment, after your abilities have been fully realized and developed. As the first teleporting super-soldier, we'd need to monitor your changing condition to insure there are no adverse side effects—at least none that would be seriously deleterious to our objectives."

If Saul had felt like a guinea pig before, he now knew why. Quite simply he was one. Because of these irreversible changes taking place in his body, he would likely have to be monitored for the rest of his life. Nothing would be the same anymore, not least of all him. Koby hadn't mentioned anything about monitoring his condition with respect to his health, only an uncertain government agenda.

"What are your objectives?" Saul asked, knowing he probably wouldn't get a straight answer.

"National defense. The United States, Canada, our other allies."

That's as straight as it gets. So much for the psychic part of my super-soldier abilities. Saul had a million questions, but the first thing that occurred to him was there was no easy way out of this conundrum. It was Hydra, a nine-headed serpent; for each head you cut off, two more would grow back in its place.

"What makes you think I would agree to any of this?"

Koby stopped twirling the pen and placed it on the table. His steely brown eyes looked through Saul. "Take a look at your situation. You're a depressed, alcoholic wannabe writer with a death wish. You would have killed yourself if it weren't for Nicholas. You're dead broke. You're wanted for murder in Canada and the Dominican Republic. There are others who want your ass six feet underground. And you have a condition that requires constant professional monitoring. There's no turning back from that. If you agree to work with us and bring Nicholas on board, as I said, we will reward you handsomely. We'll set you up with a house here in Jarabacoa and you can keep your place on Prince Edward Island, spend summers there if you want. You'll be one of us."

"What about Joella?"

"We know you love her. That's why you're here. She can move in with you. She's gut-poor and can barely feed her family, as you know. And you can't provide for her now."

Saul began to wonder if this had been a CIA-organized conspiracy from the start. Maybe he'd never know the answer. "And the cops?"

"We'll fix that—in Canada and here."

Saul went on the assumption the CIA knew everything. "And Pearla?"

"She's dead. Flattened into a pancake."

"Monica?"

"We'll take care of her. I've never met a more bat-shit crazy woman, besides Pearla, maybe."

"Met?" Did he say "met?" Leave it alone. "What if Nicholas doesn't come on board?"

"We'll cross that bridge when we get to it. But I believe you can persuade him."

"If I don't agree, what happens?"

"You can walk out of here a free man. So can your girlfriend, and Samantha. But you won't be free for long. And, until you learn to harness your abilities, you might not be alive long. And neither will Joella for that matter. She's in almost as much shit as you are."

It sounded like a veiled threat. *If it looks like a duck, quacks like a duck...*

"How long do I have to decide?"

"One hour."

Chapter Twenty-Six

Three months later, Saul crouched behind a beat-up pickup truck in San Marcos, Puerto Plata. He flexed his powerful bicep. Waiting for him to come home. Gazing out at the midnight stars, he knew it was only a matter of time. But it didn't matter. Time was on his side. Besides, it gave him a chance to reflect on how upside-down and then right-side-up his life had turned around in a short time.

Life as a CIA-sponsored soldier—or assassin, depending on your perspective—wasn't as bad as he'd thought. He had a beautiful home in the mountains of Jarabacoa. He still had his Prince Edward Island acreage. He and Joella had come to terms with their differences, and she had forgiven him about lying about being a bestselling author. She'd accepted his story about not sleeping with Monica while they were an item, but Saul didn't think she would ever believe it—even though it was the truth. But they were able to put it behind them and their love flourished, both emotionally and physically. Saul was more in love with Joella now than ever before. And it was mutual.

To this day, Joella didn't really know what Saul did for a living. But she didn't ask many questions, happy to have a stylish roof under her head, plenty of money, and even a maid and separate quarters—nanny included—for her daughters Evelyn and Jennifer. Saul had developed a loving bond with both daughters, although he had to admit Evelyn was still his favorite.

Both Joella and Saul had experienced many problems with Joella's other son, Carlos. He was ornery, disrespectful, and outright abusive to Jennifer and Evelyn. Maybe he was just a bad apple. But, since he never had a good male role model growing up, they gave him the benefit of the doubt, placing him for the time being in a special facility staffed with a child psychiatrist. The plan was to have Carlos return home to a loving family once he was properly diagnosed and treated.

Gisella, for a price, had offered to take the boy. But, given her volatile relationship with boyfriend Immanuel Perez, Joella and Saul had voted against that idea.

Which brought Saul right to where he was now. He'd heard that Emmanuel had been physically assaulting Gisella. He'd punched her repeatedly in the face and stabbed her in the stomach in a drunken stupor. Who knew what this clown was capable of? Of course, Saul already knew about Emmanuel's assault and the attempted rape of Joella. That should have been enough. But Saul had bided his time, waiting for Emmanuel to fuck up one more time.

Of course, he'd fucked up twice more. *Three strikes yer out, buckaroo,* Saul thought, seeing him pull up on his motorcycle. This was going to be easy.

Emmanuel dismounted and staggered twice before reaching his door. As he fumbled with the lock, Saul attacked from behind, throttling his neck tightly with both hands. He squeezed.

"You?" Emmanuel said, turning around, his eyes widening in horror.

"Three strikes yer out, buckaroo." Saul wrenched and twisted and tore Emmanuel's head clean off. He winced at the blood, brain matter, and guts squirting all over his hands and clothes. There were some things he would never get used to. He tossed the head through an open window. It landed on the concrete floor with a hollow thud, rolled into a table, tipping a lamp and shattering the bulb. The lights went out.

Saul allowed himself a small grin as he watched Emmanuel gyrate like a chicken with its head cut off—blood spraying from his neck like a fountain—before collapsing into a bloody heap on the dirt walkway of his shack.

I think you've lost your head, Emmanuel. All in a day's work. All in a day's work. Beam me up, Nicholas. There's no intelligent life down here.

Five seconds later, he was in Nicholas's other laboratory next to his posh home in Jarabacoa. Saul landed on target, outside the bathroom, knowing he would have to clean up. Watching Nicholas approach, he smiled. He'd have never thought that such a tight friendship could flourish, given the conditions under which they'd met.

Agent Koby Cyber had been right from the beginning. Once Saul had explained the situation fully and Nicholas grasped the nature of the nine-headed serpent, he'd made the only logical choice. Now he was in charge of the multi-faceted teleportation and super-soldier research and development program. For his life's work, Nicholas Fry was finally garnering some accolades. Although the teleportation program—code-named TSC-1—was still top secret, news of Nicholas's breakthroughs in genetic engineering—specifically his work with re-growing limbs—had leaked to the media and he was getting a lot of recognition and praise, both in the papers and on social media. He even had a Dominican girlfriend and a book in the works.

Approaching, Nicholas frowned at Saul's appearance. "You're a bloody mess. I hope it was worth it."

"Yes," Saul said, stoic. The thrill of the kill had worn off, and he wasn't musing over it anymore. It was what it was. A necessary evil, in this case. He remembered a time not so long ago when he wanted to kill himself. For now at least, those suicidal tendencies were gone. Saul would much rather kill specific others than himself.

"Get in there and get yourself cleaned up. And change your clothes. I have some good news for you."

A few minutes later, showered and changed, Saul relaxed in the lounge area adjacent to Nicholas's lab, drinking his new invention—Diablo Libre. It contained three ounces of Brugal white rum with a shot of Sprite, a twist of lime, and crushed ice. No, he hadn't been able to give up drinking; but at least now he didn't let it run or ruin his life. Grinning at the new NO SMOKING sign on the wall, he reached for his pack and lit up. "What's the news?"

Pointing to the sign, Nicholas waved an accusatory finger, then closed his hand resignedly. He took a sip of his Scotch on the rocks. "I talked to Samantha today."

Samantha and Nicholas had not only become good friends, she was now looking after Nicholas's other lab in his absence and monitoring events on Prince Edward Island. Raccoons Bob and Robbie had made complete recoveries. She looked after them and did other lab-related tasks under

Nicholas's tutelage. In spite of herself, she'd become fond of the two raccoons, claiming they behaved somewhat like people. Another positive note: she hadn't noticed any half-raccoons, half-coyotes wandering the streets lately and teleporting randomly around the globe. So far, so good.

Nicholas took another sip. "Something good about your book, *The Final Hour*. She wanted so badly to tell you in person, but she was so excited she blurted out some of it to me."

"Wow. Do you know the details?"

"I heard something about a contract."

"They're offering me a contract?" Saul had difficulty containing his excitement. He took another big pull on the Diablo Libre. He'd spent almost his entire life believing he was nothing more than a wannabe writer. And now, suddenly, his efforts had been validated by a gatekeeper publisher. Penguin was big. Huge. This called for a celebration.

"That's what she said. She wants you to call her about the details."

After some celebratory toasts and light-hearted conversation, Nicholas changed gears. "You say you don't feel any ill effects from the TSC-1?"

Saul shook his head.

"And the hairs have completely disappeared?"

"Nicholas, you examined me yourself last week. Said I'm fit as a fiddle."

"I just want to be sure. I'm a scientist."

"I know."

"And this psychic ability is getting stronger?"

Saul nodded. Lately, he'd been developing the ability to read people's thoughts seconds before they opened their mouths. Oftentimes he would finish Joella's sentences for her, or call her and know exactly what she was doing while she was doing it. On rare occasions, he'd get fleeting mental images of events unfolding in the present.

"And the nightmares?" Nicholas said.

"Still there." Now and then he woke up abruptly in the night, sweat-soaked and jittery, with a grim realization that somewhere something terrible was occurring, had occurred, or would occur. Although he had yet to substantiate any of it thus far, it continued to haunt his psyche.

"But you had them before any of this."

"Yes."

"You just can't remember if they gave you as much 'anticipatory dread,' to use your words?"

"I was a raving drunk back then. No, I don't remember."

"I don't know if much has changed in that regard. Only now, with your new-and-improved constitution, you can handle it much better."

"Come on… that's not fa—" But a horrible image stopped him mid-sentence. He saw a long nose, red-slit eyes, and a bone-chilling, evil grin.

"Saul," Nicholas said. "You're turning white again. Nothing good ever happens when you turn white."

Saul stood. "I've got to go. Joella's in trouble. Meet me at my house."

And he disappeared.

Chapter Twenty-Seven

Reappearing in the bedroom he shared with Joella, Saul didn't even have to think about who it was. He knew. It was Pearla. But the woman attacking Joella with a machete didn't much resemble Pearla anymore. It was some hellish aberration that was not of this world. Her black slithery body was grossly enlarged, with the arms and legs of an Olympic weightlifter. Her long hair was a silvery color, and it glowed in the moonlight rays seeping in from the bedroom window. She had a slithery serpent's tongue and blood-red eyes. What was familiar were her signature red panties and bra. She bounced around the bedroom, pendulous breasts heaving, swinging the machete as Joella twisted and rolled in a frantic effort to survive.

Joella's right leg was already cut and bleeding badly. So was her chest—a seven-inch gash below her left breast squirted blood.

"Help me," Joella said when she saw Saul appear in the doorway.

"It's not her you want," Saul said.

Pearla spun around and stared livid red daggers at Saul. "You. The big-shot government agent now? Killing people for a living?"

Joella's jaw dropped, her eyes widening, as she wrapped a sheet around her injured leg, trying to stem the bloody tide.

Saul curled his right index finger. "Come and get it, bitch. Come and get it."

He leaped forward and chopped the machete hand. It sprang from Pearla's hands and stuck in the wall. Pearla's eyes widened and turned to run for the weapon.

Turning to Joella, Saul said, "Get out, honey. Now!"

Joella staggered to the door, slipped in her own dripping blood, and collapsed on the floor. Loosing strength from blood loss, she crawled to the door, moaning in pain.

Saul bent down to help her, momentarily distracted.

Pearla turned and raised the machete, slicing at Saul's neck. He drove a fist up and struck the machete handle and Pearla's hand. The machete flew away, but this time Pearla reached out quickly and plucked it out of the air.

Contorting her features, she moved toward Saul. "I see your strength has increased. But so has mine."

Saul swiftly kicked the machete out of her hand. With a twang, it stuck in the ceiling.

As she reached for it, he kicked both of her legs out from under her. She landed on her ass with a loud thud, right next to Joella. Joella turned over, crawled on top of Pearla, and dug her nails into Pearla's eye sockets. Pearla screamed and flung her into the wall.

Saul leaped up, caught Joella in both hands, and laid her gently on the bed.

Then he charged Pearla, grabbed her by the neck, and began swinging her around the room. One rotation, two rotations, three rotations, four—before tossing her through the second-floor window. Glass shattered everywhere. Pearla extended her arms and legs like a professional diver, swooped down, then up, did a perfect 360-degree turn, and flew back into the bedroom, slamming into Saul and sending them both crashing into the wall.

Watching the battle, Joella's eyes slowly closed as consciousness ebbed.

Gripping each other's arms, Saul and Pearla twirled around in a macabre dance ritual, smashing ornaments, tables, lamps, and pictures. Saul chopped her hands away, clutched a clump of her hair in one hand, swung her around three times, and whipped her right into the door. "Die, you fucking bitch. Why won't you die?"

She crashed through it, flew over the railing, and landed hard on the marble floor beneath. Saul rushed to the railing and looked over. Her crumpled mass was beginning to re-grow and reform into something larger and more sinister than he'd ever seen before in his life—a black, deadly, all-consuming force of pure evil.

Just then Nicholas rushed into the living room and stopped in front of the tide of rising fury. "Go straight to hell, you bitch." He pointed something resembling a Star Trek ray gun at her changing form.

Cackling loudly, she floated up. He fired. A white beam struck her, enveloping her in a white mist. The mist turned a fiery red as she struggled for freedom, screaming horribly.

A large explosion rocketed debris and flames skyward. The last thing Saul saw was Nicholas being blown out the door by the force of the blast. Then it fanned out rapidly, burning Saul's face and blasting him clear through the hallway, through the bedroom, and out the now glassless window.

He crash-landed hard on the concrete and lay there, injured and bleeding, watching orange and red flames engulf the house. Black smoke snaked across the rising sun. Only two words entered his mind before he lost consciousness. *Black dawn.*

Chapter Twenty-Eight

The gray mist turned pitch black, enveloping the rising sun. Black dawn, sentencing time. A time for punishment. A time for retribution. Kalfu knew only too well what that meant. And he knew there was not a damn thing he could do about it.

There was no denying it. He'd not served his time well. He'd escaped the bowels of Hell many times, visiting Earth, availing himself of the lustful fruits of that mortal kingdom. And, in doing so, he'd committed unpardonable sins. Probably the worst was his attempt to usurp the Supreme Being's almighty power and authority by creating a spirit of his own—one Rubina Diaz, aka Pearla, the spirit of love and lust. A spirit he'd planned on having at his beck and call, to deliver many fruits of the flesh to satisfy his insatiable appetite for sex.

Sitting cross-legged with his head bowed, the once-powerful spirit of the crossroads between the living and the dead allowed himself a peek at his creation, the woman he'd wantonly taken, possessed, misled, and abused. She looked frightened, he thought, nothing like the disciple he'd first met and molded.

Pearla, reduced to her human form, did not acknowledge Kalfu's gaze. At one time she would've revered it, worshipped it, lusted after it. Now, she sat cross-legged, looking down, eyes half-closed, waiting for the punishment to be meted out.

Through the black mist, a small glowing white dot appeared in the distance. It grew to the size of a full moon. Black streaks swam across it, painting elongated eyes and a garish grin.

Bondye, The Supreme Being, spoke: "You have transgressed your boundaries yet again. You dare believe you can create a spirit to use as a pawn in your twisted quest for debauchery and pleasures of the flesh. Humans are not capable of entering the spirit realm, except in rare cases ordained by myself, The Supreme Being. And how this mortal woman landed here is still a mystery to me. There are some humans on Earth meddling in affairs beyond their scope. In time, they will be identified and nature will take its course, meting out punishment as it sees fit under my watchful eye. Do you understand?"

"Whatever you say," Kalfu said, raising his head, knowing but no longer caring about the breach in protocol. He knew the end was near. It suddenly didn't matter anymore. He locked eyes with The Supreme Being.

Ignoring Kalfu's gaze, The Supreme Being's garish grin turned sinister. He turned to Pearla. "What about you, woman? Do you understand?"

Pearla nodded. "Yes, Your Holiness."

"Before I mete out punishment, I have this to say. I want to hear from both of you about how you feel about your transgressions. Kalfu, you first. And make it quick. Do you feel any remorse for your sins, and what are your last words?"

Kalfu stared evil daggers at The Supreme Being. Black bloodless eyes stared back.

"No, I don't have any fucking remorse for what I did. If I could, I'd probably do it all over again. And, as for you, Mister King Shit of Turd Mountain, well you can fuck right off and rot in Hell for all I care."

"Enough," Bondye said. "You die now." A thundering boom echoed from the sky. Kalfu burst into flames. His horrible dying screams slowly faded away, along with his blood-red glow.

Bondye scowled at Pearla, who had stopped trembling. Now, she looked composed, almost serene, ready to welcome the chance to meet her maker and plummet into the black, fiery abyss of Hell.

"And you, woman? Speak."

Pearla continued to look down. This was her moment and she did not want to ruin it. It was finally time for all her lifelong struggles to end, finally time for her to go to Hell, a place she had revered, cherished, and worshipped as a young child. She'd always tilted her Voodoo worship to the dark side rather than the light. Finally, the suffering would be over. It was the end of one agenda and the beginning of another. She felt a fresh black vitality coarse through her veins as she slowly raised her head. "Your Holiness, I am deeply sorry for the pain and suffering I may have caused you, the other spirits, and the people I injured and killed on Earth. But, given the chance, I'd do it all over again."

An elongated index finger emerged from the white moon that was the face of The Supreme Being. Thunder clapped from the heavens, and Pearla burst into flames and disappeared.

Bondye frowned. Where were the anguished cries, the horrified screams of agony? Was there some new and powerful malignant force taking root? The Supreme Being did not have an answer, and this puzzled him deeply. He was supposed to be all-knowing. Something was wrong. Terribly wrong.

In an instant, he vanished with a thunderously loud boom that reverberated long and loud through the heavens.

Spiraling down a dark tunnel into the fire pit of Hell, Pearla thought, *They don't have a clue what's coming. Not a fucking clue.*

Epilogue

Watching the budgie swoop down from a tree and land on his hand, Saul reckoned this new affinity he had with nature was nothing short of a miracle. The budgie stared into his eyes, chirped a hello, and tilted its head. Saul tenderly scratched its neck and the budgie chirped again. Then it hopped up on Saul's arm and pecked him lightly on the nose. It stared straight into his eyes for a moment, and then flew away, disappearing into the orange-yellow glow of dawn.

Saul continued along the path, admiring nature's beauty. Of course there were other miracles, he thought, nearing the house that was his temporary residence until the contractors could finish his new home. As he strolled along, he held out a hand and began counting miracles.

One: Nicholas's Star Trek ray gun that had delivered Pearla to Hell.

Two: That Saul had survived the blast with only a minor concussion and a few cuts and bruises.

Three: On this day—Thursday, December 24th, Christmas Eve—he felt healthier and happier than he had in many months. How things had changed. *It wasn't so long ago I was telling myself, "You're nothing. You're a loser."* At one time he could say a lot of nasty things about himself. He already had. But now he couldn't say he was a loser. Now, he was something. "I'm a winner."

He continued walking, returning to the miracle count. *Where was I? Right.*

Four: That Joella survived. While he'd landed on concrete, Joella, who'd been crumpled on the bed and bleeding to death, had been blown clear out the window. The bed landed on the lawn upright—with her still on it—breaking her fall. If it weren't for the quick thinking of Koby Cyber, who rushed her to the hospital, she'd be dead. As it was, the machete wound missed her heart by an inch and the gash on her leg wasn't as serious as all the blood suggested. Life was a game of inches, Saul thought.

"Hey Saul." It was Nicholas, standing on the back wrap-around deck of the house. "Come on. Dinner's almost ready."

Saul waved. "Be right there."

Nicholas disappeared inside.

Five: Blasting through the door, Nicholas had landed in an outdoor water fountain, dousing his flaming body and saving his life. Along with a minor concussion, he'd suffered second and third-degree burns to his hands, arms, neck, and face. They were healing nicely and the scars gave him a certain character and charm, as well as a mad-scientist look. Angela, his twenty-six-year-old fiancé, didn't mind at all. In her words, "He's hotter now than he was before."

Saul had two hands out now. Six: Luckily the girls, Jennifer and Evelyn, were not affected by the explosion that had decimated the house. The guest quarters where they lived with the nanny were untouched by the blaze, as was the case with Nicholas's lab and residence.

Saul reached the stairs, climbed them, and stood on the porch for a moment, admiring the last sliver of sunlight as it slipped beneath the mountainous backdrop. Of course, more than just the miracles, there were some unanswered questions and wrinkles.

Monica Morales, aka The Stalker, had not been dealt with as Koby had promised. She'd not only survived—walking away scot-free after committing multiple murders and robberies—she'd thrived. She'd written a bestselling novel, *My Life as a Stalker and Back Again*, appeared on *Oprah*, *Regis and Kelly*, CBS News, and even CNN.

While he'd been mystified by these developments, Koby had assured Saul that Monica was no longer a threat to him; she was too power and fame-hungry and too narcissistic to risk losing it all by pursuing Saul. Not to mention, she wouldn't be much of a match for him anymore with his new mental and physical powers. So Saul had let it go. For the most part, Koby had delivered on his promises. He'd saved Joella's life. And before every killing assignment, Koby gave Saul the opportunity to research the targets himself so he could decide if by killing them he would indeed be ridding the world of pestilence.

Up to this point, Koby had been loyal to a fault. He was even close to being indoctrinated into friendship territory. Saul knew there were things he didn't know about Koby, about the whole plot. But there were some things he didn't want to know. In the end, happiness was fleeting. Enjoy the moment. Hang on to what you have. In a split-second, everything can change.

Of course, convincing Joella that he was making the world a better place to live in was another matter. While recovering in the hospital, she'd broken down on one occasion when he visited her bedside, saying, "My boyfriend's a murderer," and balling her eyes out. But over time, and many conversations, Saul was able to convince her that what he did was for the betterment of humankind—he was disposing of human trash.

Joella appeared at the back door. She looked ravishing in a low-cut black evening dress. She smiled at Saul and gave him that look. The one that had melted him when he'd first met her, and melted him now. "Are you all right, honey?"

He moved closer and hugged her tightly. She smelled of roses and honey. He kissed her passionately. "Better than ever, baby. Better than ever."

Opening the door, he was stunned.

"Surprise," everyone yelled, not quite in unison, but close enough for Saul.

He grinned widely. "My God, this is a surprise. I need a drink."

Everybody was there; at least, everybody who mattered. Koby and his wife Andrea; Spencer and his new girlfriend Jennifer; Samantha and her husband Thomas; of course, Nicolas and his fiancé Angela; his long-time friend Marlon, whom he hadn't talked to in ages, and the two girls, Jennifer and Evelyn, whom he now considered his daughters.

Evelyn was the first to run to him. She bounded right into his arms and he hugged her warmly. Her deep brown eyes looked into his. "It's a surprise Christmas for you, Daddy. I love you so much." Then she showed him a drawing of Superman soaring through the air in his signature costume. Underneath the flying superhero, she'd written: *My Daddy. He'll always be my superhero. Love always, Evelyn.*

"I made it for you," Evelyn said. "I love you."

Saul took the drawing. "Thank you. I love you too, honey."

Then he was swarmed by the guests, engulfed in a massive group hug. Saul's emotions got the better of him and he couldn't help wiping away a tear. "Stop it. Look what you're doing to me."

"Congratulations," Joella said, holding up a paperback copy of *The Final Hour*. "Samantha has published your book." When the others released him, she handed it over. "I'm proud of you, baby. I know I have a hard time showing it sometimes, but I really love you."

Admiring the cover, Saul turned to Samantha. "You published it?"

"Yes," she said, returning for another hug. "Congratulations. I self-published it, in your name of course. And Gail from Penguin has already read it. Now Penguin wants to offer you a contract on another book."

"I don't know what to say. Thank you so much."

Teary-eyed, Samantha released Saul and Joella took over.

To loud clapping, Joella hugged Saul and gave him a long, passionate kiss that suggested more to come. Jennifer and Evelyn clung onto a leg each. A few guests snapped photos of the happy family.

When everyone had sat down for dinner, it was Spencer who was the first to propose a toast. By then Saul had already drained three glasses of Chilean white wine. And he was just getting started. Looking at Spencer's animated, drunken smile, Saul realized the months hadn't treated his friend so well. Spencer was withered, white, and weak-looking, but trying hard to hide it. Saul had no idea how long Spencer had with this world, but he had to hand it to him—he'd go out with a thunderous explosion, guns blazing. People could learn a lot from his enjoy-the-moment attitude about life.

"I want to congratulate you, Saul, for overcoming so many fucking odds. For finishing your book, for pursuing your love interest. I think she's a great girl. I have to admit, I didn't always think that way. But I was wrong."

"Here-here," the table of guests erupted. There was a chorus of laughter.

"Wait a minute. I'm not done here," Spencer said. "I want to congratulate you for deciding you were tired of your self-serving suicide mission and for doing something about it. You crawled out of the alcoholic abyss, and you're back in flying colors. I love you for that, brother. I really do."

Applause and laughter.

"Hey, hold on. I didn't say I was finished yet," Spencer said. "Do you see me holding this wine glass to my lips? There's one last thing I wanna say, then I'll shut my mouth." Spencer locked eyes with Saul. "I know what you're doing." He waved his wine glass at Koby, who avoided eye contact. "And I hope you fuckers don't try and kill me again, but I think you're doing a damn fine job fighting the evil that will always be here. Someone's gotta do it. If I could, I would. Anyway, cheers... congratulations, bro... keep up the good work."

They toasted and drank. The applause was slow to start, but soon thundered through the room.

Saul wiped watery eyes. "Enough of this praise, already." He raised his glass. "You're gonna turn me into a blubbering idiot, just like I was before. Seriously, thank you guys for throwing this party. Thank you for coming. And thanks so much for your love, support, and friendship. I couldn't have done it without you. Now, let's eat. I'm starving. Cheers, everyone. May your fortunes be as fortunate as mine."

They ate, enjoying laughter, sarcasm, light-hearted conversation, and the odd dirty joke thrown in for good measure, until well after two in the morning.

After the guests had left and the children had been kissed goodnight and tucked in bed, Saul lay in bed, still sipping wine and studying the cover of *The Final Hour*. It depicted an apocalyptic wasteland: a city burning, destroyed by humankind's stupidity. A lone soldier, armed to the teeth, wandered through the carnage. In the background, a large skull hovered ominously, black sockets for eyes, a mouth agape in horror, flames fanning out from the skull.

Saul still couldn't believe it was his creation. He was giddy with the feeling of satisfaction that only a writer can know after embarking on—and completing—an arduous storytelling journey. Blood, sweat, and tears, but here it was, his creation, a piece of his personality, a piece of him, that would be forever immortalized.

As Joella closed the bedroom door behind her, he sighed and set the book down. *Me. A writer. An observer of human nature. Paying attention to every little nuance and documenting it.*

But as he watched Joella, he frowned, realizing how little he really knew about her. During the chaos of the last few months, perhaps he'd lost sight of what really mattered.

She cuddled up next to him. "What's wrong?"

He looked into her eyes. "I just realized I never asked you about your parents."

"That makes two of us."

"What are your parents like?"

"My father abandoned us when I was six. He wasn't a very nice man. My mother raised the family. She couldn't handle my father's rejection. She became a big drinker, an alcoholic. I'm estranged from them." Joella's eyes welled with tears.

"Sorry to hear that." Saul gently stroked Joella's face.

Joella composed herself. "It's okay. It was a long time ago. What about you? What were your parents like?"

It took some time before Saul answered. "I'm an only child. My mother left when I was six, too. My father was the one who couldn't handle the rejection. He became an alcoholic. He's dead now—car crash. I've never heard from my mother. I don't know what became of her." Saul's eyes also welled with tears.

This time it was Joella who tenderly stroked his face. "I'm sorry. Our stories are remarkably similar. Maybe that explains our insecurity issues."

Saul took a sip of wine and wiped his eyes. He kissed Joella and brightened. "Maybe, but I like to think I'm no longer a product of my upbringing. I like to think I've changed."

Joella kissed him back. "You *have* changed. And so have I."

She stood up, went over to the dresser, and plugged a CD into the stereo. She spun around, started dancing, and seductively peeling her clothes off.

Watching her mischievous smile, sexy butt, perky breasts, and naked golden flesh glowing in the candlelight, Saul recognized Bob Marley's *Is This Love?* as soon as it started:

I wanna love you and treat you right;
I wanna love you every day and every night:
We'll be together with a roof right over our heads;
We'll share the shelter of my single bed;
We'll share the same room, yeah! - for Jah provide the bread.

Is this love - is this love - is this love -
Is this love that I'm feelin'?
Is this love - is this love - is this love -
Is this love that I'm feelin'?
I wanna know - wanna know - wanna know now!
I got to know - got to know - got to know now!

After they'd made the most intense and pleasurable love that Saul could remember, he thought, *I do know. I might've missed a few things. But I know a few things now that I didn't know then.*

Once he'd thought the silent treatment worked in a relationship. Now he knew better. Communication, honesty, and trust were key. Once he'd thought bottling up his emotions and numbing them with alcohol would make his problems disappear. Now it dawned on him that vulnerability—as he'd once theorized in a drunken stupor—was the gateway to happiness.

For the first time in his life, there were no longer any nagging doubts or insecurities. It all suddenly became clear. Sure, people said that Dominican women, particularly those in the Puerto Plata area, had a money agenda. In many cases it was true. But weren't money and love inextricably linked everywhere in the world? Wouldn't it somehow always come down to money? It was never black and white. There were always shades of gray.

But if you can't provide for your woman, what the hell good are you?

Or maybe he'd realized that life was far from perfect and it wouldn't get any better than it was now. And he was sure what he had with Joella wasn't bought love.

As they lay in bed in a post-coital cuddle, he couldn't believe the words that came out of his mouth. At first he didn't even realize they were his.

"Honey?" he said.

"Yes, sweetie?"

"Will you marry me?"

"I think you already know the answer."

"I want to hear it."

"Of course I will. I thought you'd never ask."

Also by William Blackwell

Phantom Rage, Poison Rage, Infected Rage
Nightmare's Edge
Resurrection Point
Brainstorm
Rule 14
Assaulted Souls
Assaulted Souls II
Assaulted Souls III
Blood Curse
Black Dawn
The Strap
The End is Nigh
Orgon Conclusion
Freaky Franky
The Witch's Tombstone
The Dark Menace
Tales of Damnation
In Your Dreams
Macabre Alley
A Head for an Eye

The Dark Menace Preview

"*The Dark Menace* isn't just horror, it's a descent into fear, sleep, and madness. Gripping, emotional, and rooted in chilling reality. If you've ever felt watched in the dark, this story will haunt you. Absolutely compelling." -Jessica Raye

"Most thriller and horror books just follow a handful of predigested formulas because it's proven that, although they often produce mediocre results, they do work and people somehow enjoy them. This book is not like this; it is a truly original supernatural, nightmarish thriller that you will not be able to put down and that, when you finish reading it, will linger and haunt you for a long time. You will be drawn into a world where every shadow and whisper feels alive, making the experience intensely immersive. This is not for the faint-hearted, you will be immersed in horror, and you will live it. The author mixes many ideas (urban legends, demons, nightmares, madness, supernatural entities, psychopaths) in a convoluted web, and the result is explosively terrifying and wonderfully sinister. A compelling read!" -Amazon

Noah Janzen is plagued by nightmares and numerous sleep disorders; night terrors, sleepwalking, sleep talking, and a terrifying sleep paralysis that often invokes chilling images of the Shadow People and the Hat Man.

Determined to prevent his nocturnal demons from interfering with his successful career and newly formed relationship with Angela Rosewood, he meets her in a local pub. But when he sees a shadowy figure wearing a fedora and a trench coat eerily watching him through a window, he freaks out and flees.

He soon learns that a hat-wearing psycho has viciously attacked Angela, smashing in her door, trashing her apartment, and nearly killing her. Worse still, Angela suspects Noah has morphed into a conduit for evil and starts distancing herself from him. She might even think he is the Hat Man.

Desperate to save his new relationship and find answers, he seeks the aid of physicist and sleep specialist, Doctor Neil Samuelson. While remaining tight-lipped on his experiments involving the Shadow People and the Hat Man, the enigmatic doctor informs Noah that an old woman has been brutally murdered at the hands of *The Dark Menace*.

As blood-curdling reports of Shadow People and the Hat Man escalate, Noah suspects Neil has accidentally opened up a portal from another dimension, unleashing a torrent of shadowy evil entities, hell-bent on terrorizing and destroying humanity.

He's thrust into an epic battle to preserve his relationship and sanity and find answers to a strange and mysterious real-life phenomenon that has haunted and terrorized thousands of people around the world for centuries.

About the Author

Canadian dark fiction author William Blackwell studied journalism at Calgary's Mount Royal University and English literature at Vancouver's University of British Columbia. He worked as a journalist for many years before pursuing his passion for storytelling. His novels have been characterized as graphic, edgy, and at times terrifying. Currently living on a secluded acreage on Prince Edward Island, Blackwell finds much of his inspiration from Mother Nature, odd people, and traveling around the world.

Author Comments

Thank you for reading this book. I would be eternally grateful if you would post a book review on your favorite book retailer website. A positive review is the highest compliment a writer can receive. Reviews are crucial to the success of any author and they help readers discover new novels. You don't have to say much. A few sentences will suffice.

In other news, I have a gift for you. Complete the signup form below with your name and email address and download a FREE copy of *Resurrection Point*, a dark tale about the horrifying consequences of experimenting with death and resurrection. You're only agreeing to be kept up to date on blog posts, new releases, and freebies. I promise I won't spam you and you can unsubscribe at any time.

Thanks again for your support.

http://www.wblackwell.com/free-ebook/

www.ingramcontent.com/pod-product-compliance
Lightning Source LLC
Chambersburg PA
CBHW021328250626
47155CB00002B/637